St. Mawr AND

The Man Who Died

BY *D. H. Lawrence*

New York

Vintage Books

A DIVISION OF RANDOM HOUSE

VINTAGE BOOKS

are published by ALFRED A. KNOPF, INC.

and RANDOM HOUSE, INC.

Reprinted by arrangement with ALFRED A. KNOPF, INC.

Manufactured in the United States of America

Contents

St. Mawr

Lou Witt had had her own way

so long that by the age of twenty-five she didn't know where she was. Having one's own way landed one completely at sea.

To be sure, for a while she had failed in her grand love affair with Rico. And then she had had something really to despair about. But even that had worked out as she wanted. Rico had come back to her, and was dutifully married to her. And now, when she was twenty-five and he was three months older, they were a charming married couple. He flirted with other women still, to be sure. He wouldn't be the handsome Rico if he didn't. But she had "got" him. Oh, yes! You had only to see the uneasy backward glance at her, from his big blue eyes: just like a horse that is edging away from its master: to know how completely he was mastered.

She, with her odd little *museau*, not exactly pretty, but very attractive; and her quaint air of playing at being well-bred, in a sort of charade game; and her queer familiarity with foreign cities and foreign languages; and the lurking sense of being an outsider everywhere, like a sort of gipsy, who is at home anywhere and nowhere: all this made up her charm and her failure. She didn't quite belong.

Of course she was American: Louisiana family, moved down to Texas. And she was moderately rich, with no close relation except her mother. But she had been sent to school in France when she was twelve, and since she had finished school, she had drifted from Paris to Palermo, Biarritz to Vienna and back via Munich to London, then down again to Rome. Only fleeting trips to her America.

So what sort of American was she, after all?

And what sort of European was she either? She didn't "belong" anywhere. Perhaps most of all in Rome, among the artists and the Embassy people.

It was in Rome she had met Rico. He was an Australian, son of a government official in Melbourne, who had been made a baronet. So one day Rico would be Sir Henry, as he was the only son. Meanwhile he floated around Europe on a very small allowance—his father wasn't rich in capital—and was being an artist.

They met in Rome when they were twenty-two, and had a love affair in Capri. Rico was handsome, elegant, but mostly he had spots of paint on his trousers and he ruined a necktie pulling it off. He behaved in a most floridly elegant fashion, fascinating to the Italians. But at the same time he was canny and shrewd and sensible as any young poser could be, and, on principle, good-hearted, anxious. He was anxious for his future, and anxious for his place in the world, he was poor, and suddenly wasteful in spite of all his tension of economy, and suddenly spiteful in spite of all his ingratiating efforts, and suddenly ungrateful in spite of all his burden of gratitude, and suddenly rude in spite of all his good manners, and suddenly detestable in spite of all his suave, courtier-like amiability.

He was fascinated by Lou's quaint aplomb, her experiences, her "knowledge," her *gamine* knowingness, her aloneness, her pretty clothes that were sometimes an utter failure, and her southern "drawl" that was sometimes so irritating. That sing-song which was so American. Yet she used no Americanisms at all, except when she lapsed into her odd spasms of acid irony, when she was very American indeed!

And she was fascinated by Rico. They played to each other like two butterflies at one flower. They pretended to be very poor in Rome—he *was* poor: and very rich in Naples. Everybody stared their eyes out at them. And they had that love affair in Capri.

But they reacted badly on each other's nerves. She became ill. Her mother appeared. He couldn't stand Mrs. Witt, and Mrs. Witt couldn't stand him. There was a terrible fortnight. Then Lou was popped into a convent nursing-home in Umbria, and Rico dashed off to Paris. Nothing would stop him. He must go back to Australia.

He went to Melbourne, and while there his father died, leaving him a baronet's title and an income still very moderate. Lou visited America once more, as the strangest of strange lands to her. She came away disheartened, panting for Europe, and, of course, doomed to meet Rico again.

They couldn't get away from one another, even though in the course of their rather restrained correspondence he informed her that he was "probably" marrying a very dear girl, friend of his childhood, only daughter of one of the oldest families in Victoria. Not saying much.

He didn't commit the probability, but reappeared in Paris, wanting to paint his head off, terribly inspired by Cezanne and by old Renoir. He dined at the Rotonde with Lou and Mrs. Witt, who, with her queer democratic New Orleans sort of conceit, looked round the drinking-hall with savage contempt, and at Rico as part of the show. "Certainly," she said, "when these people here have got any money, they fall in love on a full stomach. And when they've got no money, they fall in love with a full pocket. I never was in a more disgusting place. They take their love like some people take after-dinner pills."

She would watch with her arching, full, strong grey eyes, sitting there erect and silent in her well-bought American clothes. And then she would deliver some such charge of grape-shot. Rico always writhed.

Mrs. Witt hated Paris: "this sordid, unlucky city," she called it. "Something unlucky is bound to happen to me in this sinister, unclean town," she said. "I feel *contagion* in the air of this place. For heaven's sake, Louise, let us go to Morocco or somewhere."

"No, mother dear, I can't now. Rico has proposed to me, and I have accepted him. Let us think about a wedding, shall we?"

"There!" said Mrs. Witt. "I said it was an unlucky city!"

And the peculiar look of extreme New Orleans annoyance came round her sharp nose. But Lou and Rico were both twenty-four years old, and beyond management. And anyhow, Lou would be Lady Carrington. But Mrs. Witt was exasperated beyond exasperation. She would almost rather have preferred Lou to elope with one of the great, evil porters at Les Halles. Mrs. Witt was at the age when the malevolent male in man, the old Adam, begins to loom above all the social tailoring. And yet—and yet—it was better to have Lady Carrington for a daughter, seeing Lou was that sort.

There was a marriage, after which Mrs. Witt departed
to America. Lou and Rico leased a little old house in Westminster, and began to settle into a certain layer of English
society. Rico was becoming an almost fashionable portrait-
painter. At least, *he* was almost fashionable, whether
his portraits were or not. And Lou too was almost
fashionable: almost a hit. There was some flaw somewhere. In spite of their appearances, both Rico and she
would never quite go down in any society. They were
the drifting artist sort. Yet neither of them was content
to be of the drifting artist sort. They wanted to fit in, to
make good.

Hence the little house in Westminster, the portraits,
the dinners, the friends, and the visits. Mrs. Witt came
and sardonically established herself in a suite in a quiet
but good-class hotel not far off. Being on the spot. And her
terrible grey eyes with the touch of a leer looked on at the
hollow mockery of things. As if *she* knew of anything better!

Lou and Rico had a curious exhausting effect on one
another: neither knew why. They were fond of one another. Some inscrutable bond held them together. But it
was a strange vibration of the nerves, rather than of the
blood. A nervous attachment, rather than a sexual love. A
curious tension of will, rather than a spontaneous passion.
Each was curiously under the domination of the other.
They were a pair—they had to be together. Yet quite soon
they shrank from one another. This attachment of the will
and the nerves was destructive. As soon as one felt strong,
the other felt ill. As soon as the ill one recovered strength,
down went the one who had been well.

And soon, tacitly, the marriage became more like a
friendship, Platonic. It was a marriage, but without sex.
Sex was shattering and exhausting, they shrank from it,
and became like brother and sister. But still they were husband and wife. And the lack of physical relation was a
secret source of uneasiness and chagrin to both of them.
They would neither of them accept it. Rico looked with
contemplative, anxious eyes at other women.

Mrs. Witt kept track of everything, watching, as it were,

from outside the fence, like a potent well-dressed demon, full of uncanny energy and a shattering sort of sense. She said little: but her small, occasionally biting remarks revealed her attitude of contempt for the *ménage*.

Rico entertained clever and well-known people. Mrs. Witt would appear, in her New York gowns and few good jewels. She was handsome, with her vigorous grey hair. But her heavy-lidded grey eyes were the despair of any hostess. They looked too many shattering things. And it was but too obvious that these clever, well-known English people got on her nerves terribly, with their finickiness and their fine-drawn discriminations. She wanted to put her foot through all these fine-drawn distinctions. She thought continually of the house of her girlhood, the plantation, the Negroes, the planters: the sardonic grimness that underlay all the big, shiftless life. And she wanted to cleave with some of this grimness of the big, dangerous America, into the safe, finicky drawing-rooms of London. So naturally she was not popular.

But being a woman of energy, she had to do *something*. During the latter part of the war she had worked with the American Red Cross in France, nursing. She loved men— real men. But, on close contact, it was difficult to define what she meant by "real" men. She never met any.

Out of the debacle of the war she had emerged with an odd piece of debris, in the shape of Geronimo Trujillo. He was an American, son of a Mexican father and a Navajo Indian mother, from Arizona. When you knew him well, you recognized the real half-breed, though at a glance he might pass as a sunburnt citizen of any nation, particularly of France. He looked like a certain sort of Frenchman, with his curiously set dark eyes, his straight black hair, his thin black moustache, his rather long cheeks, and his almost slouching, diffident, sardonic bearing. Only when you knew him, and looked right into his eyes, you saw that unforgettable glint of the Indian.

He had been badly shell-shocked, and was for a time a wreck. Mrs. Witt, having nursed him into convalescence, asked him where he was going next. He didn't know. His father and mother were dead, and he had nothing to take

him back to Phœnix, Arizona. Having had an education
in one of the Indian high schools, the unhappy fellow had
now no place in life at all. Another of the many misfits.

There was something of the Paris *Apache* in his appearance: but he was all the time withheld, and nervously
shut inside himself. Mrs. Witt was intrigued by him.

"Very well, Phœnix," she said, refusing to adopt his
Spanish name, "I'll see what I can do."

What she did was to get him a place on a sort of manor
farm, with some acquaintances of hers. He was very good
with horses, and had a curious success with turkeys and
geese and fowls.

Some time after Lou's marriage, Mrs. Witt reappeared
in London, from the country, with Phœnix in tow, and a
couple of horses. She had decided that she would ride in
the Park in the morning, and see the world that way.
Phœnix was to be her groom.

So, to the great misgiving of Rico, behold Mrs. Witt
in splendidly tailored habit and perfect boots, a smart
black hat on her smart grey hair, riding a grey gelding as
smart as she was, and looking down her conceited, inquisi-
tive, scornful, aristocratic-democratic Louisiana nose at
the people in Piccadilly, as she crossed to the Row, followed by the taciturn shadow of Phœnix, who sat on a
chestnut with three white feet as if he had grown there.

Mrs. Witt, like many other people, always expected to
find the real *beau monde* and the real *grand monde* somewhere or other. She didn't quite give in to what she saw
in the Bois de Boulogne, or in Monte Carlo, or on the Pin-
cio; all a bit shoddy, and not very *beau* and not at all
grand. There she was, with her grey eagle eye, her splendid complexion and her weapon-like health of a woman
of fifty, dropping her eyelids a little, very slightly nervous,
but completely prepared to despise the *monde* she was
entering in Rotten Row.

In she sailed, and up and down that regatta-canal of
horsemen and horsewomen under the trees of the Park.
And yes, there were lovely girls with fair hair down their
backs, on happy ponies. And awfully well-groomed papas,
and tight mammas who looked as if they were going to
pour tea between the ears of their horses, and converse

with banal skill, one eye on the teapot, one on the visitor
with whom she was talking, and all the rest of her hostess'
argus-eyes upon everybody in sight. That alert argus ca-
pability of the English matron was startling and a bit horrifying. Mrs. Witt would at once think of the old Negro
mammies, away in Louisiana. And her eyes became dag-
ger-like as she watched the clipped, shorn, mincing
young Englishmen. She refused to look at the prosperous
Jews.

It was still the days before motor-cars were allowed in
the Park, but Rico and Lou, sliding round Hyde Park Corner and up Park Lane in their car, would watch the steely
horsewoman and the saturnine groom with a sort of dismay.
Mrs. Witt seemed to be pointing a pistol at the bosom of
every other horseman or horsewoman, and announcing:
Your virility or your life! Your femininity or your life! She
didn't know herself what she really wanted them to be:
but it was something as democratic as Abraham Lincoln,
and as aristocratic as a Russian Czar, as highbrow as
Arthur Balfour, and as taciturn and unideal as Phœnix.
Everything at once.

There was nothing for it: Lou had to buy herself a horse
and ride at her mother's side, for very decency's sake. Mrs.
Witt was *so* like a smooth, levelled, gun-metal pistol, Lou
had to be a sort of sheath. And she really looked pretty,
with her clusters of dark, curly, New Orleans hair, like
grapes, and her quaint brown eyes that didn't quite
match, and that looked a bit sleepy and vague, and at the
same time quick as a squirrel's. She was slight and elegant,
and a tiny bit rakish, and somebody suggested she might
be in the movies.

Nevertheless, they were in the society columns next
morning—*two new and striking figures in the Row this
morning were Lady Henry Carrington and her mother
Mrs. Witt,* etc. And Mrs. Witt liked it, let her say what
she might. So did Lou. Lou liked it immensely. She simply
luxuriated in the sun of publicity.

"Rico dear, you must get a horse."

The tone was soft and southern and drawling, but the
overtone had a decisive finality. In vain Rico squirmed—
he had a way of writhing and squirming which perhaps

he had caught at Oxford. In vain he protested that he couldn't ride, and that he didn't care for riding. He got quite angry, and his handsome arched nose tilted and his upper lip lifted from his teeth, like a dog that is going to bite. Yet daren't quite bite.

And that was Rico. He daren't quite bite. Not that he was really afraid of the others. He was afraid of himself, once he let himself go. He might rip up in an eruption of lifelong anger all this pretty-pretty picture of a charming young wife and a delightful little home and a fascinating success as a painter of fashionable and, at the same time, "great" portraits: with colour, wonderful colour, and, at the same time, form, marvellous form. He had composed this little *tableau vivant* with great effort. He didn't want to erupt like some suddenly wicked horse—Rico was really more like a horse than a dog, a horse that might go nasty any moment. For the time, he was good, very good, dangerously good.

"Why, Rico dear, I thought you used to ride so much, in Australia, when you were young? Didn't you tell me all about it, hm?"—and as she ended on that slow, singing *hm?* which acted on him like an irritant and a drug, he knew he was beaten.

Lou kept the sorrel mare in a mews just behind the house in Westminster, and she was always slipping round to the stables. She had a funny little nostalgia for the place: something that really surprised her. She had never had the faintest notion that she cared for horses and stables and grooms. But she did. She was fascinated. Perhaps it was her childhood's Texas associations come back. Whatever it was, her life with Rico in the elegant little house, and all her social engagements, seemed like a dream, the substantial reality of which was those mews in Westminster, her sorrel mare, the owner of the mews, Mr. Saintsbury, and the grooms he employed. Mr. Saintsbury was a horsy elderly man like an old maid, and he loved the sound of titles.

"Lady Carrington!—well, I never! You've come to us for a bit of company again, I see. I don't know whatever we shall do if you go away, we shall be that lonely!" and he flashed his old-maid's smile at her. "No matter how grey the morning, your Ladyship would make a beam of sunshine. Poppy is all right, I think . . ."

Poppy was the sorrel mare with the no white feet and the startled eye, and she was all right. And Mr. Saintsbury was smiling with his old-maid's mouth, and showing all his teeth.

"Come across with me, Lady Carrington, and look at a new horse just up from the country? I think he's worth a look, and I believe you have a moment to spare, your Ladyship."

Her Ladyship had too many moments to spare. She followed the sprightly, elderly, clean-shaven man across the yard to a loose box, and waited while he opened the door.

In the inner dark she saw a handsome bay horse with his clean ears pricked like daggers from his naked head as he swung handsomely round to stare at the open doorway. He had big, black, brilliant eyes, with a sharp questioning glint, and that air of tense, alert quietness which betrays an animal that can be dangerous.

"Is he quiet?" Lou asked.

"Why—yes—my Lady! He's quiet, with those that know how to handle him. *Cup! my boy! Cup my beauty! Cup then! St. Mawr!*"

Loquacious even with the animals, he went softly forward and laid his hand on the horse's shoulder, soft and quiet as a fly settling. Lou saw the brilliant skin of the horse crinkle a little in apprehensive anticipation, like the shadow of the descending hand on a bright red-gold liquid. But then the animal relaxed again.

"Quiet with those that know how to handle him, and a bit of a ruffian with those that don't. Isn't that the ticket, eh, St. Mawr?"

"What is his name?" Lou asked.

The man repeated it, with a slight Welsh twist. "He's from the Welsh borders, belonging to a Welsh gentleman, Mr. Griffith Edwards. But they're wanting to sell him."

"How old is he?" asked Lou.

"About seven years—seven years and five months," said Mr. Saintsbury, dropping his voice as if it were a secret.

"Could one ride him in the Park?"

"Well—yes! I should say a gentleman who knew how to handle him could ride him very well and make a very handsome figure in the Park."

Lou at once decided that this handsome figure should be Rico's. For she was already half in love with St. Mawr. He was of such a lovely red-gold colour, and a dark, invisible fire seemed to come out of him. But in his big black eyes there was a lurking afterthought. Something told her that the horse was not quite happy: that somewhere deep in his animal consciousness lived a dangerous, half-revealed resentment, a diffused sense of hostility. She realized that he was sensitive, in spite of his flaming, healthy strength, and nervous with a touchy uneasiness that might make him vindictive.

"Has he got any tricks?" she asked.

"Not that I know of, my Lady: not tricks exactly. But he's one of these temperamental creatures, as they say. Though *I* say, every horse is temperamental, when you come down to it. But this one, it is as if he was a trifle raw somewhere. Touch this raw spot, and there's no answering for him."

"Where is he raw?" asked Lou, somewhat mystified. She thought he might really have some physical sore.

"Why, that's hard to say, my Lady. If he was a human being, you'd say something had gone wrong in his life. But with a horse, it's not that, exactly. A high-bred animal like St. Mawr needs understanding, and I don't know as anybody has quite got the hang of him. I confess I haven't myself. But I do realize that he is a special animal and needs a special sort of touch, and I'm willing he should have it, did I but know exactly what it is."

She looked at the glowing bay horse that stood there with his ears back, his face averted, but attending as if he were some lightning-conductor. He was a stallion. When she realized this, she became more afraid of him.

"Why does Mr. Griffith Edwards want to sell him?" she asked.

"Well—my Lady—they raised him for stud purposes— but he didn't answer. There are horses like that: don't seem to fancy the mares, for some reason. Well, anyway, they couldn't keep him for the stud. And as you see, he's a powerful, beautiful hackney, clean as a whistle, and eaten up with his own power. But there's no putting him between the shafts. He won't stand it. He's a fine saddle-horse, beautiful action, and lovely to ride. But he's got to be handled, and there you are."

Lou felt there was something behind the man's reticence.

"Has he ever made a break?" she asked, apprehensive.

"Made a break?" replied the man. "Well, if I must admit it, he's had two accidents. Mr. Griffith Edwards' son rode him a bit wild, away there in the forest of Deane, and the young fellow had his skull smashed in, against a low oak-bough. Last autumn, that was. And some time back, he crushed a groom against the side of the stall—injured him fatally. But they were both accidents, my Lady. Things will happen."

The man spoke in a melancholy, fatalistic way. The horse, with his ears laid back, seemed to be listening tensely, his face averted. He looked like something finely bred and passionate, that has been judged and condemned.

"May I say *how do you do?*" she said to the horse, drawing a little nearer in her white, summery dress, and lifting her hand that glittered with emeralds and diamonds.

He drifted away from her, as if some wind blew him. Then he ducked his head, and looked sideways at her, from his black, full eye.

"I think I'm all right," she said, edging nearer, while he watched her.

She laid her hand on his side, and gently stroked him. Then she stroked his shoulder, and then the hard, tense arch of his neck. And she was startled to feel the vivid heat of his life come through to her, through the lacquer of red-gold gloss. So slippery with vivid, hot life!

She paused, as if thinking, while her hand rested on the horse's sun-arched neck. Dimly, in her weary young-woman's soul, an ancient understanding seemed to flood in.

She wanted to buy St. Mawr.

"I think," she said to Saintsbury, "if I can, I will buy him."

The man looked at her long and shrewdly.

"Well, my Lady," he said at last, "there shall be nothing kept from you. But what would your Ladyship do with him, if I may make so bold?"

"I don't know," she replied, vaguely. "I might take him to America."

The man paused once more, then said:

"They say it's been the making of some horses, to take them over the water, to Australia or such places. It might repay you—you never know."

She wanted to buy St. Mawr. She wanted him to belong to her. For some reason the sight of him, his power, his alive, alert intensity, his unyieldingness, made her want to cry.

She never did cry: except sometimes with vexation, or to get her own way. As far as weeping went, her heart felt as dry as a Christmas walnut. What was the good of tears, anyhow? You had to keep on holding on, in this life, never give way, and never give in. Tears only left one weakened and ragged.

But now, as if that mysterious fire of the horse's body had split some rock in her, she went home and hid herself in her room, and just cried. The wild, brilliant, alert head of St. Mawr seemed to look at her out of another world. It was as if she had had a vision, as if the walls of her own world had suddenly melted away, leaving her in a great darkness, in the midst of which the large, brilliant eyes of that horse looked at her with demonish question, while his naked ears stood up like daggers from the naked lines of his inhuman head, and his great body glowed red with power.

What was it? Almost like a god looking at her terribly out of the everlasting dark, she had felt the eyes of that horse; great, glowing, fearsome eyes, arched with a question, and containing a white blade of light like a threat. What was his non-human question, and his uncanny threat? She didn't know. He was some splendid demon, and she must worship him.

She hid herself away from Rico. She could not bear the triviality and superficiality of her human relationships. Looming like some god out of the darkness was the head of that horse, with the wide, terrible, questioning eyes. And she felt that it forbade her to be her ordinary, commonplace self. It forbade her to be just Rico's wife, young Lady Carrington, and all that.

It haunted her, the horse. It had looked at her as she had never been looked at before: terrible, gleaming, questioning eyes arching out of darkness, and backed by all the fire of that great ruddy body. What did it mean, and what ban did it put upon her? She felt it put a ban on her heart: wielded some uncanny authority over her, that she dared not, could not understand.

No matter where she was, what she was doing, at the back of her consciousness loomed a great, over-aweing figure out of a dark background: St. Mawr, looking at her without really seeing her, yet gleaming a question at her, from his wide terrible eyes, and gleaming a sort of menace, doom. Master of doom, he seemed to be!

"You are thinking about something, Lou dear!" Rico said to her that evening.

He was so quick and sensitive to detect her moods—so exciting in this respect. And his big, slightly prominent blue eyes, with the whites a little bloodshot, glanced at her quickly, with searching, and anxiety, and a touch of fear, as if his conscience were always uneasy. He, too, was rather like a horse—but for ever quivering with a sort of cold, dangerous mistrust, which he covered with anxious love.

At the middle of his eyes was a central powerlessness, that left him anxious. It used to touch her to pity, that central look of powerlessness in him. But now, since she had seen the full, dark, passionate blaze of power and of different life in the eyes of the thwarted horse, the anxious powerlessness of the man drove her mad. Rico was so handsome, and he was so self-controlled, he had a gallant sort of kindness and a real worldly shrewdness. One had to admire him: at least *she* had to.

But after all, and after all, it was a bluff, an attitude. He kept it all working in himself, deliberately. It was an attitude. She read psychologists who said that everything was an attitude. Even the best of everything. But now she realized that, with men and women, everything is an attitude only when something else is lacking. Something is lacking and they are thrown back on their own devices. That black fiery flow in the eyes of the horse was not "attitude." It was something much more terrifying, and real, the only thing that was real. Gushing from the darkness in menace and question, and blazing out in the splendid body of the horse.

"Was I thinking about something?" she replied, in her slow, amused, casual fashion. As if everything was so casual and easy to her. And so it was, from the hard, polished side of herself. But that wasn't the whole story.

"I think you were, Loulina. May we offer the penny?"

"Don't trouble," she said. "I was thinking, if I was thinking of anything, about a bay horse called St. Mawr." —Her secret *almost* crept into her eyes.

"The name is awfully attractive," he said with a laugh.

"Not so attractive as the creature himself. I'm going to buy him."

"Not really!" he said. "But why?"

"He *is* so attractive. I'm going to buy him for you."

"For *me! Darling!* how you do take me for granted! He may not be in the least attractive to me. As you know, I have hardly any feeling for horses at all.—Besides, how much does he cost?"

"That I don't know, Rico dear. But I'm sure you'll love him, for my sake."—She felt, now, she was merely playing for her own ends.

"Lou dearest, *don't* spend a fortune on a horse for me, which I *don't* want. Honestly, I prefer a car."

"Won't you ride with me in the Park, Rico?"

"Honestly, dear Lou, I don't want to."

"Why not, dear boy? You'd look so beautiful. I wish you would.—And anyhow, come with me to look at St. Mawr."

Rico was divided. He had a certain uneasy feeling about horses. At the same time, he *would* like to cut a handsome figure in the Park.

They went across to the mews. A little Welsh groom was watering the brilliant horse.

"Yes, dear, he certainly *is* beautiful: such a marvellous

colour! Almost orange! But rather large, I should say, to
ride in the Park."

"No, for you he's perfect. You are so tall."

"He'd be marvellous in a composition. That colour!"

And all Rico could do was to gaze with the artist's eye
at the horse, with a glance at the groom.

"Don't you think the man is rather fascinating too?" he
said, nursing his chin artistically and penetratingly.

The groom, Lewis, was a little, quick, rather bow-
legged, loosely built fellow of indeterminate age, with a
mop of black hair and little black beard. He was grooming
the brilliant St. Mawr, out in the open. The horse was
really glorious: like a marigold, with a pure golden sheen,
a shimmer of green-gold lacquer, upon a burning red-
orange. There on the shoulder you saw the yellow lacquer
glisten. Lewis, a little scrub of a fellow, worked absorbedly, unheedingly, at the horse, with an absorption
that was almost ritualistic. He seemed the attendant
shadow of the ruddy animal.

"He goes with the horse," said Lou. "If we buy St.
Mawr, we get the man thrown in."

"They'd be *so* amusing to paint: such an extraordinary
contrast! But, darling, I *hope* you won't insist on buying
the horse. It's so frightfully expensive."

"Mother will help me.—You'd look so well on him,
Rico."

"If ever I dared take the liberty of getting on his
back——!"

"Why not?" She went quickly across the cobbled yard.

"Good morning, Lewis. How is St. Mawr?"

Lewis straightened himself and looked at her from under
the falling mop of his black hair.

"All right," he said.

He peered straight at her from under his overhanging
black hair. He had pale-grey eyes, that looked phosphores-
cent, and suggested the eyes of a wildcat peering intent
from under the darkness of some bush where it lies unseen.
Lou, with her brown, unmatched, oddly perplexed eyes,
felt herself found out.—"He's a common little fellow," she
thought to herself. "But he knows a woman and a horse,
at sight."—Aloud she said, in her southern drawl:

"How do you think he'd be with Sir Henry?"

Lewis turned his remote, coldly watchful eyes on the young baronet. Rico was tall and handsome and balanced on his hips. His face was long and well-defined, and with the hair taken straight back from the brow. It seemed as well-made as his clothing, and as perpetually presentable. You could not imagine his face dirty, or scrubby and un-shaven, or bearded, or even moustached. It was perfectly prepared for social purposes. If his head had been cut off, like John the Baptist's, it would have been a thing com-plete in itself, would not have missed the body in the least. The body was perfectly tailored. The head was one of the famous "talking heads" of modern youth, with eyebrows a trifle Mephistophelian, large blue eyes a trifle bold, and curved mouth thrilling to death to kiss.

Lewis, the groom, staring from between his bush of hair and his beard, watched like an animal from the underbrush. And Rico was still sufficiently a colonial to be uneasily aware of the underbrush, uneasy under the watchfulness of the pale-grey eyes, and uneasy in that man-to-man exposure which is characteristic of the demo-cratic colonies and of America. He knew he must ulti-mately be judged on his merits as a man, alone without a background: an ungarnished colonial.

This lack of background, this defenceless man-to-man business which left him at the mercy of every servant, was bad for his nerves. For he was *also* an artist. He bore up against it in a kind of desperation, and was easily moved to rancorous resentment. At the same time he was free of the Englishman's water tight *suffisance*. He really was aware that he would have to hold his own all alone, thrown alone on his own defences in the universe. The extreme democracy of the Colonies had taught him this.

And this the little aboriginal Lewis recognized in him. He recognized also Rico's curious hollow misgiving, fear of some deficiency in himself, beneath all his handsome, young-hero appearance.

"He'd be all right with anybody as would meet him half-way," said Lewis, in the quick Welsh manner of speech, impersonal.

"You hear, Rico!" said Lou in her sing-song, turning to her husband.

"Perfectly, darling!"

"Would you be willing to meet St. Mawr half-way, hmm?"

"All the way, darling! Mahomet would go *all* the way to that mountain. Who would dare do otherwise?"

He spoke with a laughing, yet piqued sarcasm.

"Why, I think St. Mawr would understand perfectly," she said in the soft voice of a woman haunted by love. And she went and laid her hand on the slippery, life-smooth shoulder of the horse. He, with his strange equine head lowered, its exquisite fine lines reaching a little snake-like forward, and his ears a little back, was watching her sideways, from the corner of his eye. He was in a state of absolute mistrust, like a cat crouching to spring.

"St. Mawr!" she said. "St. Mawr! What is the matter? Surely you and I are all right!"

And she spoke softly, dreamily stroked the animal's neck. She could feel a response gradually coming from him. But he would not lift up his head. And when Rico suddenly moved nearer, he sprang with a sudden jerk backwards, as if lightning exploded in his four hoofs.

The groom spoke a few low words in Welsh. Lou, frightened, stood with lifted hand arrested. She had been going to stroke him.

"Why did he do that?" she said.

"They gave him a beating once or twice," said the groom in a neutral voice, "and he doesn't forget."

She could hear a neutral sort of judgment in Lewis' voice. And she thought of the "raw spot."

Not any raw spot at all. A battle between two worlds. She realized that St. Mawr drew his hot breaths in another world from Rico's, from our world. Perhaps the old Greek horses had lived in St. Mawr's world. And the old Greek heroes, even Hippolytus, had known it.

With their strangely naked equine heads, and something of a snake in their way of looking round, and lifting their sensitive, dangerous muzzles, they moved in a prehistoric twilight where all things loomed phantasmagoric, all on one plane, sudden presences suddenly jutting out of the matrix. It was another world, an older, heavily potent world. And in this world the horse was swift and fierce and supreme, undominated and unsurpassed.—"Meet him half-way," Lewis said. But half-way across from our human world to that terrific equine twilight was not a small step. It was a step, she knew, that Rico could never take. She knew it. But she was prepared to sacrifice Rico.

St. Mawr was bought, and Lewis was hired along with him. At first, Lewis rode him behind Lou, in the Row, to get him going. He behaved perfectly.

Phœnix, the half-Indian, was very jealous when he saw the black-bearded Welsh groom on St. Mawr.

"What horse you got there?" he asked, looking at the other man with the curious unseeing stare in his hard, Navajo eyes, in which the Indian glint moved like a spark upon a dark chaos. In Phœnix's high-boned face there was all the race-misery of the dispossessed Indian, with an added blankness left by shell-shock. But at the same time, there was that unyielding, save to death, which is characteristic of his tribe: his mother's tribe. Difficult to say what subtle thread bound him to the Navajo, and made his destiny a Red Man's destiny still.

They were a curious pair of grooms, following the correct, and yet extraordinary, pair of American mistresses. Mrs. Witt and Phœnix both rode with long stirrups and straight leg, sitting close to the saddle, without posting. Phœnix looked as if he and the horse were all one piece, he never seemed to rise in the saddle at all, neither trotting nor galloping, but sat like a man riding bareback. And all the time he stared around, at the riders in the Row, at the people grouped outside the rail, chatting, at the children walking with their nurses, as if he were looking at a mirage, in whose actuality he never believed for a moment. London was all a sort of dark mirage to him. His wide, nervous-looking brown eyes, with a smallish brown pupil that showed the white all round, seemed to be focused on the far distance, as if he could not see things too near. He was watching the pale deserts of Arizona shimmer with moving light, the long mirage of a shallow lake ripple, the great pallid concave of earth and sky expanding with interchanged light. And a horse-shape loom large and portentous in the mirage, like some prehistoric beast.

That was real to him: the phantasm of Arizona. But this London was something his eye passed over, as a false mirage.

He looked too smart in his well-tailored groom's clothes, so smart, he might have been one of the satirized new-rich. Perhaps it was a sort of half-breed physical assertion that came through his clothing, the savage's physical assertion of himself. Anyhow, he looked "common," rather horsy and loud.

Except his face. In the golden suavity of his high-boned Indian face, that was hairless, with hardly any eyebrows, there was a blank, lost look that was almost touching. The same startled blank look was in his eyes. But in the smallish dark pupils the dagger-point of light still gleamed unbroken.

He was a good groom, watchful, quick, and on the spot in an instant if anything went wrong. He had a curious, quiet power over the horses, unemotional, unsympathetic, but silently potent. In the same way, watching the traffic of Piccadilly with his blank, glinting eye, he would calculate everything instinctively, as if it were an enemy, and pilot Mrs. Witt by the strength of his silent will. He threw around her the tense watchfulness of her own America, and made her feel at home.

"Phœnix," she said, turning abruptly in her saddle as they walked the horses past the sheltering policeman at Hyde Park Corner, "I can't tell you how glad I am to have something a hundred per cent American at the back of me, when I go through these gates."

She looked at him from dangerous grey eyes as if she meant it indeed, in vindictive earnest. A ghost of a smile went up to his high cheek-bones, but he did not answer.

"Why, mother?" said Lou, sing-song. "It feels to me so friendly——!"

"Yes, Louise, it does. *So* friendly! That's why I mistrust it so entirely——"

And she set off at a canter up the Row, under the green trees, her face like the face of Medusa at fifty, a weapon in itself. She stared at everything and everybody, with that stare of cold dynamite waiting to explode them all. Lou posted trotting at her side, graceful and elegant, and faintly amused. Behind came Phœnix, like a shadow, with his yellowish, high-boned face still looking sick. And at his side, on the big brilliant bay horse, the smallish, black-bearded Welshman.

Between Phœnix and Lewis there was a latent but unspoken and wary sympathy. Phœnix was terribly impressed by St. Mawr, he could not leave off staring at him. And Lewis rode the brilliant, handsome-moving stallion so very quietly, like an insinuation.

Of the two men, Lewis looked the darker, with his black beard coming up to his thick black eyebrows. He was swarthy, with a rather short nose, and the uncanny pale-grey eyes that watched everything and cared about nothing. He cared about nothing in the world, except, at the present, St. Mawr. People did not matter to him. He rode his horse and watched the world from the vantage-ground of St. Mawr, with a final indifference.

"You have been with that horse long?" asked Phœnix.

"Since he was born."

Phœnix watched the action of St. Mawr as they went. The bay moved proud and springy, but with perfect good sense, among the stream of riders. It was a beautiful June morning, the leaves overhead were thick and green; there came the first whiff of lime-tree scent. To Phœnix, however, the city was a sort of nightmare mirage, and to Lewis it was a sort of prison. The presence of people he felt as a prison around him.

Mrs. Witt and Lou were turning, at the end of the Row, bowing to some acquaintances. The grooms pulled aside. Mrs. Witt looked at Lewis with a cold eye.

"It seems an extraordinary thing to me, Louise," she said, "to see a groom with a beard."

"It isn't usual, mother," said Lou. "Do you mind?"

"Not at all. At least, I think I don't. I get very tired of modern bare-faced young men, *very!* The clean, pure boy, don't you know! Doesn't it make you tired?—No, I think a groom with a beard is quite attractive."

She gazed into the crowd defiantly, perching her finely shod toe with warlike firmness on the stirrup-iron. Then

suddenly she reined in, and turned her horse towards the
grooms.

"Lewis!" she said. "I want to ask you a question. Supposing, now, that Lady Carrington wanted you to shave
off that beard, what should you say?"

Lewis instinctively put up his hand to the said beard.

"They've wanted me to shave it off, Mam," he said.
"But I've never done it."

"But why? Tell me why."

"It's part of me, Mam."

Mrs. Witt pulled on again.

"Isn't that extraordinary, Louise?" she said. "Don't you
like the way he says *Mam*? It sounds so impossible to me.
Could any woman think of herself as Mam? Never, since
Queen Victoria! But—do you know?—it hadn't occurred
to me that a man's beard was really part of him. It always
seemed to me that men wore their beards, like they wear
their neckties, for show. I shall always remember Lewis
for saying his beard was part of him. Isn't it curious, the
way he rides? He seems to sink himself in the horse. When
I speak to him, I'm not sure whether I'm speaking to a man
or to a horse."

A few days later, Rico himself appeared on St. Mawr,
for the morning ride. He rode self-consciously, as he did
everything, and he was just a little nervous. But his
mother-in-law was benevolent. She made him ride between
her and Lou, like three ships slowly sailing abreast.

And that very day, who should come driving in an open
carriage through the Park but the Queen Mother! Dear
old Queen Alexandra, there was a flutter everywhere. And
she bowed expressly to Rico, mistaking him, no doubt, for
somebody else.

"Do you know," said Rico as they sat at lunch, he and
Lou and Mrs. Witt, in Mrs. Witt's sitting-room in the dark,
quiet hotel in Mayfair, "I really like riding St. Mawr *so*
much. He really is a noble animal.—If ever I am made a
Lord—which heaven forbid!—I shall be Lord St. Mawr."

"You mean," said Mrs. Witt, "his real lordship would
be the horse?"

"Very possible, I admit," said Rico, with a curl of his
long upper lip.

"Don't you think, mother," said Lou, "there *is* something quite noble about St. Mawr? He strikes me as the first noble thing I have ever seen."

"Certainly I've not seen any *man* that could compare with him. Because these English noblemen—well! I'd rather look at a Negro Pullman-boy, if I was looking for what *I* call nobility."

Poor Rico was getting crosser and crosser. There was a devil in Mrs. Witt. She had a hard, bright devil inside her, that she seemed to be able to let loose at will.

She let it loose the next day, when Rico and Lou joined her in the Row. She was silent but deadly with the horses, balking them in every way. She suddenly crowded over against the rail, in front of St. Mawr, so that the stallion had to rear to pull himself up. Then, having a clear track, she suddenly set off at a gallop, like an explosion, and the stallion, all on edge, set off after her.

It seemed as if the whole Park, that morning, were in a state of nervous tension. Perhaps there was thunder in the air. But St. Mawr kept on dancing and pulling at the bit, and wheeling sideways up against the railing, to the terror of the children and the onlookers, who squealed and jumped back suddenly, sending the nerves of the stallion into a rush like rockets. He reared and fought as Rico pulled him round.

Then he went on: dancing, pulling, springily progressing sideways, possessed with all the demons of perversity. Poor Rico's face grew longer and angrier. A fury rose in him, which he could hardly control. He hated his horse, and viciously tried to force him to a quiet, straight trot. Up went St. Mawr on his hind legs, to the terror of the Row. He got the bit in his teeth, and began to fight.

But Phœnix, cleverly, was in front of him.

"You get off, Rico!" called Mrs. Witt's voice, with all the calm of her wicked exultance.

And almost before he knew what he was doing, Rico had sprung lightly to the ground, and was hanging on to the bridle of the rearing stallion.

Phœnix also lightly jumped down, and ran to St. Mawr, handing his bridle to Rico. Then began a dancing and a splashing, a rearing and a plunging. St. Mawr was being wicked. But Phœnix, the indifference of conflict in his face, sat tight and immovable, without any emotion, only the heaviness of his impersonal will settling down like a weight, all the time, on the horse. There was, perhaps, a curious barbaric exultance in bare, dark will devoid of emotion or personal feeling.

So they had a little display in the Row for almost five minutes, the brilliant horse rearing and fighting. Rico, with a stiff long face, scrambled on to Phœnix's horse, and withdrew to a safe distance. Policemen came, and an officious mounted police rode up to save the situation. But it was obvious that Phœnix, detached and apparently unconcerned, but barbarically potent in his will, would bring the horse to order.

Which he did, and rode the creature home. Rico was requested not to ride St. Mawr in the Row any more, as the stallion was dangerous to public safety. The authorities knew all about him.

Where ended the first fiasco of St. Mawr.

"We didn't get on very well with his lordship this morning," said Mrs. Witt triumphantly.

"No, he didn't like his company *at all!*" Rico snarled back.

He wanted Lou to sell the horse again.

"I doubt if anyone would buy him, dear," she said. "He's a known character."

"Then make a gift of him—to your mother," said Rico with venom.

"Why to mother?" asked Lou innocently.

"She might be able to cope with him—or he with her!" The last phrase was deadly. Having delivered it, Rico departed.

Lou remained at a loss. She felt almost always a little bit dazed, as if she could not see clear nor feel clear. A curious deadness upon her, like the first touch of death. And through this cloud of numbness, or deadness, came all her muted experiences.

Why was it? She did not know. But she felt that in some way it came from a battle of wills. Her mother, Rico, herself, it was always an unspoken, unconscious battle of wills, which was gradually numbing and paralysing her. She

knew Rico meant nothing but kindness by her. She knew
her mother only wanted to watch over her. Yet always
there was this tension of will, that was so numbing. As if
at the depths of him, Rico were always angry, though he
seemed so "happy" on the top. And Mrs. Witt was organically angry. So they were like a couple of bombs, timed
to explode some day, but ticking on like two ordinary time-
pieces in the meanwhile.

She had come definitely to realize this: that Rico's anger
was wound up tight at the bottom of him, like a steel
spring that kept his works going, while he himself was
"charming," like a bomb-clock with Sèvres paintings or
Dresden figures on the outside. But his very charm was a
sort of anger, and his love was a destruction in itself. He
just couldn't help it.

And she? Perhaps she was a good deal the same herself.
Wound up tight inside, and enjoying herself being
"lovely." But wound up tight on some tension that, she
realized now with wonder, was really a sort of anger. This,
the mainspring that drove her on the round of "joys."

She used really to enjoy the tension, and the *élan* it
gave her. While she knew nothing about it. So long as she
felt it really was life and happiness, this *élan,* this tension
and excitement of "enjoying oneself."

Now suddenly she doubted the whole show. She attrib-
uted to it the curious numbness that was overcoming her,
as if she couldn't feel any more.

She wanted to come unwound. She wanted to escape
this battle of wills.

Only St. Mawr gave her some hint of the possibility.
He was so powerful, and so dangerous. But in his dark eye,
that looked, with its cloudy brown pupil, a cloud within
a dark fire, like a world beyond our world, there was a
dark vitality glowing, and within the fire, another sort of
wisdom. She felt sure of it: even when he put his ears
back, and bared his teeth, and his great eyes came bolting
out of his naked horse's head, and she saw demons upon
demons in the chaos of his horrid eyes.

Why did he seem to her like some living background,
into which she wanted to retreat? When he reared his
head and neighed from his deep chest, like deep wind-bells

resounding, she seemed to hear the echoes of another darker, more spacious, more dangerous, more splendid world than ours, that was beyond her. And there she wanted to go.

She kept it utterly a secret, to herself. Because Rico would just have lifted his long upper lip, in his bare face, in a condescending sort of "understanding." And her mother would, as usual, have suspected her of sidestepping. People, all the people she knew, seemed so entirely contained within their cardboard let's-be-happy world. Their wills were fixed like machines on happiness, or fun, or the-best-ever. This ghastly cheery-o! touch, that made all her blood go numb.

Since she had really seen St. Mawr looming fiery and terrible in an outer darkness, she could not believe the world she lived in. She could not believe it was actually happening, when she was dancing in the afternoon at Claridge's, or in the evening at the Carlton, sliding about with some suave young man who wasn't like a man at all to her. Or down in Sussex for the week-end with the Enderleys: the talk, the eating and drinking, the flirtation, the endless dancing: it all seemed far more bodiless and, in a strange way, wraithlike, than any fairy-story. She seemed to be eating Barmecide food, that had been conjured up out of thin air, by the power of words. She seemed to be talking to handsome young bare-faced unrealities, not men at all: as she slid about with them, in the perpetual dance, they too seemed to have been conjured up out of air, merely for this soaring, slithering dance-business. And she could not believe that, when the lights went out, they wouldn't melt back into thin air again, and complete nonentity. The strange nonentity of it all! Everything just conjured up, and nothing real. "*Isn't this the best ever!*" they would beamingly assert, like the wraiths of enjoyment, without any genuine substance. And she would beam back: "*Lots of fun!*"

She was thankful the season was over and everybody was leaving London. She and Rico were due to go to Scotland, but not till August. In the meantime they would go to her mother.

Mrs. Witt had taken a cottage in Shropshire, on the

Welsh border, and had moved down there with Phœnix and her horses. The open, heather-and-bilberry-covered hills were splendid for riding.

Rico consented to spend the month in Shropshire, because for near neighbours Mrs. Witt had the Manbys, at Corrabach Hall. The Manbys were rich Australians returned to the old country and set up as Squires, all in full blow. Rico had known them in Victoria: they were of good family: and the girls made a great fuss of him.

So down went Lou and Rico, Lewis, Poppy and St. Mawr, to Shrewsbury, then out into the country. Mrs. Witt's "cottage" was a tall red-brick Georgian house looking straight on to the churchyard, and the dark, looming big church.

"I never knew what a comfort it would be," said Mrs. Witt, "to have gravestones under my drawing-room windows, and funerals for lunch."

She really did take a strange pleasure in sitting in her panelled room, that was painted grey, and watching the Dean or one of the curates officiating at the graveside, among a group of black country mourners with black-bordered handkerchiefs luxuriantly in use.

"Mother!" said Lou. "I think it's gruesome!"

She had a room at the back, looking over the walled garden and the stables. Nevertheless there was the *boom! boom!* of the passing-bell, and the chiming and pealing on Sundays. The shadow of the church, indeed! A very audible shadow, making itself heard insistently.

The Dean was a big, burly, fat man with a pleasant manner. He was a gentleman, and a man of learning in his own line. But he let Mrs. Witt know that he looked down on her just a trifle—as a parvenu American, a Yankee—though she never was a Yankee: and at the same time he had a sincere respect for her, as a rich woman. Yes, a sincere respect for her, as a rich woman.

Lou knew that every Englishman, especially of the upper classes, has a wholesome respect for riches. But then, who hasn't?

The Dean was more *impressed* by Mrs. Witt than by little Lou. But to Lady Carrington he was charming: she was *almost* "one of us," you know. And he was very gracious to Rico: "your father's splendid colonial service."

Mrs. Witt had now a new pantomime to amuse her: the
Georgian house, her own pew in church—it went with the
old house: a village of thatched cottages—some of them
with corrugated iron over the thatch: the cottage people,
farm labourers and their families, with a few, very few,
outsiders: the wicked little group of cottages down at Mile
End, famous for ill living. The Mile-Enders were all Alli-
sons and Jephsons, and inbred, the Dean said: result of
working through the centuries at the quarry, and living
isolated there at Mile End.

Isolated! Imagine it! A mile and a half from the railway
station, ten miles from Shrewsbury. Mrs. Witt thought of
Texas, and said:

"Yes, they are *very* isolated, away down there!"

And the Dean never for a moment suspected sarcasm.

But there she had the whole thing staged complete for
her: English village life. Even miners breaking in to shat-
ter the rather stuffy, unwholesome harmony.—All the men
touched their caps to her, all the women did a bit of a
reverence, the children stood aside for her, if she appeared
in the street.

They were all poor again: the labourers could no longer
afford even a glass of beer in the evenings, since the Glorious War.

"Now I think that *is* terrible," said Mrs. Witt. "Not to
be able to get away from those stuffy, squalid, picturesque
cottages for an hour in the evening, to drink a glass of
beer."

"It's a pity, I do agree with you, Mrs. Witt. But Mr.
Watson has organized a men's reading-room, where the
men can smoke and play dominoes, and read if they wish."

"But that," said Mrs. Witt, "is not the same as that cosy
parlour in the 'Moon and Stars.' "

"I quite agree," said the Dean. "It isn't."

Mrs. Witt marched to the landlord of the "Moon and
Stars," and asked for a glass of cider.

"I want," she said, in her American accent, "these poor
labourers to have their glass of beer in the evenings."

"They want it themselves," said Harvey.

"Then they must have it——"

The upshot was, she decided to supply one large barrel of beer per week and the landlord was to sell it to the labourers at a penny a glass.

"My own country has gone dry," she asserted. "But not because we can't *afford* it."

By the time Lou and Rico appeared, she was deep in. She actually interfered very little: the barrel of beer was her one public act. But she *did* know everybody by sight, already, and she *did* know everybody's circumstances. And she had attended one prayer-meeting, one mother's meeting, one sewing-bee, one "social," one Sunday School meeting, one Band of Hope meeting, and one Sunday School treat. She ignored the poky little Wesleyan and Baptist chapels, and was true-blue Episcopalian.

"How strange these picturesque old villages are, Louise!" she said, with a duskiness around her sharp, well-bred nose. "How *easy* it all seems, all on a definite pattern. And how false! And underneath, *how corrupt!*"

She gave that queer, triumphant leer from her grey eyes, and queer demonish wrinkles seemed to twitter on her face.

Lou shrank away. She was beginning to be afraid of her mother's insatiable curiosity, that always looked for the snake under the flowers. Or rather, for the maggots.

Always this same morbid interest in other people and their doings, their privacies, their dirty linen. Always this air of alertness for personal happenings, personalities, personalities, personalities. Always this subtle criticism and appraisal of other people, this analysis of other people's motives. If anatomy presupposes a corpse, then psychology presupposes a world of corpses. Personalities, which means personal criticism and analysis, presupposes a whole world-laboratory of human psyches waiting to be vivisected. If you cut a thing up, of course it will smell. Hence, nothing raises such an infernal stink, at last, as human psychology.

Mrs. Witt was a pure psychologist, a fiendish psychologist. And Rico, in his way, was a psychologist too. But he had a formula. "Let's *know* the worst, dear! But let's look on the bright side, and believe the best."

"Isn't the Dean a priceless old darling!" said Rico at breakfast.

And it had begun. Work had started in the psychic vivi-section laboratory.

"Isn't he wonderful!" said Lou vaguely.

"So delightfully worldly!—*Some of us are not born to make money, dear boy. Luckily for us, we can marry it.*" —Rico made a priceless face.

"Is Mrs. Vyner so rich?" asked Lou.

"She is, quite a wealthy woman—in coal," replied Mrs. Witt. "But the Dean is surely worth his weight, even in gold. And he's a massive figure. I can imagine there would be great satisfaction in having him for a husband."

"Why, mother?" asked Lou.

"Oh, such a presence! One of these old Englishmen, that nobody can put in their pocket. You can't imagine his wife asking him to thread her needle. Something, after all, so *robust!* So different from *young* Englishmen, who all seem to me like ladies, perfect ladies."

"*Somebody* has to keep up the tradition of the perfect lady," said Rico.

"I know it," said Mrs. Witt. "And if the women won't do it, the young gentlemen take on the burden. They bear it very well."

It was in full swing, the cut and thrust. And poor Lou, who had reached the point of stupefaction in the game, felt she did not know what to do with herself.

Rico and Mrs. Witt were deadly enemies, yet neither could keep clear of the other. It might have been they who were married to one another, their duel and their duet were so relentless.

But Rico immediately started the social round: first the Manbys: then motor twenty miles to luncheon at Lady Tewkesbury's: then young Mr. Burns came flying down in his aeroplane from Chester: then they must motor to the sea, to Sir Edward Edwards' place, where there was a moonlight bathing-party. Everything intensely thrilling, and so innerly wearisome, Lou felt.

But back of it all was St. Mawr, looming like a bonfire in the dark. He really was a tiresome horse to own. He

worried the mares, if they were in the same paddock with
him, always driving them round. And with any other horse
he just fought with definite intent to kill. So he had to stay
alone.

"That St. Mawr, he's a bad horse," said Phœnix.

"Maybe!" said Lewis.

"You don't like quiet horses?" said Phœnix.

"Most horses _is_ quiet," said Lewis. "St. Mawr, he's different."

"Why don't he never get any foals?"

"Doesn't want to, I should think. Same as me."

"What good is a horse like that? Better shoot him, before he kill somebody."

"What good'll they get, shooting St. Mawr?" said Lewis.

"If he kills somebody!" said Phœnix.

But there was no answer.

The two grooms both lived over the stables, and Lou,
from her window, saw a good deal of them. They were
two quiet men, yet she was very much aware of their
presence, aware of Phœnix's rather high square shoulders
and his fine, straight, vigorous black hair that tended to
stand up assertively on his head, as he went quietly drifting about his various jobs. He was not lazy, but he did
everything with a sort of diffidence, as if from a distance,
and handled his horses carefully, cautiously, and cleverly,
but without sympathy. He seemed to be holding something back, all the time, unconsciously, as if in his very
being there was some secret. But it was a secret of _will_.
His quiet, reluctant movements, as if he never really
wanted to do anything; his long flat-stepping stride; the
permanent challenge in his high cheek-bones, the Indian
glint in his eyes, and his peculiar stare, watchful and yet
unseeing, made him unpopular with the women servants.

Nevertheless, women had a certain fascination for him:
he would stare at the pretty young maids with an intent
blank stare, when they were not looking. Yet he was rather
overbearing, domineering with them, and they resented
him. It was evident to Lou that he looked upon himself as
belonging to the Master, not to the servant class. When he
flirted with the maids, as he very often did, for he had a
certain crude ostentatiousness, he seemed to let them feel

that he despised them as inferiors, servants, while he admired their pretty charms, as fresh country maids.

"I'm fair nervous of that Phœnix," said Fanny, the fair-haired maid. "He makes you feel what he'd do to you if he could."

"He'd better not try with me," said Mabel. "I'd scratch his cheeky eyes out. Cheek!—for it's nothing else! He's nobody—common as they're made!"

"He makes you feel you was there for him to trample on," said Fanny.

"Mercy, you *are* soft! If anybody's that, it's him. Oh, my, Fanny, you've no right to let a fellow make you feel like *that!* Make *them* feel that *they're* dirt, for *you* to trample on: which they are!"

Fanny, however, being a shy little blond thing, wasn't good at assuming the trampling rôle. She was definitely nervous of Phœnix. And he enjoyed it. An invisible smile seemed to creep up his cheek-bones, and the glint moved in his eyes as he teased her. He tormented her by his very presence, as he knew.

He would come silently up when she was busy, and stand behind her perfectly still, so that she was unaware of his presence. Then, silently, he would *make* her aware. Till she glanced nervously round and, with a scream, saw him.

One day Lou watched this little play. Fanny had been picking over a bowl of black currants, sitting on the bench under the maple-tree in a corner of the yard. She didn't look round till she had picked up her bowl to go to the kitchen. Then there was a scream and a crash.

When Lou came out, Phœnix was crouching down silently gathering up the currants, which the little maid, scarlet and trembling, was collecting into another bowl. Phœnix seemed to be smiling down his back.

"Phœnix!" said Lou. "I wish you wouldn't startle Fanny!"

He looked up, and she saw the glint of ridicule in his eyes.

"Who, me?" he said.

"Yes, you. You go up behind Fanny, to startle her. You're not to do it."

He slowly stood erect, and lapsed into his peculiar invisible silence. Only for a second his eyes glanced at Lou's, and then she saw the cold anger, the gleam of malevolence and contempt. He could not bear being commanded, or reprimanded, by a woman.

Yet it was even worse with a man.

"What's that, Lou?" said Rico, appearing all handsome and in the picture, in white flannels with an apricot silk shirt.

"I'm telling Phœnix he's not to torment Fanny!"

"Oh!" and Rico's voice immediately became his father's, the important government official's. "Certainly *not!* Most certainly *not!*" He looked at the scattered currants and the broken bowl. Fanny melted into tears. "This, I suppose, is some of the results! Now look here, Phœnix, you're to leave the maids strictly alone. I shall ask them to report to me whenever, or *if* ever, you interfere with them. But I hope you *won't* interfere with them—in any way. You understand?"

As Rico became more and more Sir Henry and the government official, Lou's bones melted more and more into discomfort. Phœnix stood in his peculiar silence, the invisible smile on his cheek-bones.

"You understand what I'm saying to you?" Rico demanded, in intensified acid tones.

But Phœnix only stood there, as it were behind a cover of his own will, and looked back at Rico with a faint smile on his face and the glint moving in his eyes.

"Do you intend to answer?" Rico's upper lip lifted nastily.

"Mrs. Witt is my boss," came from Phœnix.

The scarlet flew up Rico's throat and flushed his face, his eyes went glaucous. Then quickly his face turned yellow.

Lou looked at the two men: her husband, whose rages, over-controlled, were organically terrible; the half-breed, whose dark-coloured lips were widened in a faint smile of derision, but in whose eyes caution and hate were playing against one another. She realized that Phœnix would accept *her* reprimand, or her mother's, because he could de-

spise the two of them as mere women. But Rico's bossiness
aroused murder pure and simple.

She took her husband's arm.

"Come, dear!" she said, in her half plaintive way. "I'm
sure Phœnix understands. We all understand. Go to the
kitchen, Fanny, never mind the currants. There are plenty
more in the garden."

Rico was always thankful to be drawn quickly, submis-
sively away from his own rage. He was afraid of it. He
was afraid lest he should fly at the groom in some horrible
fashion. The very thought horrified him. But in actuality
he came very near to it.

He walked stiffly, feeling paralysed by his own fury.
And those words, *Mrs. Witt is my boss,* were like hot acid
in his brain. An insult!

"By the way, Belle-Mère!" he said when they joined
Mrs. Witt—she hated being called Belle-Mère, and once
said: "If I'm the bell-mare, are you one of the colts?"—
she also hated his voice of smothered fury—"I had to
speak to Phœnix about persecuting the maids. He took
the liberty of informing me that you were his boss, so perhaps you had better speak to him."

"I certainly will. I believe they're my maids, and nobody
else's, so it's my duty to look after them. Who was he persecuting?"

"I'm the responsible one, mother," said Lou——

Rico disappeared in a moment. He must get out: get
away from the house. How? Something was wrong with
the car. Yet he must get away, away. He would go over
to Corrabach. He would ride St. Mawr. He had been talking about the horse, and Flora Manby was dying to see
him. She had said: "Oh, I can't *wait* to see that marvellous
horse of yours."

He would ride him over. It was only seven miles. He
found Lou's maid Flena, and sent her to tell Lewis. Meanwhile, to soothe himself, he dressed himself most carefully
in white riding-breeches and a shirt of purple silk crêpe,
with a flowing black tie spotted red like a ladybird, and
black riding-boots. Then he took a *chic* little white hat
with a black band.

St. Mawr was saddled and waiting, and Lewis had saddled a second horse.

"Thanks, Lewis, I'm going alone!" said Rico.

This was the first time he had ridden St. Mawr in the country, and he was nervous. But he was also in the hell of a smothered fury. All his careful dressing had not really soothed him. So his fury consumed his nervousness.

He mounted with a swing, blind and rough. St. Mawr reared.

"Stop that!" snarled Rico, and put him to the gate.

Once out in the village street, the horse went dancing sideways. He insisted on dancing at the sidewalk, to the exaggerated terror of the children. Rico, exasperated, pulled him across. But no, he wouldn't go down the centre of the village street. He began dancing and edging on to the other sidewalk, so the foot-passengers fled into the shops in terror.

The devil was in him. He would turn down every turning where he was not meant to go. He reared with panic at a furniture van. He *insisted* on going down the wrong side of the road. Rico was riding him with a martingale, and he could see the rolling, bloodshot eye.

"Damn you, *go!*" said Rico, giving him a dig with the spurs.

And away they went, down the high road, in a thunderbolt. It was a hot day, with thunder threatening, so Rico was soon in a flame of heat. He held on tight, with fixed eyes, trying all the time to rein in the horse. What he really was afraid of was that the brute would shy suddenly, as he galloped. Watching for this, he didn't care when they sailed past the turning to Corrabach.

St. Mawr flew on, in a sort of *élan*. Marvellous, the power and life in the creature! There was really a great joy in the motion. If only he wouldn't take the corners at a gallop, nearly swerving Rico off! Luckily the road was clear. To ride, to ride at this terrific gallop, on into eternity!

After several miles, the horse slowed down, and Rico managed to pull him into a lane that might lead to Corrabach. When all was said and done, it was a wonderful ride. St. Mawr could go like the wind, but with that luxurious heavy ripple of life which is like nothing else on earth. It seemed to carry one at once into another world, away from the life of the nerves.

So Rico arrived after all something of a conqueror at Corrabach. To be sure, he was perspiring, and so was his horse. But he was a hero from another, heroic world.

"Oh, such a hot ride!" he said, as he walked on to the lawn at Corrabach Hall. "Between the sun and the horse, really!—between two fires!"

"Don't you trouble, you're looking dandy, a bit hot and flushed like," said Flora Manby. "Let's go and see your horse."

And her exclamation was: "Oh, he's *lovely!* He's *fine!* I'd love to try him once——"

Rico decided to accept the invitation to stay overnight at Corrabach. Usually he was very careful, and refused to stay, unless Lou was with him. But they telephoned to the post office at Chomesbury, would Mr. Jones please send a message to Lady Carrington that Sir Henry was staying the night at Corrabach Hall, but would be home next day? Mr. Jones received the request with unction, and said he would go over himself to give the message to Lady Carrington.

Lady Carrington was in the walled garden. The peculiarity of Mrs. Witt's house was that, for grounds proper, it had the churchyard.

"I never thought, Louise, that one day I should have an old English churchyard for my lawns and shrubbery and park, and funeral mourners for my herds of deer. It's curious. For the first time in my life a funeral has become a real thing to me. I feel I could write a book on them."

But Louise only felt intimidated.

At the back of the house was a flagged court-yard, with stables and a maple-tree in a corner, and big doors opening on to the village street. But at the side was a walled garden, with fruit-trees and currant-bushes and a great bed of rhubarb, and some tufts of flowers, peonies, pink roses, sweet-williams. Phœnix, who had a certain taste for gardening, would be out there thinning the carrots or tying up the lettuce. He was not lazy. Only he would not take

work seriously, as a job. He would be quite amused tying
up lettuces, and would tie up head after head, quite pret-
tily. Then, becoming bored, he would abandon his task,
light a cigarette, and go and stand on the threshold of the
big doors, in full view of the street, watching, and yet completely indifferent.

After Rico's departure on St. Mawr, Lou went into the
garden. And there she saw Phœnix working in the onion-
bed. He was bending over, in his own silence, busy with
nimble, amused fingers among the grassy young onions.
She thought he had not seen her, so she went down another path to where a swing bed hung under the apple-
trees. There she sat with a book and a bundle of maga-
zines. But she did not read.

She was musing vaguely. Vaguely, she was glad that
Rico was away for a while. Vaguely, she felt a sense of
bitterness, of complete futility: the complete futility of
her living. This left her drifting in a sea of utter chagrin.
And Rico seemed to her the symbol of the futility.
Vaguely, she was aware that something else existed, but
she didn't know where it was or what it was.

In the distance she could see Phœnix's dark, rather tall-
built head, with its black, fine, intensely living hair tend-
ing to stand on end, like a brush with long, very fine black
bristles. His hair, she thought, betrayed him as an animal
of a different species. He was growing a little bored by
weeding onions: that also she could tell. Soon he would
want some other amusement.

Presently Lewis appeared. He was small, energetic, a
little bit bow-legged, and he walked with a slight strut.
He wore khaki riding-breeches, leather gaiters, and a blue
shirt. And, like Phœnix, he rarely had any cap or hat on
his head. His thick black hair was parted at the side and
brushed over heavily sideways, dropping on his forehead
at the right. It was very long, a real mop, under which
his eyebrows were dark and steady.

"Seen Lady Carrington?" he asked of Phœnix.

"Yes, she's sitting on that swing over there—she's been
there quite awhile."

The wretch—he had seen her from the very first!

Lewis came striding over, looking towards her with his

pale-grey eyes, from under his mop of hair.

"Mr. Jones from the post office wants to see you, my Lady, with a message from Sir Henry."

Instantly alarm took possession of Lou's soul.

"Oh!—Does he want to see me personally?—What message? Is anything wrong?"—And her voice trailed out over the last word, with a sort of anxious nonchalance.

"I don't think it's anything amiss," said Lewis reassuringly.

"Oh! You don't"—the relief came into her voice. Then she looked at Lewis with a slight, winning smile in her unmatched eyes. "I'm so afraid of St. Mawr, you know." Her voice was soft and cajoling. Phœnix was listening in the distance.

"St. Mawr's all right, if you don't do nothing to him," Lewis replied.

"I'm sure he is!—But how is one to know when one is doing something to him?—Tell Mr. Jones to come here, please," she concluded, on a changed tone.

Mr. Jones, a man of forty-five, thickset, with a fresh complexion and rather foolish brown eyes, and a big brown moustache, came prancing down the path, smiling rather fatuously, and doffing his straw hat with a gorgeous bow the moment he saw Lou sitting in her slim white frock on the coloured swing bed under the trees with their hard green apples.

"Good morning, Mr. Jones!"

"Good morning, Lady Carrington.—If I may say so, what a picture you make—a beautiful picture——"

He beamed under his big brown moustache like the greatest lady-killer.

"Do I!—Did Sir Henry say he was all right?"

"He didn't *say* exactly, but I should expect he is all right——" and Mr. Jones delivered his message, in the mayonnaise of his own unction.

"Thank you so much, Mr. Jones. It's awfully good of you to come and tell me. Now I shan't worry about Sir Henry *at all*."

"It's a great pleasure to come and deliver a satisfactory message to Lady Carrington. But it won't be kind to Sir Henry if you don't worry about him *at all* in his absence.

We all enjoy being worried about by those we love—so long as there is nothing to worry about of course!"

"Quite!" said Lou. "Now won't you take a glass of port and a biscuit, or a whisky and soda? And thank you ever so much."

"Thank *you*, my Lady. I might drink a whisky and soda, since you are so good."

And he beamed fatuously.

"Let Mr. Jones mix himself a whisky and soda, Lewis," said Lou.

"Heavens!" she thought, as the postmaster retreated a little uncomfortably down the garden path, his bald spot passing in and out of the sun, under the trees. "How ridiculous everything is, how ridiculous, ridiculous!" Yet she didn't really dislike Mr. Jones and his interlude.

Phœnix was melting away out of the garden. He had to follow the fun.

"Phœnix!" Lou called. "Bring me a glass of water, will you? Or send somebody with it."

He stood in the path looking round at her.

"All right!" he said.

And he turned away again.

She did not like being alone in the garden. She liked to have the men working somewhere near. Curious how pleasant it was to sit there in the garden when Phœnix was about, or Lewis. It made her feel she could never be lonely or jumpy. But when Rico was there, she was all aching nerve.

Phœnix came back with a glass of water, lemon juice, sugar, and a small bottle of brandy. He knew Lou liked a spoonful of brandy in her iced lemonade.

"How thoughtful of you, Phœnix!" she said. "Did Mr. Jones get his whisky?"

"He was just getting it."

"That's right.—By the way, Phœnix, I wish you wouldn't get mad if Sir Henry speaks to you. He is *really* so kind."

She looked up at the man. He stood there watching her in silence, the invisible smile on his face, and the inscrutable Indian glint moving in his eyes. What was he thinking? There was something passive and almost submissive about him, but, underneath this, an unyielding resistance and cruelty: yes, even cruelty. She felt that, on top, he was submissive and attentive, bringing her her lemonade as she liked it, without being told: thinking for her quite subtly. But underneath there was an unchanging hatred. He submitted circumstantially, he worked for a wage. And, even circumstantially, he *liked* his mistress—*la patrona*—and her daughter. But much deeper than any circumstance, or any circumstantial liking, was the categorical hatred upon which he was founded, and with which he was powerless. His liking for Lou and for Mrs. Witt, his serving them and working for a wage, was all sidetracking his own nature, which was grounded on hatred of their very existence. But what was he to do? He had to live. Therefore he had to serve, to work for a wage, and even to be faithful.

And yet *their* existence made his own existence negative. If he was to exist, positively, they would have to cease to exist. At the same time, a fatal sort of tolerance made him serve these women, and go on serving.

"Sir Henry is *so* kind to everybody," Lou insisted.

The half-breed met her eyes, and smiled uncomfortably.

"Yes, he's a kind man," he replied, as if sincerely.

"Then why do you mind if he speaks to you?"

"I don't mind," said Phœnix glibly.

"But you do. Or else you wouldn't make him so angry."

"Was he angry?—I don't know," said Phœnix.

"He was very angry. And you *do* know."

"No, I don't know if he's angry. I don't know," the fellow persisted. And there was a glib sort of satisfaction in his tone.

"That's awfully unkind of you, Phœnix," she said, growing offended in her turn.

"No, I don't know if he's angry. I don't want to make him angry. I don't know——"

He had taken on a tone of naïve ignorance, which at once gratified her pride as a woman, and deceived her.

"Well, you believe me when I tell you you *did* make him angry, don't you?"

"Yes, I believe when you tell me."

"And you promise me, won't you, not to do it again?

It's *so* bad for him—so bad for his nerves, and for his eyes.
It makes them inflamed, and injures his eyesight. And you
know, as an artist, it's terrible if anything happens to his
eyesight——"

Phœnix was watching her closely, to take it in. He still
was not good at understanding continuous, logical state-
ment. Logical connexion in speech seemed to stupefy him,
make him stupid. He understood in disconnected asser-
tions of fact. But he had gathered what she said. "He gets
mad at you. When he gets mad, it hurts his eyes. His eyes
hurt him. He can't see, because his eyes hurt him. He
wants to paint a picture, he can't. He can't paint a picture,
he can't see clear——"

Yes, he had understood. She saw he had understood.
The bright glint of satisfaction moved in his eyes.

"So now promise me, won't you, you won't make him
mad again: you won't make him angry?"

"No, I won't make him angry. I don't do anything to
make him angry," Phœnix answered, rather glibly.

"And you do understand, don't you? You do know how
kind he is: how he'd do a good turn to anybody?"

"Yes, he's a kind man," said Phœnix.

"I'm so glad you realize.—There, that's luncheon! How
nice it is to sit here in the garden, when everybody is nice
to you! No, I can carry the tray, don't you bother."

But he took the tray from her hand, and followed her
to the house. And as he walked behind her, he watched
the slim white nape of her neck, beneath the clustering of
her bobbed hair, something as a stoat watches a rabbit he
is following.

In the afternoon Lou retreated once more to her place
in the garden. There she lay, sitting with a bunch of pil-
lows behind her, neither reading nor working, just musing.
She had learned the new joy: to do absolutely nothing,
but to lie and let the sunshine filter through the leaves, to
see the bunch of red-hot-poker flowers pierce scarlet into
the afternoon, beside the comparative neutrality of some
foxgloves. The mere colour of hard red, like the big oriental poppies that had fallen, and these poker flowers,
lingered in her consciousness like a communication.

Into this peaceful indolence, when even the big, dark-grey tower of the church beyond the wall and the yew-trees was keeping its bells in silence, advanced Mrs. Witt, in a broad panama hat and a white dress.

"Don't you want to ride, or do something, Louise?" she asked ominously.

"Don't you want to be peaceful, mother?" retorted Louise.

"Yes—an *active* peace.—I can't *believe* that my daughter can be content to lie on a hammock and do *nothing*, not even read or improve her mind, the greater part of the day."

"Well, your daughter *is* content to do that. It's her greatest pleasure."

"I know it. I can see it. And it surprises me *very* much. When I was your age, I was never still. I had so much go——"

> " 'Those maids, thank God,
>   Are 'neath the sod,
>   And all their generation.'

"No, but mother, I only take life differently. Perhaps you used up that sort of *go*. I'm the harem type, mother: only I never want the men inside the lattice."

"Are you really my daughter?—Well! A woman never knows what will happen to her.—I'm an *American* woman, and I suppose I've got to remain one, no matter where I am.—What did you want, Lewis?"

The groom had approached down the path.

"If I am to saddle Poppy?" said Lewis.

"No, apparently *not!*" replied Mrs. Witt. "Your mistress prefers the hammock to the saddle."

"Thank you, Lewis. What mother says is true this afternoon, at least." And she gave him a peculiar little cross-eyed smile.

"Who," said Mrs. Witt to the man, "has been cutting at your hair?"

There was a moment of silent resentment.

"I did it myself, Mam! Sir Henry said it was too long."

"He certainly spoke the truth.—But I believe there's

a barber in the village on Saturdays—or you could ride over to Shrewsbury.—Just turn round, and let me look at the back. Is it the money?"

"No, Mam. I don't like these fellows touching my head."

He spoke coldly, with a certain hostile reserve that at once piqued Mrs. Witt.

"Don't you really!" she said. "But it's quite *impossible* for you to go about as you are. It gives you a half-witted appearance. Go now into the yard, and get a chair and a dust-sheet. I'll cut your hair."

The man hesitated, hostile.

"Don't be afraid, I know how it's done. I've cut the hair of many a poor wounded boy in hospital: and shaved them too. *You've got such a touch, nurse!* Poor fellow, he was dying, though none of us knew it.—Those are compliments I value, Louise.—Get that chair now, and a dust-sheet. I'll borrow your hair-scissors from Elena, Louise."

Mrs. Witt, happily on the war-path, was herself again. She didn't care for work, actual work. But she loved trimming. She loved arranging unnatural and pretty salads, devising new and piquant-looking ice-creams, having a turkey stuffed exactly as she knew a stuffed turkey in Louisiana, with chestnuts and butter and stuff, or showing a servant how to turn waffles on a waffle-iron, or to bake a ham with brown sugar and cloves and a moistening of rum. She liked pruning rose-trees, or beginning to cut a yew-hedge into shape. She liked ordering her own and Louise's shoes, with an exactitude and a knowledge of shoemaking that sent the salesmen crazy. She was a demon in shoes. Reappearing from America, she would pounce on her daughter. "Louise, throw those shoes away. Give them to one of the maids."—"But, mother, they are some of the best French shoes. I like them."—"Throw them away. A shoe has only two excuses for existing: perfect comfort or perfect appearance. Those have neither. I have brought you some shoes."—Yes, she had brought ten pairs of shoes from New York. She knew her daughter's foot as she knew her own.

So now she was in her element, looming behind Lewis as he sat in the middle of the yard swathed in a dust-sheet. She had on an overall and a pair of wash-leather gloves,

and she poised a pair of long scissors like one of the fates.
In her big hat she looked curiously young, but with the
youth of a bygone generation. Her heavy-lidded, laconic
grey eyes were alert, studying the groom's black mop of
hair. Her eyebrows made thin, uptilting black arches on
her brow. Her fresh skin was slightly powdered, and she
was really handsome, in a bold, bygone, eighteenth-century style. Some of the curious, adventurous stoicism of
the eighteenth century: and then a certain blatant American efficiency.

Lou, who had strayed into the yard to see, looked so
much younger and so many thousands of years older than
her mother, as she stood in her wisp-like diffidence, the
clusters of grape-like bobbed hair hanging beside her face,
with its fresh colouring and its ancient weariness, her
slightly squinting eyes, that were so disillusioned they were
becoming faun-like.

"Not too short, mother, not too short!" she remon-
strated, as Mrs. Witt, with a terrific flourish of efficiency,
darted at the man's black hair, and the thick flakes fell like
black snow.

"Now, Louise, I'm right in this job, please don't interfere.—Two things I hate to see: a man with his wool in
his neck and ears: and a bare-faced young man who looks
as if he'd bought his face as well as his hair from a men's
beauty-specialist."

And efficiently she bent down, clip—clip—clipping!
while Lewis sat utterly immobile, with sunken head, in a
sort of despair.

Phœnix stood against the stable door, with his restless,
eternal cigarette. And in the kitchen doorway the maids
appeared and fled, appeared and fled in delight. The old
gardener, a fixture who went with the house, creaked in
and stood with his legs apart, silent in intense condemnation.

"First time I ever see such a thing!" he muttered to
himself, as he creaked on into the garden. He was a bad-
tempered old soul, who thoroughly disapproved of the
household, and would have given notice, but that he knew
which side his bread was buttered: and there was butter
unstinted on his bread, in Mrs. Witt's kitchen.

Mrs. Witt stood back to survey her handiwork, holding those terrifying shears with their beak erect. Lewis lifted his head and looked stealthily round, like a creature in a trap.

"Keep still!" she said. "I haven't finished."

And she went for his front hair, with vigour, lifting up long layers and snipping off the ends artistically: till at last he sat with a black aureole upon the floor, and his ears standing out with curious new alertness from the sides of his clean-clipped head.

"Stand up," she said, "and let me look."

He stood up, looking absurdly young, with the hair all cut away from his neck and ears, left thick only on top. She surveyed her work with satisfaction.

"You look so much younger," she said, "you would be surprised. Sit down again."

She clipped the back of his neck with the shears, and then, with a very slight hesitation, she said:

"Now about the beard!"

But the man rose suddenly from the chair, pulling the dust-cloth from his neck with desperation.

"No, I'll do that myself," he said, looking her in the eyes with a cold light in his pale-grey, uncanny eyes.

She hesitated in a kind of wonder at his queer male rebellion.

"Now, listen, I shall do it much better than you—and besides," she added hurriedly, snatching at the dust-cloth he was flinging on the chair, "I haven't quite finished round the ears."

"I think I shall do," he said, again looking her in the eyes, with a cold, white gleam of finality. "Thank you for what you've done."

And he walked away to the stable.

"You'd better sweep up here," Mrs. Witt called.

"Yes, Mam," he replied, looking round at her again with an odd resentment, but continuing to walk away.

"However!" said Mrs. Witt. "I suppose he'll do."

And she divested herself of gloves and overall, and walked indoors to wash and to change. Lou went indoors too.

"It is extraordinary what hair that man has!" said Mrs.

Witt. "Did I tell you when I was in Paris I saw a woman's face in the hotel that I thought I knew? I couldn't place her, till she was coming towards me. *Aren't you Rachel Fannière?* she said. *Aren't you Janette Leroy?* We hadn't seen each other since we were girls of twelve and thirteen, at school in New Orleans. *Oh!* she said to me. *Is every illusion doomed to perish? You had such wonderful golden curls! All my life I've said: Oh, if only I had such lovely hair as Rachel Fannière! I've seen those beautiful golden curls of yours all my life. And now I meet you, you're grey!* Wasn't that terrible, Louise? Well, that man's hair made me think of it—so thick and curious. It's strange what a difference there is in hair, I suppose it's because he's just an animal—no mind! There's nothing I admire in a man like a good *mind*. Your father was a very clever man, and all the men I've admired have been clever. But isn't it curious now, I've never cared much to touch their hair. How strange life is! If it gives one thing, it takes away another.—And even those poor boys in hospital: I have shaved them, or cut their hair, like a mother, never thinking anything of it. Lovely, intelligent, clean boys most of them were. Yet it never did anything to me. I never knew before that something could happen to one from a person's *hair!* Like to Janette Leroy from my curls when I was a child. And now I'm grey, as she says.—I wonder how old a man Lewis is, Louise! Didn't he look absurdly young, with his ears pricking up?"

"I think Rico said he was forty or forty-one."

"And never been married?"

"No—not as far as I know."

"Isn't that curious now!—just an animal! no mind! A man with no mind! I've always thought that the *most* despicable thing. Yet such wonderful hair to touch. Your Henry has quite a good mind, yet I would simply shrink from touching his hair.—I suppose one likes stroking a cat's fur, just the same. Just the animal in man. Curious that I never seem to have met it, Louise. Now I come to think of it, he has the eyes of a human cat: a human tom-cat. Would you call him stupid? Yes, he's very stupid."

"No, mother, he's not stupid. He only doesn't care about our sort of things."

"Like an animal! But what a strange look he has in his eyes! a strange sort of intelligence! and a confidence in himself. Isn't that curious, Louise, in a man with as little mind as he has? Do you know, I should say he could see through a woman pretty well."

"Why, mother!" said Lou impatiently. "I think one gets so tired of your men with mind, as you call it. There are so many of that sort of clever men. And there are lots of men who aren't very clever, but are rather nice: and lots are stupid. It seems to me there's something else besides mind and cleverness, or niceness or cleanness. Perhaps it is the animal. Just think of St. Mawr! I've thought so much about him. We call him an animal, but we never know what it means. He seems a far greater mystery to me than a clever man. He's a horse. Why can't one say in the same way, of a man: *He's a man?* There seems no mystery in being a man. But there's a terrible mystery in St. Mawr."

Mrs. Witt watched her daughter quizzically.

"Louise," she said, "you won't tell me that the mere animal is all that counts in a man. I will never believe it. Man is wonderful because he is able to *think*."

"But is he?" cried Lou, with sudden exasperation. "Their thinking seems to me all so childish: like stringing the same beads over and over again. Ah, men! They and their thinking are all so *paltry*. How can you be impressed?"

Mrs. Witt raised her eyebrows sardonically.

"Perhaps I'm not—any more," she said with a grim smile.

"But," she added, "I still can't see that I am to be impressed by the mere animal in man. The animals are the same as we are. It seems to me they have the same feelings and wants as we do, in a commonplace way. The only difference is that they have no minds: no human minds, at least. And no matter what you say, Louise, lack of mind makes the commonplace."

Lou knitted her brows nervously.

"I suppose it does, mother.—But men's minds *are* so commonplace: look at Dean Vyner and his mind! Or look at Arthur Balfour, as a shining example. Isn't *that* com-

monplace, that cleverness? I would hate St. Mawr to be
spoilt by such a mind."

"Yes, Louise, so would I. Because the men you mention
are really old women, knitting the same pattern over and
over again. Nevertheless, I shall never alter my belief that
real mind is all that matters in a man, and it's *that* that we
women love."

"Yes, mother!—But what *is* real mind? The old woman
who knits the most complicated pattern? Oh, I can hear
all their needles clicking, the clever men! As a matter of
fact, mother, I believe Lewis has far more real mind than
Dean Vyner or any of the clever ones. He has a good in-
tuitive mind, he knows things without thinking them."

"That may be, Louise! But he is a servant. He is *under*.
A real man should never be under. And then you could
never be intimate with a man like Lewis."

"I don't want intimacy, mother. I'm too tired of it all.
I love St. Mawr because he isn't intimate. He stands where
one can't get at him. And he burns with life. And where
does his life come from, to him? That's the mystery. That
great burning life in him, which never is dead. Most men
have a deadness in them that frightens me so, because of
my own deadness. Why can't men get their life straight,
like St. Mawr, and then think? Why can't they think quick,
mother: quick as a woman: only farther than we do? Why
isn't men's thinking quick like fire, mother? Why is it so
slow, so dead, so deadly dull?"

"I can't tell you, Louise. My own opinion of the men of
to-day has grown very small. But I can live in spite of it."

"No, mother. We seem to be living off old fuel, like the
camel when he lives off his hump. Life doesn't rush into
us, as it does even into St. Mawr, and he's a dependent
animal. I can't live, mother. I just can't."

"I don't see why not. *I'm* full of life."

"I know you are, mother. But I'm not, and I'm your
daughter.—And don't misunderstand me, mother. I don't
want to be an animal like a horse or a cat or a lioness,
though they all fascinate me, the way they get their life
straight, not from a lot of old tanks, as we do. I don't admire the cave-man, and that sort of thing. But think,

mother, if we could get our lives straight from the source, as the animals do, and still be ourselves. You don't like men yourself. But you've no idea how men just tire me out: even the very thought of them. You say they are too animal. But they're not, mother. It's the animal in them has gone perverse, or cringing, or humble, or domesticated, like dogs. I don't know one single man who is a proud living animal. I know they've left off really thinking. But then men always do leave off really thinking, when the last bit of wild animal dies in them."

"Because we have minds——"

"We have no minds once we are tame, mother. Men are all women, knitting and crocheting words together."

"I can't altogether agree, you know, Louise."

"I know you don't.—You like clever men. But clever men are mostly such unpleasant *animals*. As animals, so very unpleasant. And in men like Rico, the animal has gone queer and wrong. And in those nice clean boys you liked so much in the war, there is no wild animal left in them. They're all tame dogs, even when they're brave and well-bred. They're all tame dogs, mother, with human masters. There's no mystery in them."

"What do you want, Louise? You *do* want the caveman who'll knock you on the head with a club."

"Don't be silly, mother. That's much more your subconscious line, you admirer of Mind.—I don't consider the cave-man is a real human animal at all. He's a brute, a degenerate. A pure animal man would be as lovely as a deer or a leopard, burning like a flame fed straight from underneath. And he'd be part of the unseen, like a mouse is, even. And he'd never cease to wonder, he'd breathe silence and unseen wonder, as the partridges do, running in the stubble. He'd be all the animals in turn, instead of one fixed, automatic thing, which he is now, grinding on the nerves.—Ah, no, mother, I want the wonder back again, or I shall die. I don't want to be like you, just criticizing and annihilating these dreary people, and enjoying it."

"My dear daughter, whatever else the human animal might be, he'd be a dangerous commodity."

"I wish he would, mother. I'm dying of these empty, dangerless men, who are only sentimental and spiteful."

"Nonsense, you're not dying."

"I am, mother. And I should be dead if there weren't St. Mawr and Phœnix and Lewis in the world."

"St. Mawr and Phœnix and Lewis! I thought you said they were servants!"

"That's the worst of it. If only they were masters! If only there were some men with as much natural life as they have, and their brave, quick minds that commanded instead of serving!"

"There are no such men," said Mrs. Witt, with a certain grim satisfaction.

"I know it. But I'm young, and I've got to live. And the thing that is offered me as life just starves me, starves me to death, mother. What am I to do? You enjoy shattering people like Dean Vyner. But I am young, I can't live that way."

"That may be."

It had long ago struck Lou how much more her mother realized and understood than ever Rico did. Rico was afraid, always afraid of realizing. Rico, with his good manners and his habitual kindness, and that peculiar imprisoned sneer of his.

He arrived home next morning on St. Mawr, rather flushed and gaudy, and over-kind, with an *empressé* anxiety about Lou's welfare which spoke too many volumes. Especially as he was accompanied by Flora Manby, and by Flora's sister Elsie, and Elsie's husband, Frederick Edwards. They all came on horseback.

"Such awful ages since I saw you!" said Flora to Lou. "Sorry if we burst in on you. We're only just saying *How do you do?* and going on to the inn. They've got rooms all ready for us there. We thought we'd stay just one night over here, and ride to-morrow to the Devil's Chair. Won't you come? Lots of fun! Isn't Mrs. Witt at home?"

Mrs. Witt was out for the moment. When she returned she had on her curious stiff face, yet she greeted the newcomers with a certain cordiality: she felt it would be diplomatic, no doubt.

"There *are* two rooms here," she said, "and if you care to poke into them, why, we shall be *delighted* to have you. But I'll show them to you first, because they are poor, inconvenient rooms, with no running water and *miles* from the baths."

Flora and Elsie declared that they were "perfectly darling sweet rooms—not overcrowded."

"Well," said Mrs. Witt, "the conveniences certainly don't fill up much space. But if you like to take them for what they are——"

"Why, we feel absolutely overwhelmed, don't we, Elsie! —But we've no clothes——!"

Suddenly the silence had turned into a house-party. The Manby girls appeared to lunch in fine muslin dresses, bought in Paris, fresh as daisies. Women's clothing takes up so little space, especially in summer! Fred Edwards was one of those blond Englishmen with a little brush moustache and those strong blue eyes which were always attempting the sentimental, but which Lou, in her prejudice, considered cruel: upon what grounds, she never analysed. However, he took a gallant tone with her at once, and she had to seem to simper. Rico, watching her, was so relieved when he saw the simper coming.

It had begun again, the whole clockwork of "lots of fun!"

"Isn't Fred flirting perfectly outrageously with Lady Carrington!—She looks so *sweet!*" cried Flora, over her coffee-cup. "Don't you mind, Harry!"

They called Rico "Harry"! His boy-name.

"Only a very little," said Harry. "*L'uomo é cacciatore.*"

"Oh, now, what does that mean?" cried Flora, who always thrilled to Rico's bits of affectation.

"It means," said Mrs. Witt, leaning forward and speaking in her most suave voice, "that man is a hunter."

Even Flora shrank under the smooth acid of the irony.

"Oh, well now!" she cried. "If he is, then what is woman?"

"The hunted," said Mrs. Witt, in a still smoother acid.

"At least," said Rico, "she is always *game!*"

"Ah, is she though!" came Fred's manly, well-bred tones. "I'm not so sure."

Mrs. Witt looked from one man to the other, as if she were dropping them down the bottomless pit.

Lou escaped to look at St. Mawr. He was still moist

where the saddle had been. And he seemed a little bit extinguished, as if virtue had gone out of him.

But when he lifted his lovely naked head, like a bunch of flames, to see who it was had entered, she saw he was still himself. For ever sensitive and alert, his head lifted like the summit of a fountain. And within him the clean bones striking to the earth, his hoofs intervening between him and the ground like lesser jewels.

He knew her and did not resent her. But he took no notice of her. He would never "respond." At first she had resented it. Now she was glad. He would never be intimate, thank heaven.

She hid herself away till tea-time, but she could not hide from the sound of voices. Dinner was early, at seven. Dean Vyner came—Mrs. Vyner was an invalid—and also an artist who had a studio in the village and did etchings. He was a man of about thirty-eight, and poor, just beginning to accept himself as a failure, as far as making money goes. But he worked at his etchings and studied esoteric matters like astrology and alchemy. Rico patronized him, and was a little afraid of him. Lou could not quite make him out. After knocking about Paris and London and Munich, he was trying to become staid, and to persuade himself that English village life, with squire and dean in the background, humble artist in the middle, and labourer in the common foreground, was a genuine life. His self-persuasion was only moderately successful. This was betrayed by the curious arrest in his body: he seemed to have to force himself into movement: and by the curious duplicity in his yellow-grey, twinkling eyes, that twinkled and expanded like a goat's; with mockery, irony, and frustration.

"Your face is curiously like Pan's," said Lou to him at dinner.

It was true, in a commonplace sense. He had the tilted eyebrows, the twinkling goaty look, and the pointed ears of a goat-Pan.

"People have said so," he replied. "But I'm afraid it's not the face of the Great God Pan. Isn't it rather the Great Goat Pan!"

"I say, that's good!" cried Rico. "The Great Goat Pan!"

"I have always found it difficult," said the Dean, "to see the Great God Pan in that goat-legged old father of satyrs. He may have a good deal of influence—the world will always be full of goaty old satyrs. But we find them somewhat vulgar. Even our late King Edward. The goaty old satyrs are too comprehensible to me to be venerable, and I fail to see a Great God in the father of them all."

"Your ears should be getting red," said Lou to Cartwright. She, too, had an odd squinting smile that suggested nymphs, so irresponsible and unbelieving.

"Oh, no, nothing personal!" cried the Dean.

"I am not sure," said Cartwright, with a small smile. "But don't you imagine Pan once *was* a Great God, before the anthropomorphic Greeks turned him into half a man?"

"Ah!—maybe. That is very possible. But—I have noticed the limitation in myself—my mind has no grasp whatsoever of Europe before the Greeks arose. Mr. Wells' Outline does not help me there, either," the Dean added with a smile.

"But what was Pan before he was a man with goat legs?" asked Lou.

"Before he looked like me?" said Cartwright, with a faint grin. "I should say he was the God that is hidden in everything. In those days you saw the thing, you never saw the God in it: I mean in the tree or the fountain or the animal. If you ever saw the God instead of the thing, you died. If you saw it with the naked eye, that is. But in the night you might see the God. And you knew it was there."

"The modern pantheist not only sees the God in everything, he takes photographs of it," said the Dean.

"Oh, and the divine pictures he paints!" cried Rico.

"Quite!" said Cartwright.

"But if they never *saw* the God in the thing, the old ones, how did they know he was there? How did they have any Pan at all?" said Lou.

"Pan was the hidden mystery—the hidden cause. That's how it was a Great God. Pan wasn't *he* at all: not even a Great God. He was Pan. All: what you see when you see in full. In the daytime you see the thing. But if your third eye is open, which sees only the things that can't be seen, you may see Pan within the thing, hidden: you may see with your third eye, which is darkness."

"Do you think I might see Pan in a horse, for example?"

"Easily. In St. Mawr!"—Cartwright gave her a knowing look.

"But," said Mrs. Witt, "it would be difficult, I should say, to open the third eye and see Pan in a man."

"Probably," said Cartwright, smiling. "In man he is over-visible: the old satyr: the fallen Pan."

"Exactly!" said Mrs. Witt. And she fell into a muse. "The fallen Pan!" she re-echoed. "Wouldn't a man be wonderful in whom Pan hadn't fallen!"

Over the coffee in the grey drawing-room she suddenly asked:

"Supposing, Mr. Cartwright, one *did* open the third eye and see Pan in an actual man—I wonder what it would be like."

She half lowered her eyelids and tilted her face in a strange way, as if she were tasting something, and not quite sure.

"I wonder!" he said, smiling his enigmatic smile. But she could see he did not understand.

"Louise!" said Mrs. Witt at bedtime. "Come into my room for a moment, I want to ask you something."

"What is it, mother?"

"You, you *get* something from what Mr. Cartwright said, about seeing Pan with the third eye? Seeing Pan in something?"

Mrs. Witt came rather close, and tilted her face with strange insinuating question at her daughter.

"I think I do, mother."

"In what?"—The question came as a pistol-shot.

"I think, mother," said Lou reluctantly, "in St. Mawr."

"In a horse!"—Mrs. Witt contracted her eyes slightly. "Yes, I can see that. I know what you mean. It *is* in St. Mawr. It *is!* But in St. Mawr it makes me *afraid*——" she dragged out the word. Then she came a step closer. "But, Louise, did you ever see it in a man?"

"What, mother?"

"Pan. Did you ever see Pan in a man, as you see Pan in St. Mawr?"

Louise hesitated.

"No, mother, I don't think I did. When I look at men with my third eye, as you call it—I think I see—mostly—a sort of—pancake." She uttered the last word with a despairing grin, not knowing quite what to say.

"Oh, Louise, isn't that it! Doesn't one always see a pancake!—Now listen, Louise. Have you ever been in love?"

"Yes, as far as I understand it."

"Listen now. Did you ever see Pan in the man you loved? Tell me if you did."

"As I see Pan in St. Mawr?—no, mother." And suddenly her lips began to tremble and the tears came to her eyes.

"Listen, Louise.—I've been in love innumerable times—and *really* in love twice. Twice!—yet for fifteen years I've left off wanting to have anything to do with a man, really. For fifteen years! And why?—Do you know?—Because I couldn't see that peculiar hidden Pan in any of them. And I became that I needed to. I needed it. But it wasn't there. Not in any man. Even when I was in love with a man, it was for other things: because I *understood* him so well, or he understood me, or we had such sympathy. Never the hidden Pan.—Do you understand what I mean? Unfallen Pan!"

"More or less, mother."

"But now my third eye is coming open, I believe. I am tired of all these men like breakfast cakes, with a teaspoonful of mind or a teaspoonful of spirit in them, for baking-powder. Isn't it extraordinary that young man Cartwright talks about Pan, but he knows nothing of it all? He knows nothing of the unfallen Pan: only the fallen Pan with goat legs and a leer—and that sort of power, don't you know——"

"But what do you know of the unfallen Pan, mother?"

"Don't ask me, Louise! I feel all of a tremble, as if I was just on the verge."

She flashed a little look of incipient triumph, and said good night.

An excursion on horseback had been arranged for the next day, to two old groups of rocks, called the Angel's

Chair and the Devil's Chair, which crowned the moor-like hills looking into Wales, ten miles away. Everybody was going—they were to start early in the morning, and Lewis would be the guide, since no one exactly knew the way.

Lou got up soon after sunrise. There was a summer scent in the trees of early morning, and monkshood flowers stood up dark and tall, with shadows. She dressed in the green linen riding-skirt her maid had put ready for her, with a close bluish smock.

"Are you going out already, dear?" called Rico from his room.

"Just to smell the roses before we start, Rico."

He appeared in the doorway in his yellow silk pyjamas. His large blue eyes had that rolling irritable look and the slightly bloodshot whites which made her want to escape.

"Booted and spurred!—the *energy!*" he cried.

"It's a lovely day to ride," she said.

"A lovely day to do anything *except* ride!" he said. "Why spoil the day riding!"—A curious bitter-acid escaped into his tone. It was evident he hated the excursion.

"Why, we needn't go if you don't want to, Rico."

"Oh, I'm sure I shall love it, once I get started. It's all this business of *starting*, with horses and paraphernalia——"

Lou went into the yard. The horses were drinking at the trough under the pump, their colours strong and rich in the shadow of the tree.

"You're not coming with us, Phœnix?" she said.

"Lewis, he's riding my horse."

She could tell Phœnix did not like being left behind.

By half past seven everybody was ready. The sun was in the yard, the horses were saddled. They came swishing their tails. Lewis brought out St. Mawr from his separate box, speaking to him very quietly in Welsh: a murmuring, soothing little speech. Lou, alert, could see that he was uneasy.

"How is St. Mawr this morning?" she asked.

"He's all right. He doesn't like so many people. He'll be all right once he's started."

The strangers were in the saddle: they moved out to the deep shade of the village road outside. Rico came to

his horse to mount. St. Mawr jumped away as if he had
seen the devil.

"Steady, fool!" cried Rico.

The bay stood with his four feet spread, his neck
arched, his big dark eye glancing sideways with that
watchful, frightening look.

"You shouldn't be irritable with him, Rico!" said Lou.
"Steady then, St. Mawr! Be steady."

But a certain anger rose also in her. The creature was so
big, so brilliant, and so stupid, standing there with his
hind legs spread, ready to jump aside or to rear terrifically,
and his great eye glancing with a sort of suspicious frenzy.
What was there to be suspicious of, after all?—Rico would
do him no harm.

"No one will harm you, St. Mawr," she reasoned, a bit
exasperated.

The groom was talking quietly, murmuringly, in Welsh.
Rico was slowly advancing again, to put his foot in the
stirrup. The stallion was watching from the corner of his
eye, a strange glare of suspicious frenzy burning stupidly.
Any moment his immense physical force might be let loose
in a frenzy of panic—or malice. He was really very irritating.

"Probably he doesn't like that apricot shirt," said Mrs.
Witt, "although it tones into him wonderfully well."

She pronounced it *ap*-ricot, and it irritated Rico terribly.

"Ought we to have *asked* him before we put it on?" he
flashed, his upper lip lifting venomously.

"I should say you should," replied Mrs. Witt coolly.

Rico turned with a sudden rush to the horse. Back
went the great animal, with a sudden splashing crash of
hoofs on the cobble-stones, and Lewis hanging on like a
shadow. Up went the forefeet, showing the belly.

"The thing is accursed," said Rico, who had dropped
the reins in sudden shock, and stood marooned. His rage
overwhelmed him like a black flood.

"Nothing in the world is so irritating as a horse that
is acting up," thought Lou.

"Say, Harry!" called Flora from the road. "Come out
here into the road to mount him."

Lewis looked at Rico and nodded. Then, soothing the

big, quivering animal, he led him springily out to the road under the trees, where the three friends were waiting. Lou and her mother got quickly into the saddle to follow. And in another moment Rico was mounted and bouncing down the road in the wrong direction, Lewis following on the chestnut. It was some time before Rico could get St. Mawr round. Watching him from behind, those waiting could judge how the young Baronet hated it.

But at last they set off—Rico ahead, unevenly but quietly, with the two Manby girls, Lou following with the fair young man who had been in a cavalry regiment and who kept looking round for Mrs. Witt.

"Don't look round for me," she called. "I'm riding behind, out of the dust."

Just behind Mrs. Witt came Lewis. It was a whole cavalcade trotting in the morning sun past the cottages and the cottage gardens, round the field that was the recreation ground, into the deep hedges of the lane.

"Why is St. Mawr so bad at starting? Can't you get him into better shape?" she asked over her shoulder.

"Beg your pardon, Mam!"

Lewis trotted a little nearer. She glanced over her shoulder at him, at his dark, unmoved face, his cool little figure.

"I think *Mam!* is so ugly. Why not leave it out!" she said. Then she repeated her question.

"St. Mawr doesn't trust anybody," Lewis replied.

"Not you?"

"Yes, he trusts me—mostly."

"Then why not other people?"

"They're different."

"All of them?"

"About all of them."

"How are they different?"

He looked at her with his remote, uncanny grey eyes.

"Different," he said, not knowing how else to put it.

They rode on slowly, up the steep rise of the wood, then down into a glade where ran a little railway built for hauling some mysterious mineral out of the hill, in wartime, and now already abandoned. Even on this countryside the dead hand of the war lay like a corpse decomposing.

They rode up again, past the foxgloves under the trees. Ahead the brilliant St. Mawr and the sorrel and grey horses were swimming like butterflies through the sea of bracken, glittering from sun to shade, shade to sun. Then once more they were on a crest, and through the thinning trees could see the slopes of the moors beyond the next dip.

Soon they were in the open, rolling hills, golden in the morning and empty save for a couple of distant bilberry-pickers, whitish figures pick—pick—picking with curious, rather disgusting assiduity. The horses were on an old trail which climbed through the pinky tips of heather and ling, across patches of green bilberry. Here and there were tufts of harebells blue as bubbles.

They were out, high on the hills. And there to west lay Wales, folded in crumpled folds, goldish in the morning light, with its moor-like slopes and patches of corn uncannily distinct. Between was a hollow, wide valley of summer haze, showing white farms among trees, and grey slate roofs.

"Ride beside me," she said to Lewis. "Nothing makes me want to go back to America like the old look of these little villages.—You have never been to America?"

"No, Mam."

"Don't you ever want to go?"

"I wouldn't mind going."

"But you're not just crazy to go?"

"No, Mam."

"Quite content as you are?"

He looked at her, and his pale, remote eyes met hers.

"I don't fret myself," he replied.

"Not about anything at all—ever?"

His eyes glanced ahead, at the other riders.

"No, Mam!" he replied, without looking at her.

She rode a few moments in silence.

"What is that over there?" she asked, pointing across the valley. "What is it called?"

"Yon's Montgomery."

"Montgomery! And is that *Wales*——?" She trailed the ending curiously.

"Yes, Mam."

"Where you come from?"

"No, Mam! I come from Merioneth."

"Not from Wales? I thought you were Welsh?"

"Yes, Mam. Merioneth *is* Wales."

"And you are Welsh?"

"Yes, Mam."

"I had a Welsh grandmother. But I come from Louisiana, and when I go back home, the Negroes still call me Miss Rachel. *Oh, my, it's little Miss Rachel come back home. Why, ain't I mighty glad to see you—u, Miss Rachel!* That gives me such a strange feeling, you know."

The man glanced at her curiously, especially when she imitated the Negroes.

"Do you feel strange when you go home?" she asked.

"I was brought up by an aunt and uncle," he said. "I never go to see them."

"And you don't have any home?"

"No, Mam."

"No wife nor anything?"

"No, Mam."

"But what do you do with your life?"

"I keep to myself."

"And care about nothing?"

"I mind St. Mawr."

"But you've not always had St. Mawr—and you won't always have him.—Were you in the war?"

"Yes, Mam."

"At the front?"

"Yes, Mam—but I was a groom."

"And you came out all right?"

"I lost my little finger from a bullet."

He held up his small, dark left hand, from which the little finger was missing.

"And did you like the war—or didn't you?"

"I didn't like it."

Again his pale-grey eyes met hers, and they looked so non-human and uncommunicative, so without connexion, and inaccessible, she was troubled.

"Tell me," she said. "Did you never want a wife and a home and children, like other men?"

"No, Mam. I never wanted a home of my own."

"Nor a wife of your own?"

"No, Mam."

"Nor children of your own?"

"No, Mam."

She reined in her horse.

"Now wait a minute," she said. "Now tell me why."

His horse came to standstill, and the two riders faced one another.

"Tell me why—I must know why you never wanted a wife and children and a home. I must know why you're not like other men."

"I never felt like it," he said. "I made my life with horses."

"Did you hate people very much? Did you have a very unhappy time as a child?"

"My aunt and uncle didn't like me, and I didn't like them."

"So you've never liked anybody?"

"Maybe not," he said. "Not to get as far as marrying them."

She touched her horse and moved on.

"Isn't that curious!" she said. "I've loved people, at various times. But I don't believe *I've* ever liked anybody, except a few of our Negroes. I don't like Louise, though she's my daughter and I love her. But I don't really *like* her.—I think you're the first person I've ever liked since I was on our plantation, and we had some *very fine* Negroes. —And I think that's very curious.—Now I want to know if you like *me*."

She looked at him searchingly, but he did not answer.

"Tell me," she said. "I don't mind if you say no. But tell me if you like me. I feel I must know."

The flicker of a smile went over his face—a very rare thing with him.

"Maybe I do," he said. He was thinking that she put him on a level with a Negro slave on a plantation: in his idea, Negroes were still slaves. But he did not care where she put him.

"Well, I'm glad—I'm glad if you like me. Because you *don't* like most people, I know that."

They had passed the hollow where the old Aldecar

Chapel hid in damp isolation, beside the ruined mill, over
the stream that came down from the moors. Climbing the
sharp slope, they saw the folded hills like great shut fingers,
with steep, deep clefts between. On the near sky-line was
a bunch of rocks; and away to the right another bunch.

"Yon's the Angel's Chair," said Lewis, pointing to the
nearer rocks. "And yon's the Devil's Chair, where we're
going."

"Oh!" said Mrs. Witt. "And aren't we going to the
Angel's Chair?"

"No, Mam."

"Why not?"

"There's nothing to see there. The other's higher, and
bigger, and that's where folks mostly go."

"Is that so!—They give the Devil the higher seat in this
country, do they? I think they're right."—And as she got
no answer, she added: "You believe in the Devil, don't
you?"

"I never met him," he answered, evasively.

Ahead, they could see the other horses twinkling in a
cavalcade up the slope, the black, the bay, the two greys
and the sorrel, sometimes bunching, sometimes straggling.
At a gate all waited for Mrs. Witt. The fair young man fell
in beside her, and talked hunting at her. He had hunted
the fox over these hills, and was vigorously excited locat-
ing the spot where the hounds gave the first cry, etc.

"Really!" said Mrs. Witt. "*Really!* Is that so!"

If irony could have been condensed to prussic acid,
the fair young man would have ended his life's history
with his reminiscences.

They came at last, trotting in file along a narrow
track between heather, along the saddle of a hill, to where
the knot of pale granite suddenly cropped out. It was one
of those places where the spirit of aboriginal England still
lingers, the old savage England, whose last blood flows
still in a few Englishmen, Welshmen, Cornishmen. The
rocks, whitish with weather of all the ages, jutted against
the blue August sky, heavy with age-moulded round-
nesses.

Lewis stayed below with the horses, the party scrambled rather awkwardly, in their riding-boots, up the foot-

worn boulders. At length they stood in the place called the
Chair, looking west, west towards Wales, that rolled in
golden folds upwards. It was neither impressive nor a very
picturesque landscape: the hollow valley with farms, and
then the rather bare upheaval of hills, slopes with corn
and moor and pasture, rising like a barricade, seemingly
high, slantingly. Yet it had a strange effect on the imagina-
tion.

"Oh, mother," said Lou, "doesn't it make you feel old,
old, older than anything ever was?"

"It certainly does seem aged," said Mrs. Witt.

"It makes me want to die," said Lou. "I feel we've
lasted almost too long."

"Don't say that, Lady Carrington. Why, you're a spring
chicken yet: or shall I say an unopened rosebud?" re-
marked the fair young man.

"No," said Lou. "All these millions of ancestors have
used all the life up. We're not really alive, in the sense that
they were alive."

"But who?" said Rico. "Who are *they?*"

"The people who lived on these hills, in the days gone
by."

"But the same people still live on the hills, darling. It's
just the same stock."

"No, Rico. That old fighting stock that worshipped
devils among these stones—I'm sure they did——"

"But look here, do you mean they were any better
than we are?" asked the fair young man.

Lou looked at him quizzically.

"We don't exist," she said, squinting at him oddly.

"I jolly well know *I* do," said the fair young man.

"I consider these days are the best ever, especially for
girls," said Flora Manby. "And anyhow they're our own
days, so I don't jolly well see the use of crying them down."

They were all silent, with the last echoes of emphatic
joie de vivre trumpeting on the air, across the hills of
Wales.

"Spoken like a brick, Flora," said Rico. "Say it again,
we may not have the Devil's Chair for a pulpit next time."

"I do," reiterated Flora. "I think this is the best age

there ever was for a girl to have a good time in. I read all
through H. G. Wells' history, and I shut it up and thanked
my stars I live in nineteen-twenty odd, not in some other
beastly date when a woman had to cringe before mouldy
domineering men."

After this they turned to scramble to another part of
the rocks, to the famous Needle's Eye.

"Thank you so much, I am really better without help,"
said Mrs. Witt to the fair young man, as she slid downwards till a piece of grey silk stocking showed above her
tall boot. But she got her toe in a safe place, and in a moment stood beside him, while he caught her arm protectingly. He might as well have caught the paw of a mountain
lion protectingly.

"I should like *so* much to know," she said suavely, looking into his eyes with a demonish straight look, "what
makes you so certain that you exist."

He looked back at her, and his jaunty blue eyes went
baffled. Then a slow, hot, salmon-coloured flush stole over
his face, and he turned abruptly round.

The Needle's Eye was a hole in the ancient grey rock,
like a window, looking to England: England at the moment in shadow. A stream wound and glinted in the flat
shadow, and beyond that the flat, insignificant hills
heaped in mounds of shade. Cloud was coming—the English side was in shadow. Wales was still in the sun, but the
shadow was spreading. The day was going to disappoint
them. Lou was a tiny bit chilled already.

Luncheon was still several miles away. The party hastened down to the horses. Lou picked a few sprigs of ling,
and some harebells, and some straggling yellow flowers:
not because she wanted them, but to distract herself. The
atmosphere of "enjoying ourselves" was becoming cruel
to her: it sapped all the life out of her. "Oh, if only
I needn't enjoy myself," she moaned inwardly. But the
Manby girls were enjoyng themselves so much. "I think
it's frantically lovely up here," said the other one—not
Flora—Elsie.

"It *is* beautiful, isn't it! I'm *so* glad you like it," replied
Rico. And he was really relieved and gratified, because

the other one said she was enjoying it so frightfully. He dared not say to Lou, as he wanted to: "I'm afraid, Lou darling, you don't love it as much as we do."—He was afraid of her answer: "No, dear, I don't love it at all! I want to be away from these people."

Slightly piqued, he rode on with the Manby group, and Lou came behind with her mother. Cloud was covering the sky with grey. There was a cold wind. Everybody was anxious to get to the farm for luncheon, and be safely home before rain came.

They were riding along one of the narrow little foot-tracks, mere groves of grass between heather and bright green bilberry. The blond young man was ahead, then his wife, then Flora, then Rico. Lou, from a little distance, watched the glossy, powerful haunches of St. Mawr swaying with life, always too much life, like a menace. The fair young man was whistling a new dance tune.

"That's an awfully attractive tune," Rico called. "Do whistle it again, Fred, I should like to memorize it."

Fred began to whistle it again.

At that moment St. Mawr exploded again, shied sideways as if a bomb had gone off, and kept backing through the heather.

"Fool!" cried Rico, thoroughly unnerved: he had been terribly sideways in the saddle, Lou had feared he was going to fall. But he got his seat, and pulled the reins viciously, to bring the horse to order, and put him on the track again. St. Mawr began to rear: his favourite trick. Rico got him forward a few yards, when up he went again.

"Fool!" yelled Rico, hanging in the air.

He pulled the horse over backwards on top of him.

Lou gave a loud, unnatural, horrible scream: she heard it herself, at the same time as she heard the crash of the falling horse. Then she saw a pale gold belly, and hoofs that worked and flashed in the air, and St. Mawr writhing, straining his head terrifically upwards, his great eyes starting from the naked lines of his nose. With a great neck arching cruelly from the ground, he was pulling frantically at the reins, which Rico still held tight.—Yes, Rico, lying strangely sideways, his eyes also starting from his yellow-white face, among the heather, still clutched the reins.

Young Edwards was rushing forward, and circling round the writhing, immense horse, whose pale-gold, inverted bulk seemed to fill the universe.

"Let him get up, Carrington! Let him get up!" he was yelling, darting warily near, to get the reins.—Another spasmodic convulsion of the horse.

Horror! The young man reeled backwards with his face in his hands. He had got a kick in the face. Red blood running down his chin!

Lewis was there, on the ground, getting the reins out of Rico's hands. St. Mawr gave a great curve like a fish, spread his forefeet on the earth and reared his head, looking round in a ghastly fashion. His eyes were arched, his nostrils wide, his face ghastly in a sort of panic. He rested thus, seated with his forefeet planted and his face in panic, almost like some terrible lizard, for several moments. Then he heaved sickeningly to his feet, and stood convulsed, trembling.

There lay Rico, crumpled and rather sideways, staring at the heavens from a yellow, dead-looking face. Lewis, glancing round in a sort of horror, looked in dread at St. Mawr again. Flora had been hovering.—She now rushed screeching to the prostrate Rico:

"Harry! Harry! you're not dead! Oh, Harry! Harry! Harry!"

Lou had dismounted.—She didn't know when. She stood a little way off, as if spellbound, while Flora cried *Harry! Harry! Harry!*

Suddenly Rico sat up.

"Where is the horse?" he said.

At the same time an added whiteness came on his face, and he bit his lip with pain, and he fell prostrate·again in a faint. Flora rushed to put her arm round him.

Where was the horse? He had backed slowly away, in an agony of suspicion, while Lewis murmured to him in vain. His head was raised again, the eyes still starting from their sockets, and a terrible guilty, ghostlike look on his face. When Lewis drew a little nearer, he twitched and shrank like a shaken steel spring, away—not to be

touched. He seemed to be seeing legions of ghosts, down
the dark avenues of all the centuries that have lapsed since
the horse became subject to man.

And the other young man? He was still standing, at a
little distance, with his face in his hands, motionless, the
blood falling on his white shirt, and his wife at his side,
pleading, distracted.

Mrs. Witt too was there, as if cast in steel, watching.
She made no sound and did not move, only, from a fixed,
impassive face, watched each thing.

"Do tell me what you think is the matter?" Lou
pleaded, distracted, to Flora, who was supporting Rico
and weeping torrents of unknown tears.

Then Mrs. Witt came forward and began in a very prac-
tical manner to unclose the shirt-neck and feel the young
man's heart. Rico opened his eyes again, said *"Really!"*
and closed his eyes once more.

"It's fainting!" said Mrs. Witt. "We have no brandy."

Lou, too weary to be able to feel anything, said:

"I'll go and get some."

She went to her alarmed horse, who stood among the
others with her head down, in suspense. Almost unconsciously Lou mounted, set her face ahead, and was riding
away.

Then Poppy shied too, with a sudden start, and Lou
pulled up. "Why?" she said to her horse. "Why did you
do that?"

She looked around, and saw in the heather a glimpse
of yellow and black.

"A snake!" she said wonderingly.

And she looked closer.

It was a dead adder that had been drinking at a reedy
pool in a little depression just off the road, and had been
killed with stones. There it lay, also crumpled, its head
crushed, its gold-and-yellow back still glittering dully,
and a bit of pale-blue belly showing, killed that morning.

Lou rode on, her face set towards the farm. An
unspeakable weariness had overcome her. She could not
even suffer. Weariness of spirit left her in a sort of apathy.

And she had a vision, a vision of evil. Or not strictly a
vision. She became aware of evil, evil, evil, rolling in great

waves over the earth. Always she had thought there was no such thing—only a mere negation of good. Now, like an ocean to whose surface she had risen, she saw the dark-grey waves of evil rearing in a great tide.

And it had swept mankind away without mankind's knowing. It had caught up the nations as the rising ocean might lift the fishes, and was sweeping them on in a great tide of evil. They did not know. The people did not know. They did not even wish it. They wanted to be good and to have everything joyful and enjoyable. Everything joyful and enjoyable: for everybody. This was what they wanted, if you asked them.

But at the same time, they had fallen under the spell of evil. It was a soft, subtle thing, soft as water, and its motion was soft and imperceptible, as the running of a tide is invisible to one who is out on the ocean. And they were all out on the ocean, being borne along in the current of the mysterious evil, creatures of the evil principle, as fishes are creatures of the sea.

There was no relief. The whole world was enveloped in one great flood. All the nations, the white, the brown, the black, the yellow, all were immersed in the strange tide of evil that was subtly, irresistibly rising. No one, perhaps, deliberately wished it. Nearly every individual wanted peace and a good time all round: everybody to have a good time.

But some strange thing had happened, and the vast, mysterious force of positive evil was let loose. She felt that from the core of Asia the evil welled up, as from some strange pole, and slowly was drowning earth.

It was something horrifying, something you could not escape from. It had come to her as in a vision, when she saw the pale-gold belly of the stallion upturned, the hoofs working wildly, the wicked curved hams of the horse, and then the evil straining of that arched, fish-like neck, with the dilated eyes of the head. Thrown backwards, and working its hoofs in the air. Reversed, and purely evil.

She saw the same in people. They were thrown backwards, and writhing with evil. And the rider, crushed, was still reining them down.

What did it mean? Evil, evil, and a rapid return to the

sordid chaos. Which was wrong, the horse or the rider?
Or both?

She thought with horror of St. Mawr, and of the look
on his face. But she thought with horror, a colder horror,
of Rico's face as he snarled *Fool!* His fear, his impotence
as a master, as a rider, his presumption. And she thought
with horror of those other people, so glib, so glibly evil.

What did they want to do, those Manby girls? Undermine, undermine, undermine. They wanted to undermine
Rico, just as that fair young man would have liked to undermine her. Believe in nothing, care about nothing: but
keep the surface easy, and have a good time. *Let us undermine one another. There is nothing to believe in, so let us
undermine everything. But look out! No scenes, no spoiling the game. Stick to the rules of the game. Be sporting,
and don't do anything that would make a commotion. Keep
the game going smooth and jolly, and bear your bit like a
sport. Never, by any chance, injure your fellow man
openly. But always injure him secretly. Make a fool of him,
and undermine his nature. Break him up by undermining
him, if you can. It's good sport.*

The evil! The mysterious potency of evil. She could see
it all the time, in individuals, in society, in the press. There
it was in socialism and bolshevism: the same evil. But
bolshevism made a mess of the outside of life, so turn it
down. Try fascism. Fascism would keep the surface of
life intact, and carry on the undermining business all the
better. All the better sport. Never draw blood. Keep the
hæmorrhage internal, invisible.

And as soon as fascism makes a break—which it
is bound to, because all evil works up to a break—then
turn it down. With gusto, turn it down.

Mankind, like a horse, ridden by a stranger, smooth-
faced, evil rider. Evil himself, smooth-faced and pseudo-
handsome, riding mankind past the dead snake, to the last
break.

Mankind no longer its own master. Ridden by this
pseudo-handsome ghoul of outward loyalty, inward
treachery, in a game of betrayal, betrayal, betrayal. The
last of the gods of our era, Judas supreme!

People performing outward acts of loyalty, piety, self-sacrifice. But inwardly bent on undermining, betraying. Directing all their subtle evil will against any positive living thing. Masquerading as the ideal, in order to poison the real.

Creation destroys as it goes, throws down one tree for the rise of another. But ideal mankind would abolish death, multiply itself million upon million, rear up city upon city, save every parasite alive, until the accumulation of mere existence is swollen to a horror. But go on saving life, the ghastly salvation army of ideal mankind. At the same time secretly, viciously, potently undermine the natural creation, betray it with kiss after kiss, destroy it from the inside, till you have the swollen rottenness of our teeming existence. —But keep the game going. Nobody's going to make another bad break, such as Germany and Russia made.

Two bad breaks the secret evil has made: in Germany and in Russia. Watch it! Let evil keep a policeman's eye on evil! The surface of life must remain unruptured. Production must be heaped upon production. And the natural creation must be betrayed by many more kisses, yet. Judas is the last God, and, by heaven, the most potent.

But even Judas made a break: hanged himself, and his bowels gushed out. Not long after his triumph.

Man must destroy as he goes, as trees fall for trees to rise. The accumulation of life and things means rottenness. Life must destroy life, in the unfolding of creation. We save up life at the expense of the unfolding, till all is full of rottenness. Then at last, we make a break.

What's to be done? Generally speaking, nothing. The dead will have to bury their dead, while the earth stinks of corpses. The individual can but depart from the mass, and try to cleanse himself. Try to hold fast to the living thing, which destroys as it goes, but remains sweet. And in his soul fight, fight, fight to preserve that which is life in him from the ghastly kisses and poison-bites of the myriad evil ones. Retreat to the desert, and fight. But in his soul adhere to that which is life itself, creatively destroying as it goes: destroying the stiff old thing to let the new bud come through. The one passionate principle of crea-

tive being, which recognizes the natural good, and has a
sword for the swarms of evil. Fights, fights, fights to protect itself. But with itself, is strong and at peace.

Lou came to the farm, and got brandy, and asked the
men to come out to carry in the injured.

It turned out that the kick in the face had knocked a
couple of young Edward's teeth out, and would disfigure
him a little.

"To go through the war, and then get this!" he mum-
bled, with a vindictive glance at St. Mawr.

And it turned out that Rico had two broken ribs and a
crushed ankle. Poor Rico, he would limp for life.

"I want St. Mawr *shot!*" was almost his first word, when
he was in bed at the farm and Lou was sitting beside him.

"What good would that do, dear?" she said.

"The brute is evil. I want him *shot!*"

Rico could make the last word sound like the spitting
of a bullet.

"Do you want to shoot him yourself?"

"No. But I want to have him shot. I shall never be easy
till I know he has a bullet through him. He's got a wicked
character. I don't feel you are safe, with him down there.
I shall get one of the Manbys' gamekeepers to shoot him.
You might tell Flora—or I'll tell her myself, when she
comes."

"Don't talk about it now, dear. You've got a tempera-
ture."

Was it true, St. Mawr was evil? She would never forget
him writhing and lunging on the ground, nor his awful
face when he reared up. But then that noble look of his:
surely he was not mean? Whereas all evil had an inner
meanness, mean! Was he mean? Was he meanly treacherous? Did he know he could kill, and meanly wait his opportunity?

She was afraid. And if this were true, then he *should*
be shot. Perhaps he ought to be shot.

This thought haunted her. Was there something mean
and treacherous in St. Mawr's spirit, the vulgar evil? If so,
then have him shot. At moments, an anger would rise in
her, as she thought of his frenzied rearing, and his mad,
hideous writhing on the ground, and in the heat of her

anger she would want to hurry down to her mother's house
and have the creature shot at once. It would be a satisfaction, and a vindication of human rights. Because, after all,
Rico was considerate of the brutal horse. But not a spark
of consideration did the stallion have for Rico. No, it was
the slavish malevolence of a domesticated creature that
kept cropping up in St. Mawr. The slave, taking his slavish vengeance, then dropping back into subservience.

All the slaves of this world, accumulating their prep-
arations for slavish vengeance, and then, when they have
taken it, ready to drop back into servility. Freedom! Most
slaves can't be freed, no matter how you let them loose.
Like domestic animals, they are, in the long run, more
afraid of freedom than of masters: and freed by some generous master, they will at last crawl back to some mean
boss, who will have no scruples about kicking them. Because, for them, far better kicks and servility than the
hard, lonely responsibility of real freedom.

The wild animal is at every moment intensely self-
disciplined, poised in the tension of self-defence, self-
preservation, and self-assertion. The moments of relaxation
are rare and most carefully chosen. Even sleep is watchful, guarded, unrelaxing, the wild courage pitched one
degree higher than the wild fear. Courage, the wild thing's
courage to maintain itself alone and living in the midst of
a diverse universe.

Did St. Mawr have this courage?

And did Rico?

Ah, Rico! He was one of mankind's myriad conspirators,
who conspire to live in absolute physical safety, whilst
willing the minor disintegration of all positive living.

But St. Mawr? Was it the natural wild thing in him
which caused these disasters? Or was it the slave, asserting
himself for vengeance?

If the latter, let him be shot. It would be a great satisfaction to see him dead.

But if the former——

When she could leave Rico with the nurse, she motored down to her mother for a couple of days. Rico lay in
bed at the farm.

Everything seemed curiously changed. There was a

new silence about the place, a new coolness. Summer had
passed with several thunderstorms, and the blue, cool
touch of autumn was about the house. Dahlias and peren-
nial yellow sunflowers were out, the yellow of ending summer, the red coals of early autumn. First mauve tips of
Michaelmas daisies were showing. Something suddenly
carried her away to the great bare spaces of Texas, the
blue sky, the flat, burnt earth, the miles of sunflowers.
Another sky, another silence, towards the setting sun.

And suddenly, she craved again for the more absolute
silence of America. English stillness was so soft, like an inaudible murmur of voices, of presences. But the silence in
the empty spaces of America was still unutterable, almost
cruel.

St. Mawr was in a small field by himself: she could not
bear that he should be always in stable. Slowly she went
through the gate towards him. And he stood there looking at her, the bright bay creature.

She could tell he was feeling somewhat subdued, after
his late escapade. He was aware of the general human
condemnation: the human damning. But something ob-
stinate and uncanny in him made him not relent.

"Hello! St. Mawr!" she said, as she drew near, and he
stood watching her, his ears pricked, his big eyes glancing
sideways at her.

But he moved away when she wanted to touch him.

"Don't trouble," she said. "I don't want to catch you
or do anything to you."

He stood still, listening to the sound of her voice, and
giving quick, small glances at her. His underlip trembled.
But he did not blink. His eyes remained wide and unrelenting. There was a curious malicious obstinacy in him which
aroused her anger.

"I don't want to touch you," she said. "I only want
to look at you, and even you can't prevent that."

She stood gazing hard at him, wanting to know, to
settle the question of his meanness or his spirit. A thing
with a brave spirit is not mean.

He was uneasy as she watched him. He pretended to
hear something, the mares two fields away, and he lifted

his head and neighed. She knew the powerful, splendid sound so well: like bells made of living membrane. And he looked so noble again, with his head tilted up, listening, and his male eyes looking proudly over the distance, eagerly.

But it was all a bluff.

He knew, and became silent again. And as he stood there a few yards away from her, his head lifted and wary, his body full of power and tension, his face slightly averted from her, she felt a great animal sadness come from him. A strange animal atmosphere of sadness, that was vague and disseminated through the air, and made her feel as though she breathed grief. She breathed it into her breast, as if it were a great sigh down the ages, that passed into her breast. And she felt a great woe: the woe of human unworthiness. The race of men judged in the consciousness of the animals they have subdued, and there found unworthy, ignoble.

Ignoble men, unworthy of the animals they have sub-jugated, bred the woe in the spirit of their creatures. St. Mawr, that bright horse, one of the kings of creation in the order below man, it had been a fulfilment for him to serve the brave, reckless, perhaps cruel men of the past, who had a flickering, rising flame of nobility in them. To serve that flame of mysterious further nobility. Nothing matters but that strange flame, of inborn nobility that obliges men to be brave, and onward plunging. And the horse will bear him on.

But now where is the flame of dangerous, forward-pressing nobility in men? Dead, dead, guttering out in a stink of self-sacrifice whose feeble light is a light of ex-haustion and *laissez-faire*.

And the horse, is he to go on carrying man forward into this?—this gutter?

No! Man wisely invents motor-cars and other machines, automobile and locomotive. The horse is superannuated, for man.

But alas, man is even more superannuated, for the horse.

Dimly in a woman's muse, Lou realized this, as she breathed the horse's sadness, his accumulated vague

woe from the generations of latter-day ignobility. And a
grief and a sympathy flooded her, for the horse. She realized now how his sadness recoiled into these frenzies of
obstinacy and malevolence. Underneath it all was grief,
an unconscious, vague, pervading animal grief, which perhaps only Lewis understood, because he felt the same.
The grief of the generous creature which sees all ends
turning to the morass of ignoble living.

She did not want to say any more to the horse: she did
not want to look at him any more. The grief flooded her
soul, that made her want to be alone. She knew now what
it all amounted to. She knew that the horse, born to serve
nobly, had waited in vain for someone noble to serve. His
spirit knew that nobility had gone out of men. And this left
him high and dry, in a sort of despair.

As she walked away from him, towards the gate, slowly
he began to walk after her.

Phœnix came striding through the gate towards her.
"You not afraid of that horse?" he asked sardonically, in
his quiet, subtle voice.

"Not at the present moment," she replied, even more
quietly, looking direct at him. She was not in any mood
to be jeered at.

And instantly the sardonic grimace left his face, followed by the sudden blankness, and the look of race-
misery in the keen eyes.

"Do you want me to be afraid?" she said, continuing
to the gate.

"No, I don't want it," he replied, dejected.

"Are you afraid of him yourself?" she said, glancing
round. St. Mawr had stopped, seeing Phœnix, and had
turned away again.

"I'm not afraid of no horses," said Phœnix.

Lou went on quietly. At the gate, she asked him:

"Don't you like St. Mawr, Phœnix?"

"I like him. He's a very good horse."

"Even after what he's done to Sir Henry?"

"That don't make no difference to him being a good
horse."

"But suppose he'd done it to you?"

"I don't care. I say it my own fault."

"Don't you think he is wicked?"

"I don't think so. He don't kick anybody. He don't bite anybody. He don't pitch, he don't buck, he don't do nothing."

"He rears," said Lou.

"Well, what is rearing!" said the man, with a slow, contemptuous smile.

"A good deal, when a horse falls back on you."

"That horse don't want to fall back on you, if you don't make him. If you know how to ride him.—That horse want his own way sometime. If you don't let him, you got to fight him. Then look out!"

"Look out he doesn't kill you, you mean!"

"Look out you don't let him," said Phœnix, with his slow, grim, sardonic smile.

Lou watched the smooth, golden face with its thin line of moustache and its sad eyes with the glint in them. Cruel —there was something cruel in him, right down in the abyss of him. But at the same time, there was an aloneness, and a grim little satisfaction in a fight, and the peculiar courage of an inherited despair. People who inherit despair may at last turn it into greater heroism. It was almost so with Phœnix. Three quarters of his blood was probably Indian and the remaining quarter, that came through the Mexican father, had the Spanish-American despair to add to the Indian. It was almost complete enough to leave him free to be heroic.

"What are we going to do with him, though?" she asked.

"Why don't you and Mrs. Witt go back to America— you never been West. You go West."

"Where, to California?"

"No. To Arizona or New Mexico or Colorado or Wyoming, anywhere. Not to California."

Phœnix looked at her keenly, and she saw the desire dark in him. He wanted to go back. But he was afraid to go back alone, empty-handed, as it were. He had suffered too much, and in that country his sufferings would overcome him, unless he had some other background. He had been too much in contact with the white world, and his

own world was too dejected, in a sense, too hopeless for
his own hopelessness. He needed an alien contact to give
him relief.

But he wanted to go back. His necessity to go back
was becoming too strong for him.

"What is it like in Arizona?" she asked. "Isn't it all pale-
coloured sand and alkali, and a few cactuses, and terribly
hot and deathly?"

"No!" he cried. "I don't take you there. I take you to
the mountains—trees—" he lifted up his hand and looked
at the sky—"big trees—pine! *Pino—real* and *pinovetes*,
smell good. And then you come down, *piñon*, not very tall,
and *cedro*, cedar, smell good in the fire. And then you see
the desert, away below, go miles and miles, and where
the canyon go, the crack where it look red! I know, I been
there, working a cattle ranch."

He looked at her with a haunted glow in his dark eyes.
The poor fellow was suffering from nostalgia. And as he
glowed at her in that queer mystical way, she too seemed
to see that country, with its dark, heavy mountains holding in their lap the great stretches of pale, creased, silent
desert that still is virgin of idea, its word unspoken.

Phœnix was watching her closely and subtly. He
wanted something of her. He wanted it intensely, heavily,
and he watched her as if he could force her to give it him.
He wanted her to take him back to America, because,
rudderless, he was afraid to go back alone. He wanted her
to take him back: avidly he wanted it. She was to be the
means to his end.

Why shouldn't he go back by himself? Why should he
crave for her to go too? Why should he want her there?

There was no answer, except that he did.

"Why, Phœnix," she said, "I might possibly go back
to America. But you know, Sir Henry would never go
there. He doesn't like America, though he's never been.
But I'm sure he'd never go there to live."

"Let him stay here," said Phœnix abruptly, the sardonic look on his face as he watched her face. "You come,
and let him stay here."

"Ah, that's a whole story!" she said, and moved away.
As she went, he looked after her, standing silent and

arrested and watching as an Indian watches.—It was not love. Personal love counts so little when the greater griefs, the greater hopes, the great despairs and the great resolutions come upon us.

She found Mrs. Witt rather more silent, more firmly closed within herself, than usual. Her mouth was shut tight, her brows were arched rather more imperiously than ever, she was revolving some inward problem about which Lou was far too wise to enquire.

In the afternoon Dean Vyner and Mrs. Vyner came to call on Lady Carrington.

"What bad luck this is, Lady Carrington!" said the Dean. "Knocks Scotland on the head for you this year, I'm afraid. How did you leave your husband?"

"He seems to be doing as well as he could do!" said Lou.

"But how *very* unfortunate!" murmured the invalid Mrs. Vyner. "Such a handsome young man, in the bloom of youth! Does he suffer much pain?"

"Chiefly his foot," said Lou.

"Oh, I *do* so hope they'll be able to restore the ankle. Oh, how dreadful to be lamed at his age!"

"The doctor doesn't know. There *may* be a limp," said Lou.

"That horse has certainly left his mark on two good-looking young fellows," said the Dean. "If you don't mind my saying so, Lady Carrington, I think he's a bad egg."

"Who, St. Mawr?" said Lou, in her American sing-song.

"Yes, Lady Carrington," murmured Mrs. Vyner, in her invalid's low tone. "Don't you think he ought to be put away? He seems to me the incarnation of cruelty. His neigh. It goes through me like knives. Cruel! Cruel! Oh, I think he should be put away."

"How put away?" murmured Lou, taking on an invalid's low tone herself.

"Shot, I suppose," said the Dean.

"It is quite painless. He'll know nothing," murmured Mrs. Vyner hastily. "And think of the harm he has done already! Horrible! Horrible!" she shuddered. "Poor Sir Henry lame for life, and Eddy Edwards disfigured. Besides all that has gone before. Ah, no, such a creature ought not to live!"

"To live, and have a groom to look after him and feed him," said the Dean. "It's a bit thick, while he's smashing up the very people that give him bread—or oats, since he's a horse. But I suppose you'll be wanting to get rid of him?"

"Rico does," murmured Lou.

"Very naturally. So should I. A vicious horse is worse than a vicious man—except that you are free to put him six feet underground, and end his vice finally, by your own act."

"Do you think St. Mawr is vicious?" said Lou.

"Well, of course—if we're driven to definitions!—I *know* he's dangerous."

"And do you think we ought to shoot everything that is dangerous?" asked Lou, her colour rising.

"But, Lady Carrington, have you consulted your husband? Surely his wish should be law, in a matter of this sort! And on such an occasion! For *you*, who are a woman, it is enough that the horse is cruel, cruel, evil! I felt it long before anything happened. That evil male cruelty! Ah!" and Mrs. Vyner clasped her hands convulsively.

"I suppose," said Lou slowly, "that St. Mawr is really Rico's horse: I gave him to him, I suppose. But I don't believe I could let him shoot him, for all that."

"Ah, Lady Carrington," said the Dean breezily, "you can shift the responsibility. The horse is a public menace, put it at that. We can get an order to have him done away with, at the public expense. And among ourselves we can find some suitable compensation for you, as a mark of sympathy. Which, believe me, is very sincere! One hates to have to destroy a fine-looking animal. But I would sacrifice a dozen rather than have our Rico limping."

"Yes, indeed," murmured Mrs. Vyner.

"Will you excuse me one moment, while I see about tea?" said Lou, rising and leaving the room. Her colour was high, and there was a glint in her eye. These people almost roused her to hatred. Oh, these awful, house-bred, house-inbred human beings, how repulsive they were!

She hurried to her mother's dressing-room. Mrs. Witt was very carefully putting a touch of red on her lips.

"Mother, they want to shoot St. Mawr," she said.

"I know," said Mrs. Witt, as calmly as if Lou had said tea was ready.

"Well—" stammered Lou, rather put out, "don't you think it cheek?"

"It depends, I suppose, on the point of view," said Mrs. Witt dispassionately, looking closely at her lips. "I don't think the English climate agrees with me. I need something to stand up against, no matter whether it's great heat or great cold. This climate, like the food and the people, is most always lukewarm or tepid, one or the other. And the tepid and the lukewarm are not really my line." She spoke with a slow drawl.

"But they're in the drawing-room, mother, trying to force me to have St. Mawr killed."

"What about tea?" said Mrs. Witt.

"I don't care," said Lou.

Mrs. Witt worked the bell-handle.

"I suppose, Louise," she said, in her most beaming eighteenth-century manner, "that these are your guests, so you will preside over the ceremony of pouring out."

"No, mother, you do it. I can't smile to-day."

"I can," said Mrs. Witt.

And she bowed her head slowly, with a faint, ceremoniously effusive smile, as if handing a cup of tea.

Lou's face flickered to a smile.

"Then you pour out for them. You can stand them better than I can."

"Yes," said Mrs. Witt. "I saw Mrs. Vyner's hat coming across the churchyard. It looks so like a crumpled cup and saucer, that I have been saying to myself ever since: *Dear Mrs. Vyner, can't I fill your cup?*—and then pouring tea into that hat. And I hear the Dean responding: *My head is covered with cream, my cup runneth over.*—That is the way they make *me* feel."

They marched downstairs, and Mrs. Witt poured tea with that devastating correctness which made Mrs. Vyner, who was utterly impervious to sarcasm, pronounce her "indecipherably vulgar."

But the Dean was the old bulldog, and he had set his teeth in a subject.

"I was talking to Lady Carrington about that stallion, Mrs. Witt."

"Did you say stallion?" asked Mrs. Witt, with perfect neutrality.

"Why, yes, I presume that's what he is."

"I presume so," said Mrs. Witt colourlessly.

"I'm afraid Lady Carrington is a little sensitive on the wrong score," said the Dean.

"I beg your pardon," said Mrs. Witt, leaning forward in her most colourless polite manner. "You mean stallion's score?"

"Yes," said the Dean testily. "The horse St. Mawr."

"The stallion St. Mawr," echoed Mrs. Witt, with utmost mild vagueness. She completely ignored Mrs. Vyner, who felt plunged like a specimen into methylated spirit. There was a moment's full stop.

"Yes?" said Mrs. Witt naïvely.

"You agree that we can't have any more of these accidents to your young men?" said the Dean rather hastily.

"I certainly do!" Mrs. Witt spoke very slowly, and the Dean's lady began to look up. She might find a loophole through which to wriggle into the contest. "You know, Dean, that my son-in-law calls me, for preference, *belle-mère!* It sounds so awfully English when he says it; I always see myself as an old grey mare with a bell round her neck, leading a bunch of horses." She smiled a prim little smile, *very* conversationally. "Well!" and she pulled herself up from the aside. "Now, as the bell-mare of the bunch of horses, I shall see to it that my son-in-law doesn't go too near that stallion again. That stallion won't stand mischief."

She spoke so earnestly that the Dean looked at her with round wide eyes, completely taken aback.

"We all know, Mrs. Witt, that the author of the mischief is St. Mawr himself," he said, in a loud tone.

"Really! you think *that?*" Her voice went up in American surprise. "Why, how *strange*——!" and she lingered over the last word.

"Strange, eh?—After what's just happened?" said the Dean, with a deadly little smile.

"Why, yes! Most strange! I saw with my own eyes my

son-in-law pull that stallion over backwards, and hold him down with the reins as tight as he could hold them; pull St. Mawr's head backwards on to the ground, till the groom had to crawl up and force the reins out of my son-in-law's hands. Don't you think that was mischievous on Sir Henry's part?"

The Dean was growing purple. He made an apoplectic movement with his hand. Mrs. Vyner was turned to a seated pillar of salt, strangely dressed up.

"Mrs. Witt, you are playing on words."

"No, Dean Vyner, I am not. My son-in-law pulled that horse over backwards and pinned him down with the reins."

"I am sorry for the horse," said the Dean, with heavy sarcasm.

"I am *very*," said Mrs. Witt, "sorry for that stallion: *very!*"

Here Mrs. Vyner rose as if a chair-spring had suddenly propelled her to her feet. She was streaky pink in the face.

"Mrs. Witt," she panted, "you misdirect your sympathies. That poor young man—in the beauty of youth!"

"Isn't he *beautiful*——" murmured Mrs. Witt, extravagantly in sympathy. "He is my daughter's husband!" And she looked at the petrified Lou.

"Certainly!" panted the Dean's wife. "And you can defend that—that——"

"That stallion," said Mrs. Witt. "But you see, Mrs. Vyner," she added, leaning forward female and confidential, "if the old grey mare doesn't defend the stallion, who will? All the blooming young ladies will defend my beautiful son-in-law. You feel so *warmly* for him yourself! I'm an American woman, and I always have to stand up for the accused. And I stand up for that stallion. I say it is not right. He was pulled over backwards and then pinned down by my son-in-law—who may have meant to do it, or may not. And now people abuse him.—Just tell everybody, Mrs. Vyner and Dean Vyner"—she looked round at the Dean—"that the *belle-mère's* sympathies are with the stallion."

She looked from one to the other with a faint and gracious little bow, her black eyebrows arching in her eighteenth-century face like black rainbows, and her full, bold grey eyes absolutely incomprehensible.

"Well, it's a peculiar message to have to hand round, Mrs. Witt," the Dean began to boom, when she interrupted him by laying her hand on his arm and leaning forward, looking up into his face like a clinging, pleading female.

"Oh, but *do* hand it, Dean, *do* hand it," she pleaded, gazing intently into his face.

He backed uncomfortably from that gaze.

"Since you wish it," he said, in a chest voice.

"I most certainly *do*——" she said, as if she were wishing the sweetest wish on earth. Then, turning to Mrs. Vyner:

"Good-bye, Mrs. Vyner. We *do* appreciate your coming, my daughter and I."

"I came out of kindness——" said Mrs. Vyner.

"Oh, I know it, I know it," said Mrs. Witt. "Thank you *so* much. Good-bye! Good-bye, Dean! Who is taking the morning service on Sunday? I hope it is you, because I want to come."

"It *is* me," said the Dean. "Good-bye! Well, good-bye, Lady Carrington. I shall be going over to see our young man to-morrow, and will gladly take you or anything you have to send."

"Perhaps mother would like to go," said Lou, softly, plaintively.

"Well, we shall see," said the Dean. "Good-bye for the present!"

Mother and daughter stood at the window watching the two cross the churchyard. Dean and wife knew it, but daren't look round, and daren't admit the fact to one another.

Lou was grinning with a complete grin that gave her an odd, dryad or faun look, intensified.

"It was almost as good as pouring tea into her hat," said Mrs. Witt serenely. "People like that tire me out. I shall take a glass of sherry."

"So will I, mother.—It was even better than pouring tea in her hat.—You meant, didn't you, if you poured tea in her hat, to put cream and sugar in first?"

"I did," said Mrs. Witt.

But after the excitement of the encounter had passed away, Lou felt as if her life had passed away too. She went to bed, feeling she could stand no more.

In the morning she found her mother sitting at a window watching a funeral. It was raining heavily, so that some of the mourners even wore mackintosh coats. The funeral was in the poorer corner of the churchyard, where another new grave was covered with wreaths of sodden, shrivelling flowers.—The yellowish coffin stood on the wet earth, in the rain: the curate held his hat, in a sort of permanent salute, above his head, like a little unbrella as he hastened on with the service. The people seemed too wet to weep more wet.

It was a long coffin.

"Mother, do you really *like* watching?" asked Lou irritably, as Mrs. Witt sat in complete absorption.

"I do, Louise, I really enjoy it."

"Enjoy, mother!"—Lou was almost disgusted.

"I'll tell you why. I imagine I'm the one in the coffin— this is a girl of eighteen, who died of consumption—and those are my relatives, and I'm watching them put me away. And you know, Louise, I've come to the conclusion that hardly anybody in the world really lives, and so hardly anybody really dies. They may well say: *O Death, where is thy sting-a-ling-a-ling?* Even Death can't sting those that have never really lived.—I always used to want that—to die without death stinging me.—And I'm sure the girl in the coffin is saying to herelf: *Fancy Aunt Emma putting on a drab slicker, and wearing it while they bury me. Doesn't show much respect. But then my mother's family always were common!* I feel there should be a solemn burial of a roll of newspapers containing the account of the death and funeral, next week. It would be just as serious: the grave of all the world's remarks———"

"I don't want to think about it, mother. One ought to be able to laugh at it. I want to laugh at it."

"Well, Louise, I think it's just as great a mistake to laugh at everything as to cry at everything. Laughter's not the one panacea, either. I should *really* like, before I do come to be buried in a box, to know where I am. That young girl in that coffin never was anywhere—any more than the newspaper remarks on her death and burial. And I begin to wonder if I've ever been anywhere. I seem to have been a daily sequence of newspaper remarks, myself. I'm sure I never really conceived you and gave you birth. It all happened in newspaper notices. It's a newspaper fact that you are my child, and that's about all there is to it."

Lou smiled as she listened.

"I always knew you were philosophic, mother. But I never dreamed it would come to elegies in a country churchyard, written to your motherhood."

"*Exactly*, Louise! Here I sit and sing the elegy to my own motherhood. I never had any motherhood, except in newspaper fact. I never was a wife, except in newspaper notices. I never was a young girl, except in newspaper remarks. Bury everything I ever said or that was said about me, and you've buried *me*. But since Kind Words Can Never Die, I can't be buried, and death has no sting-a-ling-a-ling for *me!*—Now listen to me, Louise: I want death to be real to me—not as it was to that young girl. I *want* it to hurt me, Louise. If it hurts me enough, I shall know I was alive."

She set her face and gazed under half-dropped lids at the funeral, stoic, fate-like, and yet, for the first time, with a certain pure wistfulness of a young, virgin girl. This frightened Lou very much. She was so used to the matchless Amazon in her mother, that when she saw her sit there still, wistful, virginal, tender as a girl who has never taken armour, wistful at the window that only looked on graves, a serious terror took hold of the young woman. The terror of *too late!*

Lou felt years, centuries older than her mother, at that moment, with the tiresome responsibility of youth to protect and guide their elders.

"What can we do about it, mother?" she asked protectively.

"Do nothing, Louise. I'm not going to have anybody wisely steering my canoe, now I feel the rapids are near. I shall go with the river. Don't you pretend to do anything for me. I've done enough mischief myself, that way. I'm going down the stream, at last."

There was a pause.

"But in actuality, what?" asked Lou, a little ironically.

"I don't quite know. Wait awhile."

"Go back to America?"

"That is possible."

"I may come too."

"I've always waited for you to go back of your own will."

Lou went away, wandering round the house. She was so unutterably tired of everything—weary of the house, the graveyard, weary of the thought of Rico. She would have to go back to him to-morrow, to nurse him. Poor old Rico, going on like an amiable machine from day to day. It wasn't his fault. But his life was a rattling nullity, and her life rattled in null correspondence. She had hardly strength enough to stop rattling and be still. Perhaps she had not strength enough.

She did not know. She felt so weak that unless something carried her away, she would go on rattling her bit in the great machine of human life till she collapsed, and her rattle rattled itself out, and there was a sort of barren silence where the sound of her had been.

She wandered out in the rain, to the coach-house where Lewis and Phœnix were sitting facing one another, one on a bin, the other on the inner door-step.

"Well," she said, smiling oddly. "What's to be done?"

The two men stood up. Outside, the rain fell steadily on the flagstones of the yard, past the leaves of trees. Lou sat down on the little iron step of the dogcart.

"That's cold," said Phœnix. "You sit here." And he threw a yellow horse-blanket on the box where he had been sitting.

"I don't want to take your seat," she said.

"All right, you take it."

He moved across and sat gingerly on the shaft of the dogcart.—Lou seated herself, and loosened her soft tartan shawl. Her face was pink and fresh, and her dark hair curled almost merrily in the damp. But under her eyes were the finger-prints of deadly weariness.

She looked up at the two men, again smiling in her odd fashion.

"What are we going to do?" she asked.

They looked at her closely, seeking her meaning.

"What about?" said Phœnix, a faint smile reflecting on his face, merely because she smiled.

"Oh, everything," she said, hugging her shawl again. "You know what they want? They want to shoot St. Mawr."

The two men exchanged glances.

"Who want it?" said Phœnix.

"Why—all our *friends!*" she made a little *moue*. "Dean Vyner does."

Again the men exchanged glances. There was a pause. Then Phœnix said, looking aside:

"The boss is selling him."

"Who?"

"Sir Henry."—The half-breed always spoke the title with difficulty, and with a sort of sneer. "He sell him to Miss Manby."

"How do you know?"

"The man from Corrabach told me last night. Flora, she say it."

Lou's eyes met the sardonic, empty-seeing eyes of Phœnix direct. There was too much sarcastic understanding. She looked aside.

"What else did he say?" she asked.

"I don't know," said Phœnix, evasively. "He say they cut him—else shoot him. Think they cut him—and if he die, he die."

Lou understood. He meant they would geld St. Mawr —at his age.

She looked at Lewis. He sat with his head down, so she could not see his face.

"Do you think it is true?" she asked. "Lewis? Do you think they would try to geld St. Mawr—to make him a gelding?"

Lewis looked up at her. There was a faint deadly glimmer of contempt on his face.

"Very likely, Mam," he said.

She was afraid of his cold, uncanny pale eyes, with their uneasy grey dawn of contempt. These two men, with their silent, deadly inner purpose, were not like other men. They seemed like two silent enemies of all the other men she

knew. Enemies in the great white camp, disguised as servants, waiting the incalculable opportunity. What the opportunity might be, none knew.

"Sir Henry hasn't mentioned anything to me about
selling St. Mawr to Miss Manby," she said.

The derisive flicker of a smile came on Phœnix's face.

"He sell him first, and tell you then," he said, with his
deadly impassive manner.

"But do you really think so?" she asked.

It was extraordinary how much corrosive contempt
Phœnix could convey, saying nothing. She felt it almost
as an insult. Yet it was a relief to her.

"You know, I can't believe it. I can't believe Sir Henry
would want to have St. Mawr mutilated. I believe he'd
rather shoot him."

"You think so?" said Phœnix, with a faint grin.

Lou turned to Lewis.

"Lewis, will you tell me what you truly think?"

Lewis looked at her with a hard, straight, fearless British
stare.

"That man Philips was in the 'Moon and Stars' last
night. He said Miss Manby told him she was buying St.
Mawr, and she asked him if he thought it would be safe
to cut him, and make a horse of him. He said it would be
better, take some of the nonsense out of him. He's no good
for a sire, anyhow——"

Lewis dropped his head again, and tapped a tattoo with
the toe of his rather small foot.

"And what do you think?" said Lou.—It occurred to
her how sensible and practicable Miss Manby was, so
much more so than the Dean.

Lewis looked up at her with his pale eyes.

"It won't have anything to do with me," he said. "I
shan't go to Corrabach Hall."

"What will you do, then?"

Lewis did not answer. He looked at Phœnix.

"Maybe him and me go to America," said Phœnix, looking at the void.

"Can he get in?" said Lou.

"Yes, he can. I know how," said Phœnix.

"And the money?" she said.

"We got money."

There was a silence, after which she asked of Lewis:

"You'd leave St. Mawr to his fate?"

"I can't help his fate," said Lewis. "There's too many people in the world for me to help anything."

"Poor St. Mawr!"

She went indoors again, and up to her room: then higher, to the top rooms of the tall Georgian house. From one window she could see the fields in the rain. She could see St. Mawr himself, alone as usual, standing with his head up, looking across the fences. He was streaked dark with rain. Beautiful, with his poised head and massive neck, and his supple hindquarters. He was neighing to Poppy. Clear on the wet wind came the sound of his bell-like, stallion's calling, that Mrs. Vyner called cruel. It was a strange noise, with a splendour that belonged to another world-age. The mean cruelty of Mrs. Vyner's humanitar-ianism, the barren cruelty of Flora Manby, the eunuch cruelty of Rico. Our whole eunuch civilization, nasty-minded as eunuchs are, with their kind of sneaking, steril-izing cruelty.

Yet even she herself, seeing St. Mawr's conceited march along the fence, could not help addressing him:

"Yes, my boy! If you knew what Miss Flora Manby was preparing for you! *She'll* sharpen a knife that will settle you."

And Lou called her mother.

The two American women stood high at the window, overlooking the wet, close, hedged-and-fenced English landscape. Everything enclosed, enclosed, to stifling. The very apples on the trees looked so shut in, it was impos-sible to imagine any speck of "Knowledge" lurking inside them. Good to eat, good to cook, good even for show. But the wild sap of untamable and inexhaustible knowledge— no! Bred out of them. Geldings, even the apples.

Mrs. Witt listened to Lou's half-humorous statements.

"You must admit, mother, Flora is a sensible girl," she said.

"I admit it, Louise."

"She goes straight to the root of the matter."

"And eradicates the root. Wise girl! And what is your answer?"

"I don't know, mother. What would you say?"

"I know what *I* should say."

"Tell me."

"I should say: *Miss Manby, you may have my husband, but not my horse. My husband won't need emasculating, and my horse I won't have you meddle with. I'll preserve one last male thing in the museum of this world, if I can.*"

Lou listened, smiling faintly.

"That's what I will say," she replied at length. "The funny thing is, mother, they think all their men with their bare faces or their little quotation-marks moustaches *are* so tremendously male. That fox-hunting one!"

"I know it. Like little male motor-cars. Give him a little gas, and start him on the low gear, and away he goes: all his male gear rattling, like a cheap motor-car."

"I'm afraid I dislike men altogether, mother."

"You may, Louise. Think of Flora Manby, and how you love the fair sex."

"After all, St. Mawr is better. And I'm glad if he gives them a kick in the face."

"Ah, Louise!" Mrs. Witt suddenly clasped her hands with wicked passion. "*Ay, qué gozo!* as our Juan used to say, on your father's ranch in Texas." She gazed in a sort of wicked ecstasy out of the window.

They heard Lou's maid softly calling Lady Carrington from below. Lou went to the stairs.

"What is it?"

"Lewis wants to speak to you, my Lady."

"Send him into the sitting-room."

The two women went down.

"What is it, Lewis?" asked Lou.

"Am I to bring in St. Mawr, in case they send for him from Corrabach?"

"No," said Lou swiftly.

"Wait a minute," put in Mrs. Witt. "What makes you think they will send for St. Mawr from Corrabach, Lewis?" she asked, suave as a grey leopard cat.

"Miss Manby went up to Flints Farm with Dean Vyner

this morning, and they've just come back. They stopped
the car, and Miss Manby got out at the field gate, to look
at St. Mawr. I'm thinking if she made the bargain with
Sir Henry, she'll be sending a man over this afternoon,
and if I'd better brush St. Mawr down a bit, in case."

The man stood strangely still, and the words came like
shadows of his real meaning. It was a challenge.

"I see," said Mrs. Witt slowly.

Lou's face darkened. She too saw.

"So that is her game," she said. "That is why they got
me down here."

"Never mind, Louise," said Mrs. Witt. Then to Lewis:
"Yes, please bring in St. Mawr. You wish it, don't you,
Louise?"

"Yes," hesitated Lou. She saw by Mrs. Witt's closed
face that a counter-move was prepared.

"And, Lewis," said Mrs. Witt, "my daughter may
wish you to ride St. Mawr this afternoon—not to Corrabach Hall."

"Very good, Madam."

Mrs. Witt sat silent for some time, after Lewis had gone,
gathering inspiration from the wet, grisly gravestones.

"Don't you think it's time we made a move, daughter?"
she asked.

"Any move," said Lou desperately.

"Very well then.—My dearest friends, and my *only*
friends, in this country, are in Oxfordshire. I will set off
to *ride* to Merriton this afternoon, and Lewis will ride with
me on St. Mawr."

"But you can't ride to Merriton in an afternoon," said
Lou.

"I know it. I shall ride across country. I shall *enjoy* it,
Louise.—Yes.—I shall consider I am on my way back to
America. I am most deadly tired of this country. From
Merriton I shall make my arrangements to go to
America, and take Lewis and Phœnix and St. Mawr along
with me. I think they want to go.—You will decide for
yourself."

"Yes, I'll come too," said Lou casually.

"Very well. I'll start immediately after lunch, for I can't

breathe in this place any longer. Where are Henry's automobile maps?"

Afternoon saw Mrs. Witt, in a large waterproof cape, mounted on her horse, Lewis, in another cape, mounted on St. Mawr, trotting through the rain, splashing in the puddles, moving slowly southwards. They took the open country, and would pass quite near to Flints Farm. But Mrs. Witt did not care. With great difficulty she had managed to fasten a small waterproof roll behind her, containing her night things. She seemed to breathe the first breath of freedom.

And sure enough, an hour or so after Mrs. Witt's departure, arrived Flora Manby in a splashed-up motor-car, accompanied by her sister, and bringing a groom and a saddle.

"Do you know, Harry sold me St. Mawr," she said. "I'm just wild to get that horse in hand."

"How?" said Lou.

"Oh, I don't know. There are ways. Do you mind if Philips rides him over now, to Corrabach?—Oh, I forgot, Harry sent you a note."

"Dearest Loulina: Have you been gone from here two days or two years? It seems the latter. You are terribly missed. Flora wanted so much to buy St. Mawr, to save us further trouble, that I have sold him to her. She is giving me what we paid: rather, what you paid; so of course the money is yours. I am thankful we are rid of the animal, and that he falls into competent hands—I asked her please to remove him from your charge to-day. And I can't tell how much easier I am in my mind, to think of him gone. You are coming back to me to-morrow, aren't you? I shall think of nothing else but you, till I see you. A *rivederti*, darling dear! R."

"I'm so sorry," said Lou. "Mother went on horseback to see some friends, and Lewis went with her on St. Mawr. He knows the road."

"She'll be back this evening?" said Flora.

"I don't know. Mother is so uncertain. She may be away a day or two."

"Well, here's the cheque for St. Mawr."

"No, I won't take it now—no, thank you—not till mother comes back with the goods."

Flora was chagrined. The two women knew they hated one another. The visit was a brief one.

Mrs. Witt rode on in the rain, which abated as the afternoon wore down, and the evening came without rain, and with a suffusion of pale yellow light. All the time she had trotted in silence, with Lewis just behind her. And she scarcely saw the heather-covered hills with the deep clefts between them, nor the oak-woods, nor the lingering foxgloves, nor the earth at all. Inside herself she felt a profound repugnance for the English country: she preferred even the crudeness of Central Park in New York.

And she felt an almost savage desire to get away from Europe, from everything European. Now she was really *en route,* she cared not a straw for St. Mawr or for Lewis or anything. Something just writhed inside her, all the time, against Europe. That closeness, that sense of cohesion, that sense of being fused into a lump with all the rest—no matter how much distance you kept—this drove her mad. In America the cohesion was a matter of choice and will. But in Europe it was organic, like the helpless particles of one sprawling body. And the great body in a state of incipient decay.

She was a woman of fifty-one: and she seemed hardly to have lived a day. She looked behind her—the thin trees and swamps of Louisiana, the sultry, sub-tropical excitement of decaying New Orleans, the vast bare dryness of Texas, with mobs of cattle in an illumined dust! The half-European thrills of New York! The false stability of Boston! A clever husband, who was a brilliant lawyer, but who was far more thrilled by his cattle ranch than by his law: and who drank heavily and died. The years of first widowhood in Boston, consoled by a self-satisfied sort of intellectual courtship from clever men.—For curiously enough, while she wanted it, she had always been able to compel men to pay court to her. All kinds of men.—Then a rather dashing time in New York—when she was in her early forties. Then the long *visual* philandering in Europe. She left off "loving," save through the eye, when she came to Europe. And when she made her trips to America, she found it was finished there also, her "loving."

What was the matter? Examining herself, she had long ago decided that her nature was a destructive force. But then, she justified herself, she had only destroyed that which was destructible. If she could have found something indestructible, especially in men, though she would have fought against it, she would have been glad at last to be defeated by it.

That was the point. She really wanted to be defeated, in her own eyes. And nobody had ever defeated her. Men were never really her match. A woman of terrible strong health, she felt even that in her strong limbs there was far more electric power than in the limbs of any man she had met. That curious fluid electric force, that could make any man kiss her hand, if she so willed it. A queen, as far as she wished. And not having been very clever at school, she always had the greatest respect for the mental powers. Her own were not mental powers. Rather electric, as of some strange physical dynamo within her. So she had been ready to bow before Mind.

But alas! After a brief time, she had found Mind, at least the man who was supposed to have the mind, bowing before her. Her own peculiar dynamic force was stronger than the force of Mind. She could make Mind kiss her hand.

And not by any sensual tricks. She did not really care about sensualities, especially as a younger woman. Sex was a mere adjunct. She cared about the mysterious, intense, dynamic sympathy that could flow between her and some "live" man—a man who was highly conscious, a real live wire. That she cared about.

But she had never rested until she had made the man she admired: and admiration was the root of her attraction to any man: made him kiss her hand. In both senses, actual and metaphorical. Physical and metaphysical. Conquered his country.

She had always succeeded. And she believed that, if she cared, she always *would* succeed. In the world of living men. Because of the power that was in her, in her arms, in her strong, shapely, but terrible hands, in all the great dynamo of her body.

For this reason she had been so terribly contemptuous of Rico, and of Lou's infatuation. Ye Gods! What was Rico in the scale of men!

Perhaps she despised the younger generation too easily. Because she did not see its sources of power, she concluded it was powerless. Whereas perhaps the power of accommodating oneself to any circumstance and committing oneself to no circumstance is the last triumph of mankind.

Her generation had had its day. She had had her day. The world of her men had sunk into a sort of insignificance. And with a great contempt she despised the world that had come into place instead: the world of Rico and Flora Manby, the world represented, to her, by the Prince of Wales.

In such a world there was nothing even to conquer. It gave everything and gave nothing to everybody and anybody all the time. *Dio benedetto!* as Rico would say. A great complicated tangle of nonentities ravelled in nothingness. So it seemed to her.

Great God! This was the generation she had helped to bring into the world.

She had had her day. And, as far as the mysterious battle of life went, she had won all the way. Just as Cleopatra, in the mysterious business of a woman's life, won all the way.

Though that bald tough Cæsar had drawn his iron from the fire without losing much of its temper. And he had gone his way. And Antony surely was splendid to die with.

In her life there had been no tough Cæsar to go his way in cold blood, away from her. Her men had gone from her like dogs on three legs, into the crowd. And certainly there was no gorgeous Antony to die for and with.

Almost she was tempted in her heart to cry: "Conquer me, O God, before I die!"—But then she had a terrible contempt for the God that was supposed to rule this universe. She felt she could make *Him* kiss her hand. Here she was, a woman of fifty-one, past the change of life.

And her great dread was to die an empty, barren death. Oh, if only Death might open dark wings of mystery and consolation! To die an easy, barren death. To pass out as she had passed in, without mystery or the rustling of darkness! That was her last, final, ashy dread.

"Old!" she said to herself. "I am not *old!* I have lived many years, that is all. But I am as timeless as an hourglass that turns morning and night, and spills the hours of sleep one way, the hours of consciousness the other way, without itself being affected. Nothing in all my life has ever truly affected me.—I believe Cleopatra only tried the asp, as she tried her pearls in wine, to see if it would really, really have any effect on her. Nothing had ever really had any effect on her, neither Cæsar nor Antony nor any of them. Never once had she really been lost, lost to herself. Then try death, see if that trick would work. If she would lose herself to herself that way.—Ah, death——!"

But Mrs. Witt mistrusted death too. She felt she might pass out as a bed of asters passes out in autumn, to mere nothingness.—And something in her longed to die, at least, *positively:* to be folded then at last into throbbing wings of mystery, like a hawk that goes to sleep. Not like a thing made into a parcel and put into the last rubbish-heap.

So she rode trotting across the hills, mile after mile, in silence. Avoiding the roads, avoiding everything, avoiding everybody, just trotting forwards, towards night.

And by nightfall they had travelled twenty-five miles. She had motored around this country, and knew the little towns and the inns. She knew where she would sleep.

The morning came beautiful and sunny. A woman so strong in health, why should she ride with the fact of death before her eyes? But she did.

Yet in sunny morning she must do something about it.

"Lewis!" she said. "Come here and tell me something, please! Tell me," she said, "do you believe in God?"

"In God!" he said, wondering. "I never think about it."

"But do you say your prayers?"

"No, Mam!"

"Why don't you?"

He thought about it for some minutes.

"I don't like religion. My aunt and uncle were religious."

"You don't like religion," she repeated. "And you don't believe in God.—Well, then——"

"Nay!" he hesitated. "I never said I didn't believe in God.—Only I'm sure I'm not a Methodist. And I feel a fool in a proper church. And I feel a fool saying my prayers.—And I feel a fool when ministers and parsons come getting at me.—I never think about God, if folks don't try to make me." He had a small, sly smile, almost gay.

"And you don't like feeling a fool?" She smiled rather patronizingly.

"No, Mam."

"Do I make you feel a fool?" she asked, dryly.

He looked at her without answering.

"Why don't you answer?" she said, pressing.

"I think you'd like to make a fool of me sometimes," he said.

"Now?" she pressed.

He looked at her with that slow, distant look.

"Maybe!" he said, rather unconcernedly.

Curiously, she couldn't touch him. He always seemed to be watching her from a distance, as if from another country. Even if she made a fool of him, something in him would all the time be far away from her, not implicated.

She caught herself up in the personal game, and returned to her own isolated question. A vicious habit made her start the personal tricks. She didn't want to, really.

There was something about this little man—sometimes, to herself, she called him *Little Jack Horner, Sat in a corner*—that irritated her and made her want to taunt him. His peculiar little inaccessibility, that was so tight and easy.

Then again, there was something, his way of looking at her as if he looked from out of another country, a country of which he was an inhabitant, and where she had never been: this touched her strangely. Perhaps behind this little man was the mystery. In spite of the fact that in actual life, in her world, he was only a groom, almost *chétif*, with his legs a little bit horsy and bowed; and of no education, saying *Yes, Mam!* and *No, Mam!* and accomplishing nothing, simply nothing at all on the face of the earth. Strictly a nonentity.

And yet, what made him perhaps the only real entity to her, his seeming to inhabit another world than hers. A world dark and still, where language never ruffled the growing leaves, and seared their edges like a bad wind.

Was it an illusion, however? Sometimes she thought it was. Just bunkum, which she had faked up, in order to have something to mystify about.

But then, when she saw Phœnix and Lewis silently together, she knew there *was* another communion, silent, excluding her. And sometimes when Lewis was alone with St. Mawr: and once, when she saw him pick up a bird that had stunned itself against a wire: she had realized another world, silent, where each creature is alone in its own aura of silence, the mystery of power: as Lewis had power with St. Mawr, and even with Phœnix.

The visible world, and the invisible. Or rather, the audible and the inaudible. She had lived so long, and so completely, in the visible, audible world. She would not easily admit that other, inaudible. She always wanted to jeer, as she approached the brink of it.

Even now, she wanted to jeer at the little fellow, because of his holding himself inaccessible within the inaudible, silent world. And she knew he knew it.

"Did you never want to be rich, and be a gentleman, like Sir Henry?" she asked.

"I would many times have liked to be rich. But I never exactly wanted to be a gentleman," he said.

"Why not?"

"I can't exactly say. I should be uncomfortable if I was like they are."

"And are you comfortable now?"

"When I'm let alone."

"And do they let you alone? Does the world let you alone?"

"No, they don't."

"Well, then——"

"I keep to myself all I can."

"And are you comfortable, as you call it, when you keep to yourself?"

"Yes, I am."

"But when you keep to yourself, what do you keep to? What precious treasure have you to keep to?"

He looked, and saw she was jeering.

"None," he said. "I've got nothing of that sort."

She rode impatiently on ahead.

And the moment she had done so, she regretted it. She might put the little fellow, with contempt, out of her reckoning. But no, she would not do it.

She had put so much out of her reckoning: soon she would be left in an empty circle, with her empty self at the centre.

She reined in again.

"Lewis!" she said. "I don't want you to take offence at anything I say."

"No, Mam."

"I don't want you to say just *No, Mam!* all the time!" she cried impulsively. "Promise me."

"Yes, Mam!"

"But really! Promise me you won't be offended at whatever I say."

"Yes, Mam!"

She looked at him searchingly. To her surprise, she was almost in tears. A woman of her years! And with a servant!

But his face was blank and stony, with a stony, distant look of pride that made him inaccessible to her emotions. He met her eyes again: with that cold, distant look, looking straight into her hot, confused, pained self. So cold and as if merely refuting her. He didn't believe her, nor trust her, nor like her even. She was an attacking enemy to him. Only he stayed really far away from her, looking down at her from a sort of distant hill where her weapons could not reach: not quite.

And at the same time, it hurt him in a dumb, living way, that she made these attacks on him. She could see the cloud of hurt in his eyes, no matter how distantly he looked at her.

They bought food in a village shop, and sat under a

tree near a field where men were already cutting oats, in a warm valley. Lewis had stabled the horses for a couple of hours, to feed and rest. But he came to join her under the tree, to eat.—He sat at a little distance from her, with the bread and cheese in his small brown hands, eating silently, and watching the harvesters. She was cross with him, and therefore she was stingy, would give him nothing to eat but dry bread and cheese. Herself, she was not hungry.—So all the time he kept his face a little averted from her. As a matter of fact, he kept his whole being averted from her, away from her. He did not want to touch her, nor to be touched by her. He kept his spirit there, alert, on its guard, but out of contact. It was as if he had unconsciously accepted the battle, the old battle. He was her target, the old object of her deadly weapons. But he refused to shoot back. It was as if he caught all her missiles in full flight, before they touched him, and silently threw them on the ground behind him. And in some essential part of himself he ignored her, staying in another world.

That other world! Mere male armour of artificial imperviousness! It angered her.

Yet she knew, by the way he watched the harvesters, and the grasshoppers popping into notice, that it was another world. And when a girl went by, carrying food to the field, it was at him she glanced. And he gave that quick, animal little smile that came from him unawares. Another world!

Yet also, there was a sort of meanness about him: a *suffisance!* A keep-yourself-for-yourself, and don't give yourself away.

Well!—she rose impatiently.

It was hot in the afternoon, and she was rather tired. She went to the inn and slept, and did not start again till tea-time.

Then they had to ride rather late. The sun sank, among a smell of cornfields, clear and yellow-red behind motionless dark trees. Pale smoke rose from cottage chimneys. Not a cloud was in the sky, which held the upward-floating like a bowl inverted on purpose. A new moon sparkled and was gone. It was beginning of night.

Away in the distance, they saw a curious pinkish glare
of fire, probably furnaces. And Mrs. Witt thought she
could detect the scent of furnace smoke, or factory smoke.
But then she always said that of the English air: it was
never quite free of the smell of smoke, coal-smoke.

They were riding slowly on a path through fields, down
a long slope. Away below was a puther of lights. All the
darkness seemed full of half-spent crossing lights, a curious
uneasiness. High in the sky a star seemed to be walking.
It was an aeroplane with a light. Its buzz rattled above.
Not a space, not a speck of this country that wasn't hu-
manized, occupied by the human claim. Not even the sky.

They descended slowly through a dark wood, which
they had entered through a gate. Lewis was all the time
dismounting and opening gates, letting her pass, shutting
the gate and mounting again.

So, in a while she came to the edge of the wood's darkness, and saw the open pale concave of the world beyond.
The darkness was never dark. It shook with the concus-
sion of many invisible lights, lights of towns, villages,
mines, factories, furnaces, squatting in the valleys and behind all the hills.

Yet, as Rachel Witt drew rein at the gate emerging from
the wood, a very big, soft star fell in heaven, cleaving the
hubbub of this human night with a gleam from the
greater world.

"See! a star falling!" said Lewis, as he opened the gate.

"I saw it," said Mrs. Witt, walking her horse past him.

There was a curious excitement of wonder, or magic,
in the little man's voice. Even in this night something
strange had stirred awake in him.

"You ask me about God," he said to her, walking his
horse alongside in the shadow of the wood's edge, the
darkness of the old Pan, that kept our artificially lit world
at bay. "I don't know about God. But when I see a star fall
like that out of long-distance places in the sky: and the
moon sinking saying Good-bye! Good-bye! Good-bye! and
nobody listening: I think I hear something, though I
wouldn't call it God."

"What then?" said Rachel Witt.

"And you smell the smell of oak-leaves now," he said,

"now the air is cold. They smell to me more alive than people. The trees hold their bodies hard and still, but they watch and listen with their leaves. And I think they say to me: *Is that you passing there, Morgan Lewis? All right, you pass quickly, we shan't do anything to you. You are like a holly-bush.*"

"Yes," said Rachel Witt, dryly. *"Why?"*

"All the time, the trees grow, and listen. And if you cut a tree down without asking pardon, trees will hurt you some time in your life, in the night-time."

"I suppose," said Rachel Witt, "that's an old superstition."

"They say that ash-trees don't like people. When the other people were most in the country—I mean like what they call fairies, that have all gone now—they liked ash-trees best. And you know the little green things with little small nuts in them, that come flying down from ash-trees —*pigeons,* we call them—they're the seeds—the other people used to catch them and eat them before they fell to the ground. And that made the people so they could hear trees living and feeling things.—But when all these people that there are now came to England, they liked the oak-trees best, because their pigs ate the acorns. So now you can tell the ash-trees are mad, they want to kill all these people. But the oak-trees are many more than the ash-trees."

"And do you eat the ash-tree seeds?" she asked.

"I always ate them when I was little. Then I wasn't frightened of ash-trees, like most of the others. And I wasn't frightened of the moon. If you didn't go near the fire all day, and if you didn't eat any cooked food nor anything that had been in the sun, but only things like turnips or radishes or pig-nuts, and then went without any clothes on, in the full moon, then you could see the people in the moon, and go with them. They never have fire, and they never speak, and their bodies are clear almost like jelly. They die in a minute if there's a bit of fire near them. But they know more than we. Because unless fire touches them, they never die. They see people live and they see people perish, and they say people are only like twigs on a tree, you break them off the tree, and kindle with them.

You make a fire of them, and they are gone, the fire is gone, everything is gone. But the people of the moon don't die, and fire is nothing to them. They look at it from the distance of the sky, and see it burning things up, people all appearing and disappearing like twigs that come in spring and you cut them in autumn and make a fire of them and they are gone. And they say: what do people matter? If you want to matter, you must become a moon-boy. Then, all your life, fire can't blind you and people can't hurt you. Because at full moon you can join the moon people, and go through the air and pass any cool places, pass through rocks and through the trunks of trees, and when you come to people lying warm in bed, you punish them."

"How?"

"You sit on the pillow where they breathe, and you put a web across their mouth, so they can't breathe the fresh air that comes from the moon. So they go on breathing the same air again and again, and that makes them more and more stupefied. The sun gives out heat, but the moon gives out fresh air. That's what the moon people do: they wash the air clean with moonlight."

He was talking with a strange eager naïveté that amused Rachel Witt, and made her a little uncomfortable in her skin. Was he after all no more than a sort of imbecile?

"Who told you all this stuff?" she asked abruptly.

And, as abruptly, he pulled himself up.

"We used to say it, when we were children."

"But you don't believe it? It *is* only childishness, after all."

He paused a moment or two.

"No," he said, in his ironical little day-voice. "I know I shan't make anything but a fool of myself, with that talk. But all sorts of things go through our heads, and some seem to linger, and some don't. But you asking me about God put it into my mind, I suppose. I don't know what sort of things I believe in: only I know it's not what the chapel-folks believe in. We, none of us believe in them when it comes to earning a living, or, with you people, when it comes to spending your fortune. Then we know that bread costs money, and even your sleep you have to pay for.—That's work. Or, with you people, it's just owning property and seeing you get your value for your money.—But a man's mind is always full of things. And some people's minds, like my aunt and uncle, are full of religion and hell for everybody except themselves. And some people's minds are all money, money, money, and how to get hold of something they haven't got hold of yet. And some people, like you, are always curious about what everybody else in the world is after. And some people are all for enjoying themselves and being thought much of, and some, like Lady Carrington, don't know what to do with themselves. Myself, I don't want to have in my mind the things other people have in their minds. I'm one that likes my own things best. And if, when I see a bright star fall, like to-night, I think to myself: *There's movement in the sky. The world is going to change again. They're throwing something to us from the distance, and we've got to have it, whether we want it or not. To-morrow there will be a difference for everybody, thrown out of the sky upon us, whether we want it or not:* then that's how I want to think, so let me please myself."

"You know what a shooting star actually is, I suppose? —and that there are always many in August, because we pass through a region of them?"

"Yes, Mam, I've been told. But stones don't come at us from the sky for nothing. Either it's like when a man tosses an apple to you out of his orchard, as you go by, or it's like when somebody shies a stone at you, to cut your head open. You'll never make me believe the sky is like an empty house with a slate falling from the roof. The world has its own life, the sky has a life of its own, and never is it like stones rolling down a rubbish-heap and falling into a pond. Many things twitch and twitter within the sky, and many things happen beyond us. My own way of thinking is my own way."

"I never knew you talk so much."

"No, Mam. It's your asking me that about God. Or else it's the night-time. I don't believe in God and being good and going to heaven. Neither do I worship idols, so I'm not a heathen, as my aunt called me. Never from a boy did I want to believe the things they kept grinding in their guts at home, and at Sunday School, and at school. A man's mind has to be full of something, so I keep to what we used to think as lads. It's childish nonsense, I know it. But it suits me. Better than other people's stuff. Your man Phœnix is about the same, when he lets on.—Anyhow, its my own stuff, that we believed as lads, and I like it better than other people's stuff.—You asking about God made me let on. But I would never belong to any club, or trades-union, and God's the same to my mind."

With this he gave a little kick to his horse, and St. Mawr went dancing excitedly along the highway they now entered, leaving Mrs. Witt to trot after as rapidly as she could.

When she came to the hotel, to which she had telegraphed for rooms, Lewis disappeared, and she was left thinking hard.

It was not till they were twenty miles from Merriton, riding through a slow morning mist, and she had a rather far-away, wistful look on her face, unusual for her, that she turned to him in the saddle and said:

"Now don't be surprised, Lewis, at what I am going to say. I am going to ask you, now, supposing I wanted to marry you, what should you say?"

He looked at her quickly, and was at once on his guard.

"That you didn't mean it," he replied hastily.

"Yes,"—she hesitated, and her face looked wistful and tired.—"Supposing I *did* mean it. Supposing I did *really*, from my heart, want to marry you and be a wife to you—" she looked away across the fields—"then what should you say?"

Her voice sounded sad, a little broken.

"Why, Mam!" he replied, knitting his brow and shaking his head a little. "I should say you didn't mean it, you know. Something would have come over you."

"But supposing I *wanted* something to come over me?"

He shook his head.

"It would never do, Mam! Some people's flesh and blood is kneaded like bread: and that's me. And some are rolled like fine pastry, like Lady Carrington. And some are mixed with gunpowder. They're like a cartridge you put in a gun, Mam."

She listened impatiently.

"Don't talk," she said, "about bread and cakes and pastry, it all means nothing. You used to answer short enough, *Yes, Mam! No, Mam!* That will do now. Do you mean *Yes!* or *No?*"

His eyes met hers. She was again hectoring.

"No, Mam!" he said, quite neutral.

"Why?"

As she waited for his answer, she saw the foundations of his loquacity dry up, his face go distant and mute again, as it always used to be, till these last two days, when it had had a funny touch of inconsequential merriness.

He looked steadily into her eyes, and his look was neutral, sombre, and hurt. He looked at her as if infinite seas, infinite spaces divided him and her. And his eyes seemed to put her away beyond some sort of fence. An anger congealed cold like lava, set impassive against her and all her sort.

"No, Mam. I couldn't give my body to any woman who didn't respect it."

"But I do respect it, I do!"—she flushed hot like a girl.

"No, Mam. Not as *I* mean it," he replied.

There was a touch of anger against her in his voice, and a distance of distaste.

"And how do *you* mean it?" she replied, the full sarcasm coming back into her tones. She could see that as a woman to touch and fondle he saw her as repellent: only repellent.

"I have to be a servant to women now," he said, "even to earn my wage. I could never touch with my body a woman whose servant I was."

"You're not my servant: my daughter pays your wages. —And all that is beside the point, between a man and a woman."

"No woman who I touched with my body should ever speak to me as you speak to me, or think of me as you think of me," he said.

"But—" she stammered, "I think of you—with love. And can you be so unkind as to notice the way I speak? You know it's only my way."

"You, as a woman," he said, "you have no respect for a man."

"Respect! Respect!" she cried. "I'm likely to lose what respect I have left. I know I can *love* a man. But whether a man can love a woman——"

"No," said Lewis. "I never could, and I think I never shall. Because I don't want to. The thought of it makes me feel shame."

"What do you mean?" she cried.

"Nothing in the world," he said, "would make me feel such shame as to have a woman shouting at me, or mocking at me, as I see women mocking and despising the men they marry. No woman shall touch my body, and mock me or despise me. No woman."

"But men must be mocked, or despised even, sometimes."

"No. Not this man. Not by the woman I touch with my body."

"Are you perfect?"

"I don't know. But if I touch a woman with my body, it must put a lock on her, to respect what I will never have despised: never!"

"What will you never have despised?"

"My body! And my touch upon the woman."

"Why insist so on your body?"—And she looked at him with a touch of contemptuous mockery, raillery.

He looked her in the eyes, steadily, and coldly, putting her away from him, and himself far away from her.

"Do you expect that any woman will stay your humble slave to-day?" she asked cuttingly.

But he only watched her, coldly, distant, refusing any connexion.

"Between men and women, it's a question of give and take. A man can't expect *always* to be humbly adored."

He watched her still, cold, rather pale, putting her far from him. Then he turned his horse and set off rapidly along the road, leaving her to follow.

She walked her horse and let him go, thinking to herself:

"There's a little bantam cock. And a groom! Imagine it! Thinking he can dictate to a woman!"

She was in love with him. And he, in an odd way, was in love with her. She had known it by the odd, uncanny merriment in him, and his unexpected loquacity. But he would not have her come physically near him. Unapproachable there as a cactus, guarding his "body" from her contact. As if contact with her would be mortal insult and fatal injury to his marvellous "body."

What a little cock-sparrow!

Let him ride ahead. He would have to wait for her somewhere.

She found him at the entrance to the next village. His face was pallid and set. She could tell he felt he had been insulted, so he had congealed into stiff insentience.

"At the bottom of all men is the same," she said to herself: "An empty, male conceit of themselves."

She too rode up with a face like a mask, and straight on to the hotel.

"Can you serve dinner to myself and my servant?" she asked at the inn: which, fortunately for her, accommodated motorists, otherwise they would have said *No!*

"I think," said Lewis as they came in sight of Merriton, "I'd better give Lady Carrington a week's notice."

A complete little stranger! And an impudent one.

"Exactly as you please," she said.

She found several letters from her daughter at Marshall Place.

"Dear Mother: No sooner had you gone off than Flora appeared, not at all in the bud, but rather in full blow. She demanded her victim: Shylock demanding the pound of flesh: and wanted to hand over the shekels.

"Joyfully I refused them. She said 'Harry' was much better, and invited him and me to stay at Corrabach Hall till he was quite well: it would be less strain on your household while he was still in bed and helpless. So the plan is that he shall be brought down on Friday, if he is really fit for the journey, and we drive straight to Corrabach. I am packing his bags and mine, clearing up our traces: his trunks to go to Corrabach, mine to stay here and make up their minds.—I am going to Flints Farm again to-morrow, dutifully, though I am no flower for the bedside.—I do so want to know if Rico has already called her Fiorita: or perhaps Florecita. It reminds me of old William's joke: *Now yuh tell me, little Missy: which is the*

best posy that grow? And the hushed whisper in which
he said the answer: *The Collyposy!* Oh, dear, I am so
tired of feeling spiteful, but how else is one to feel?

"You looked most prosaically romantic, setting off in a
rubber cape, followed by Lewis. Hope the roads were
not very slippery, and that you had a good time, *á la
Mademoiselle de Maupin*. Do remember, dear, not to de-
vour little Lewis before you have got half-way———"

"Dear Mother: I half expected word from you before I
left, but nothing came. Forrester drove me up here just
before lunch. Rico seems much better, almost himself,
and a little more than that. He broached our staying at
Corrabach very tactfully. I told him Flora had asked me,
and it seemed a good plan. Then I told him about St.
Mawr. He was a little piqued, and there was a pause of
very disapproving silence. Then he said: *Very well, darling. If you wish to keep the animal, do so by all means. I
make a present of him again.* Me: *That's so good of you,
Rico. Because I know revenge is sweet.* Rico: *Revenge,
Loulina! I don't think I was selling him for vengeance!
Merely to get rid of him to Flora, who can keep better
hold over him.* Me: *But you know, dear, she was going to
geld him!* Rico: *I don't think anybody knew it. We only
wondered if it were possible, to make him more amenable.
Did she tell you?* Me: *No—Phœnix did. He had it from
a groom.* Rico: *Dear me! A concatenation of grooms! So
your mother rode off with Lewis, and carried St. Mawr
out of danger! I understand! Let us hope worse won't be-
fall.* Me: *Whom?* Rico: *Never mind, dear! It's so lovely
to see you. You are looking rested. I thought those Coun-
tess of Witton roses the most marvellous things in the
world, till you came, now they're quite in the background.*
He had some very lovely red roses, in a crystal bowl: the
room smelled of roses. Me: *Where did they come from?*
Rico: *Oh, Flora brought them!* Me: *Bowl and all?* Rico:
Bowl and all! Wasn't it dear of her? Me: *Why, yes! But
then she's the goddess of flowers, isn't she?* Poor darling,
he was offended that I should twit him while he is ill, so
I relented. He has had a couple of marvellous invalid's
bed-jackets sent from London: one a pinkish yellow, with
rose-arabesque facings: this one in fine cloth. But un-

fortunately he has already dropped soup on it. The other is a lovely silvery and blue and green soft brocade. He had that one on to receive me, and I at once complimented him on it. He has got a new ring too: sent by Aspasia Weingartner, a rather lovely <u>intaglio</u> of Priapus under an apple bough, at least so he says it is. He made a naughty face, and said: *The Priapus stage is rather advanced for poor me.* I asked what the Priapus stage, was, but he said: *Oh, nothing!* Then nurse said: *There's a big classical dictionary that Miss Manby brought up, if you wish to see it.* So I have been studying the Classical Gods. The world always was a queer place. It's a very queer one when Rico is the god Priapus. He would go round the orchard painting lifelike apples on the trees, and inviting nymphs to come and eat them. And the nymphs would pretend they were real: *Why, Sir Prippy, what stunningly naughty apples!* There's nothing so artificial as sinning nowadays. I suppose it once was real.

"I'm bored here: wish I had my horse."

"Dear Mother: I'm so glad you are enjoying your ride. I'm sure it is like riding into history, like the Yankee at the Court of King Arthur, in those old by-lanes and Roman roads. They still fascinate me: at least, more before I get there than when I am actually there. I begin to feel real American and to resent the past. Why doesn't the past decently bury itself, instead of sitting waiting to be admired by the present?

"Phœnix brought Poppy. I am so fond of her: rode for five hours yesterday. I was glad to get away from this farm. The doctor came, and said Rico would be able to go down to Corrabach to-morrow. Flora came to hear the bulletin, and sailed back full of zest. Apparently Rico is going to do a portrait of her, sitting up in bed. What a mercy the bed-clothes won't be mine when Priapus wields his palette from the pillow.

"Phœnix thinks you intend to go to America with St. Mawr, and that I am coming too, leaving Rico this side. —I wonder. I feel so unreal, nowadays, as if I too were nothing more than a painting by Rico on a mill-board. I feel almost too unreal even to make up my mind to anything. It is terrible when the life-flow dies out of one, and everything is like cardboard, and oneself is like cardboard. I'm sure it is worse than being dead. I realized it yesterday when Phœnix and I had a picnic lunch by a stream. You see I must imitate you in all things. He found me some water-cresses, and they tasted so damp and *alive*, I knew how deadened I was. Phœnix wants us to go and have a ranch in Arizona, and raise horses, with St. Mawr, if willing, for Father Abraham. I wonder if it matters what one does: if it isn't all the same thing over again. Only Phœnix, his funny blank face, makes my heart melt and go sad. But I believe he'd be cruel too. I saw it in his face when he didn't know I was looking. Anything though, rather than this deadness and this paint-Priapus business. *Au revoir*, mother dear! Keep on having a good time——"

"Dear Mother: I had your letter from Merriton: am so glad you arrived safe and sound in body and temper. There was such a funny letter from Lewis, too: I enclose it. What makes him take this extraordinary line? But I'm writing to tell him to take St. Mawr to London, and wait for me there. I have telegraphed Mrs. Squire to get the house ready for me. I shall go straight there.

"Things developed here as they were bound to. I just couldn't bear it. No sooner was Rico put in the automobile than a self-conscious importance came over him, like when the wounded hero is carried into the middle of the stage. *Why so solemn, Rico dear?* I asked him, trying to laugh him out of it. *Not solemn, dear, only feeling a little transient.* I don't think he knew himself what he meant. Flora was on the steps as the car drew up, dressed in severe white. She only needed an apron, to become a nurse: or a veil, to become a bride. Between the two, she had an unbearable air of a woman in seduced circumstances, as the *Times* said. She ordered two menservants about in subdued, you would have said hushed, but competent tones. And then I saw there was a touch of the priestess about her as well: Cassandra preparing for her violation: Iphigenia, with Rico for Orestes, on a stretcher: he looking like Adonis, fully prepared to be an unconscionable time in dying. They had given him a lovely room, downstairs, with doors opening on to a little garden all of its own. I believe it was Flora's boudoir. I left nurse

and the men to put him to bed. Flora was hovering anxiously in the passage outside. *Oh, what a marvellous room!
Oh, how colourful, how beautiful!* came Rico's tones, the
hero behind the scenes. I must say, it was like a harvest
festival, with roses and gaillardias in the shadow, and corn-
flowers in the light, and a bowl of grapes, and nectarines
among leaves. *I'm so anxious that he should be happy,*
Flora said to me in the passage. *You know him best. Is
there anything else I could do for him?* Me: *Why, if you
went to the piano and sang, I'm sure he'd love it. Couldn't
you sing: Oh, my love is like a rred, rred rrose!*—You
know how Rico imitates Scotch!

"Thank goodness I have a bedroom upstairs: nurse
sleeps in a little antechamber to Rico's room. The Edwards
are still here, the blond young man with some very fu-
turistic plaster on his face. *Awfully good of you to come!*
he said to me, looking at me out of one eye, and holding
my hand fervently. How's that for cheek? *It's awfully
good of Miss Manby to let me come,* said I. He: *Ah, but
Flora is always a sport, a topping good sport!*

"I don't know what's the matter, but it just all put me
into a fiendish temper. I felt I couldn't sit there at luncheon with that bright, youthful company, and hear about
their tennis and their polo and their hunting and have
their flirtatiousness making me sick. So I asked for a tray in
my room. Do as I might, I couldn't help being horrid.

"Oh, and Rico! He really is too awful. Lying there in
bed with every ear open, like Adonis waiting to be per-
suaded not to die. Seizing a hushed moment to take Flora's
hand and press it to his lips, murmuring: *How awfully
good you are to me, dear Flora!* And Flora: *I'd be better
if I knew how, Harry!* So cheerful with it all! No, it's too
much. My sense of humour is leaving me: which means,
I'm getting into too bad a temper to be able to ridicule it
all. I suppose I feel in the minority. It's an awful thought,
to think that most all the young people in the world are
like this: so bright and cheerful, and *sporting*, and so
brimming with *libido*. How awful!

"I said to Rico: *You're very comfortable here, aren't
you?* He: *Comfortable! It's comparative heaven.* Me:
Would you mind if I went away? A deadly pause. He is

deadly afraid of being left alone with Flora. He feels safe
so long as I am about, and he can take refuge in his marriage ties. He: *Where do you want to go, dear?* Me: *To
mother. To London. Mother is planning to go to America,
and she wants me to go.* Rico: *But you don't want to go
t—he—e—re—e!* You know, mother, how Rico can put a
venomous emphasis on a word, till it suggests pure poison.
It nettled me. *I'm not sure,* I said. Rico: *Oh, but you
can't stand that awful America.* Me: *I want to try again.*
Rico: *But, Lou dear, it will be winter before you get
there. And this is absolutely the wrong moment for me
to go over there. I am only just making headway over
here. When I am absolutely sure of a position in England,
then we nip across the Atlantic and scoop in a few dollars,
if you like. Just now, even when I am well, would be fatal.
I've only just sketched in the outline of my success in
London, and one ought to arrive in New York ready-made
as a famous and important Artist.* Me: *But mother and I
didn't think of going to New York. We thought we'd sail
straight to New Orleans—if we could: or to Havana. And
then go West to Arizona.* The poor boy looked at me in
such distress. *But, Loulina darling, do you mean you want
to leave me in the lurch for the winter season? You can't
mean it. We're just getting on so splendidly, really!*—I was
surprised at the depth of feeling in his voice: how tremendously his career as an artist—a popular artist—matters to him. I can never believe it.—You know, mother,
you and I feel alike about daubing paint on canvas: every
possible daub that can be daubed has already been done,
so people ought to leave off. Rico is so shrewd. I always
think he's got his tongue in his cheek, and I'm always stag-
gered once more to find that he takes it absolutely seriously. His career! The Modern British Society of Painters:
perhaps even the Royal Academy! Those people we see
in London, and those portraits Rico does! He may even
be a second Laslow, or a thirteenth Orpen, and die happy!
Oh! mother! How can it really matter to *anybody!*

"But I was really rather upset, when I realized how his
heart was fixed on his career, and that I might be spoiling
everything for him. So I went away to think about it. And
then I realized how unpopular you are, and how un-

popular I shall be myself, in a little while. A sort of hatred
for people has come over me. I hate their ways and their
bunk, and I feel like kicking them in the face, as St.
Mawr did that young man. Not that I should ever do it.
And I don't think I should ever have made my final an-
nouncement to Rico, if he hadn't been such a beautiful
pig in clover, here at Corrabach Hall. He has known the
Manbys all his life; they and he are sections of one engine.
He would be far happier with Flora: or I won't say happier, because there is something in him which rebels:
but he would on the whole fit much better. I myself am at
the end of my limit, and beyond it. I can't 'mix' any more,
and I refuse to. I feel like a bit of eggshell in the mayonnaise: the only thing is to take it out, you can't beat it in.
I *know* I shall cause a fiasco, even in Rico's career, if I
stay. I shall go on being rude and hateful to people as I
am at Corrabach, and Rico will lose all his nerve.

"So I have told him. I said this evening, when no one
was about: *Rico dear, listen to me seriously. I can't stand
these people. If you ask me to endure another week of
them, I shall either become ill or insult them, as mother
does. And I don't want to do either. Rico: But, darling,
isn't everybody perfect to you!* Me: *I tell you, I shall just
make a break, like St. Mawr, if I don't get out. I simply
can't stand people.*—The poor darling, his face goes so
blank and anxious. He knows what I mean, because, except that they tickle his vanity all the time, he hates them
as much as I do. But his vanity is the chief thing to him.
He: *Lou darling, can't you wait till I get up, and we can
go away to the Tyrol or somewhere for a spell?* Me: *Won't
you come with me to America, to the South-west? I believe it's marvellous country.*—I saw his face switch into
hostility; quite vicious. He: *Are you so keen on spoiling everything for me? Is that what I married you for? Do
you do it deliberately?* Me: *Everything is already spoilt
for me. I tell you I can't stand people, your Floras and
your Aspasias, and your forthcoming young Englishmen.
After all, I am an American, like mother, and I've got to
go back.* He: *Really! And am I to come along as part of
the luggage, Labelled cabin!* Me: *You do as you wish,
Rico.* He: *I wish to God you did as you wished, Lou*

*dear. I'm afraid you do as Mrs. Witt wishes. I've always
heard that the holiest thing in the world was a mother.*
Me: *No, dear, it's just that I can't stand people.* He
(with a snarl): *And I suppose I'm lumped in as* PEOPLE!
And when he'd said it, it was true. We neither of us said
anything for a time. Then he said, calculating: *Very well,
dear! You take a trip to the land of stars and stripes, and
I'll stay here and go on with my work. And when you've
seen enough of their stars and tasted enough of their
stripes, you can come back and take your place again with
me.*—We left it at that.

"You and I are supposed to have important business
connected with our estates in Texas—it sounds so well
—so we are making a hurried trip to the States, as they
call them. I shall leave for London early next week——"

Mrs. Witt read this long letter with satisfaction. She
herself had one strange craving: to get back to America.
It was not that she idealized her native country: she was
a tartar of restlessness there, quite as much as in Europe.
It was not that she expected to arrive at any blessed abid-
ing-place. No, in America she would go on fuming and
chafing the same. But at least she would be in America,
in her own country. And that was what she wanted.

She picked up the sheet of poor paper, that had been
folded in Lou's letter. It was the letter from Lewis, quite
nicely written. "Lady Carrington, I write to tell you and
Sir Henry that I think I had better quit your service, as
it would be more comfortable all round. If you will write
and tell me what you want me to do with St. Mawr, I
will do whatever you tell me. With kind regards to Lady
Carrington and Sir Henry, I remain, Your obedient servant, Morgan Lewis."

Mrs. Witt put the letter aside, and sat looking out of
the window. She felt, strangely, as if already her soul had
gone away from her actual surroundings. She was there,
in Oxfordshire, in the body, but her spirit had departed
elsewhere. A listlessness was upon her. It was with an
effort she roused herself, to write to her lawyer in London,
to get her release from her English obligations. Then she
wrote to the London hotel.

For the first time in her life she wished she had a

maid, to do little things for her. All her life, she had had
too much energy to endure anyone hanging round her,
personally. Now she gave up. Her wrists seemed numb,
as if the power in her were switched off.

When she went down, they said Lewis had asked to
speak to her. She had hardly seen him since they had arrived at Merriton.

"I've had a letter from Lady Carrington, Mam. She says
will I take St. Mawr to London and wait for her there.
But she says I am to come to you, Mam, for definite or-
ders."

"Very well, Lewis. I shall be going to London in a few
days' time. You arrange for St. Mawr to go up one day
this week, and you will take him to the Mews. Come to
me for anything you want. And don't talk of leaving my
daughter. We want you to go with St. Mawr to America,
with us and Phœnix."

"And your horse, Mam?"

"I shall leave him here at Merriton. I shall give him to
Miss Atherton."

"Very good, Mam!"

"Dear Daughter: I shall be in my old quarters in Mayfair next Saturday, calling the same day at your house to
see if everything is ready for you. Lewis has fixed up
with the railway: he goes to town to-morrow. The reason
of his letter was that I had asked him if he would care to
marry me, and he turned me down with emphasis. But I
will tell you about it. You and I are the scribe and the
Pharisee; I never could write a letter, and you could never
leave off——"

"Dearest Mother: I smelt something rash, but I know
it's no use saying: How *could* you? I only wonder, though,
that you should think of marriage. You know, dear, I ache
in every fibre to be left alone, from all that sort of thing. I
feel all bruises, like one who has been assassinated. I do
so understand why Jesus said: *Noli me tangere.* Touch me
not, I am not yet ascended unto the Father. Everything
had hurt him so much, wearied him so beyond endurance,
he felt he could not bear one little human touch on his
body. I am like that. I can hardly bear even Elena to hand
me a dress. As for a man—and marriage—ah, no! *Noli me*

tangere, homo! I am not yet ascended unto the Father. Oh, leave me alone, leave me alone! That is all my cry to all the world.

"Curiously, I feel that Phœnix understands what I feel. He leaves me so understandingly alone, he almost gives me my sheath of aloneness: or at least, he protects me in my sheath. I am grateful for him.

"Whereas Rico feels my aloneness as a sort of shame to himself. He wants at least a blinding *pretence* of intimacy. Ah, intimacy! The thought of it fills me with aches, and the pretence of it exhausts me beyond myself.

"Yes, I long to go away to the West, to be away from the world like one dead and in another life, in a valley that life has not yet entered.

"Rico asked me: What are you doing with St. Mawr? When I said we were taking him with us, he said: *Oh, the corpus delicti!* Whether that means anything I don't know. But he has grown sarcastic beyond my depth.

"I shall see you to-morrow——"

Lou arrived in town, at the dead end of August, with her maid and Phœnix. How wonderful it seemed to have London empty of all her set: her own little house to herself, with just the housekeeper and her own maid. The fact of being alone in those surroundings was so wonderful. It made the surroundings themselves seem all the more ghostly. Everything that had been actual to her was turning ghostly: even her little drawing-room was the ghost of a room, belonging to the dead people who had known it, or to all the dead generations that had brought such a room into being, evolved it out of their quaint domestic desires. And now, in herself, those desires were suddenly spent: gone out like a lamp that suddenly dies. And then she saw her pale, delicate room with its little green agate bowl and its two little porcelain birds and its soft, roundish chairs, turned into something ghostly, like a room set out in a museum. She felt like fastening little labels on the furniture: *Lady Louise Carrington Lounge Chair, Last used August, 1923.* Not for the benefit of posterity: but to remove her own self into another world, another realm of existence.

"My house, my house, my house, how can I ever have

taken so much pains about it!" she kept saying to herself. It was like one of her old hats, suddenly discovered neatly put away in an old hatbox. And what a horror: an old "fashionable" hat!

Lewis came to see her, and he sat there in one of her delicate mauve chairs, with his feet on a delicate old carpet from Turkestan, and she just wondered. He wore his leather gaiters and khaki breeches as usual, and a faded blue shirt. But his beard and hair were trimmed, he was tidy. There was a certain fineness of contour about him, a certain subtle gleam, which made him seem, apart from his rough boots, not at all gross, or coarse, in that setting of rather silky, oriental furnishings. Rather he made the Asiatic, sensuous exquisiteness of her old rugs and her old white Chinese figures seem a weariness. Beauty! What was beauty, she asked herself? The oriental exquisiteness seemed to her all like dead flowers whose hour had come, to be thrown away.

Lou could understand her mother's wanting, for a moment, to marry him. His detachedness and his acceptance of something in destiny which people cannot accept. Right in the middle of him he accepted something from destiny, that gave him a quality of eternity. He did not care about persons, people, even events. In his own odd way, he was an aristocrat, unaccessible in his aristocracy. But it was the aristocracy of the invisible powers, the greater influences, nothing to do with human society.

"You don't really want to leave St. Mawr, do you?" Lou asked him. "You don't really want to quit, as you said?"

He looked at her steadily, from his pale-grey eyes, without answering, not knowing what to say.

"Mother told me what she said to you.—But she doesn't mind, she says you are entirely within your rights. She has a real regard for you. But we mustn't let our regards run us into actions which are beyond our scope, must we? That makes everything unreal. But you will come with us to America with St. Mawr, won't you? We depend on you."

"I don't want to be uncomfortable," he said.

"Don't be," she smiled. "I myself hate unreal situations—I feel I can't stand them any more. And most marriages are unreal situations. But apart from anything exaggerated, you like being with mother and me, don't you?"

"Yes, I do. I like Mrs. Witt as well. But not——"

"I know. There won't be any more of that——"

"You see, Lady Carrington," he said, with a little heat, "I'm not by nature a marrying man. And I should feel I was selling myself."

"Quite!—Why do you think you are not a marrying man, though?"

"Me! I don't feel myself after I've been with women." He spoke in a low tone, looking down at his hands. "I feel messed up. I'm better to keep to myself.—Because——" and here he looked up with a flare in his eyes—"women —they only want to make you give in to them, so that they feel almighty, and you feel small."

"Don't you like feeling small?" Lou smiled. "And don't you want to make them give in to you?"

"Not me," he said. "I don't want nothing. Nothing, I want."

"Poor mother!" said Lou. "She thinks if she feels moved by a man, it must result in marriage—or that kind of thing. Surely she makes a mistake. I think you and Phœnix and mother and I might live somewhere in a far-away wild place, and make a good life: so long as we didn't begin to mix up marriage, or love or that sort of thing, into it. It seems to me men and women have really hurt one another so much, nowadays, that they had better stay apart till they have learned to be gentle with one another again. Not all this forced passion and destructive philandering. Men and women should stay apart, till their hearts grow gentle towards one another again. Now, it's only each one fighting for his own—or her own—underneath the cover of tenderness."

"*Dear!—darling!—Yes, my love!*" mocked Lewis, with a faint smile of amused contempt.

"Exactly. People always say *dearest!* when they hate each other most."

Lewis nodded, looking at her with a sudden sombre gloom in his eyes. A queer bitterness showed on his mouth. But even then, he was so still and remote.

The housekeeper came and announced The Honourable Laura Ridley. This was like a blow in the face of Lou. She rose hurriedly—and Lewis rose, moving to the door.

"Don't go, please, Lewis," said Lou—and then Laura Ridley appeared in the doorway. She was a woman a few years older than Lou, but she looked younger. She might have been a shy girl of twenty-two, with her fresh complexion, her hesitant manner, her round, startled brown eyes, her bobbed hair.

"Hello!" said the new-comer. "Imagine your being back! I saw you in Paddington."

Those sharp eyes would see everything.

"I thought everyone was out of town," said Lou. "This is Mr. Lewis."

Laura gave him a little nod, then sat on the edge of her chair.

"No," she said. "I did go to Ireland to my people, but I came back. I prefer London when I can be more or less alone in it. I thought I'd just run in for a moment, before you're gone again.—Scotland, isn't it?"

"No, mother and I are going to America."

"America! Oh, I thought it was Scotland."

"It was. But we have suddenly to go to America."

"I see!—And what about Rico?"

"He is staying on in Shropshire. Didn't you hear of his accident?"

Lou told about it briefly.

"But how awful!" said Laura. "But there! I knew it! I had a premonition when I saw that horse. We had a horse that killed a man. Then my father got rid of it. But ours was a mare, that one. Yours is a boy."

"A full-grown man, I'm afraid."

"Yes, of course, I remember.—But how awful! I suppose you won't ride in the Row. The awful people that ride there nowadays, anyhow! Oh, aren't they awful! Aren't people monstrous, really! My word, when I see the horses crossing Hyde Park corner, on a wet day, and coming down smash on those slippery stones, giving their riders a fractured skull!—No joke!"

She enquired details of Rico.

"Oh, I suppose I shall see him when he gets back," she said. "But I'm sorry you are going. I shall miss you, I'm afraid. Though you won't be staying long in America. No one stays there longer than they can help."

"I think the winter through, at least," said Lou.

"Oh, all the winter! So long? I'm sorry to hear *that*. You're one of the few, very few people one can talk *really* simply with. Extraordinary, isn't it, how few really simple people there are! And they get fewer and fewer. I stayed a fortnight with my people, and a week of that I was in bed. It was really horrible. They really try to take the life out of one, *really!* Just because one won't be as they are, and play their game. I simply refused, and came away."

"But you can't cut yourself off altogether," said Lou.

"No, I suppose not. One has to see somebody. Luckily one has a few artists for friends. They're the only real people, anyhow——" She glanced round inquisitively at Lewis, and said, with a slight, impertinent elvish smile on her virgin face:

"Are you an artist?"

"No, Mam!" he said. "I'm a groom."

"Oh, I see!" She looked him up and down.

"Lewis is St. Mawr's master," said Lou.

"Oh, the horse! the terrible horse!" She paused a moment. Then again she turned to Lewis with that faint smile, slightly condescending, slightly impertinent, slightly flirtatious.

"Aren't you afraid of him?" she asked.

"No, Mam."

"Aren't you *really!*—And can you always master him?"

"Mostly. He knows me."

"Yes! I suppose that's it."—She looked him up and down again, then turned away to Lou.

"What have you been painting lately?" said Lou. Laura was not a bad painter.

"Oh, hardly anything. I haven't been able to get on at all. This is one of my bad intervals."

Here Lewis rose, and looked at Lou.

"All right," she said. "Come in after lunch, and we'll finish those arrangements."

Laura gazed after the man, as he dived out of the room, as if her eyes were gimlets that could bore into his secret.

In the course of the conversation she said:

"What a curious little man that was!"

"Which?"

"The groom who was here just now. *Very* curious! Such peculiar eyes. I shouldn't wonder if he had psychic powers."

"What sort of psychic powers?" said Lou.

"Could *see* things.—And hypnotic too. He might have hypnotic powers."

"What makes you think so?"

"He gives me that sort of feeling. Very curious! Probably he hypnotizes the horse.—Are you leaving the horse here, by the way, in stable?"

"No, taking him to America."

"Taking him to America! How extraordinary!"

"It's mother's idea. She thinks he might be valuable as a stock horse on a ranch. You know we still have interest in a ranch in Texas."

"Oh, I see! Yes, probably he'd be very valuable, to improve the breed of the horses over there.—My father has some very lovely hunters. Isn't it disgraceful, he would never let me ride!"

"Why?"

"Because we girls weren't important, in his opinion.— So you're taking the horse to America! With the little man?"

"Yes, St. Mawr will hardly behave without him."

"I see!—I see—ee—ee! Just you and Mrs. Witt and the little man. I'm sure you'll find he has psychic powers."

"I'm afraid I'm not so good at finding things out," said Lou.

"Aren't you? No, I suppose not. I am. I have a flair. I sort of *smell* things.—Then the horse is already here, is he? When do you think you'll sail?"

"Mother is finding a merchant boat that will go to Galveston, Texas, and take us along with the horse. She

knows people who will find the right thing. But it takes
time."

"What a much nicer way to travel than on one of those
great liners! Oh, how awful they are! So vulgar! Floating
palaces they call them! My word, the people inside the
palaces!—Yes, I should say that would be a much pleasanter way of travelling: on a cargo boat."

Laura wanted to go down to the Mews to see St. Mawr.
The two women went together.

St. Mawr stood in his box, bright and tense as usual.

"Yes!" said Laura Ridley, with a slight hiss. "Yes! Isn't
he beautiful! Such very perfect legs!"—She eyed him
round with those gimlet, sharp eyes of hers. "Almost a
pity to let him go out of England. We need some of his
perfect *bone,* I feel.—But his eye! Hasn't he got a look
in it, my word!"

"I can never see that he looks wicked," said Lou.

"Can't you!"—Laura had a slight hiss in her speech,
a sort of aristocratic decision in her enunciation, that got
on Lou's nerves.—"He looks wicked to me!"

"He's not *mean,*" said Lou. "He'd never do anything
mean to you."

"Oh, mean! I dare say not. No! I'll grant him that, he
gives fair warning. His eye says *Beware!*—But isn't he a
beauty, *isn't* he!" Lou could feel the peculiar reverence
for St. Mawr's breeding, his show qualities. Herself, all
she cared about was the horse himself, his real nature.
"Isn't it extraordinary," Laura continued, "that you never
get a *really,* perfectly satisfactory animal! There's always
something wrong. And in men too. Isn't it curious? there's
always something—something wrong—or something missing. Why is it?"

"I don't know," said Lou. She felt unable to cope with
any more. And she was glad when Laura left her.

The days passed slowly, quietly, London almost empty
of Lou's acquaintances. Mrs. Witt was busy getting all
sorts of papers and permits: such a fuss! The battle light
was still in her eye. But about her nose was a dusky,
pinched look that made Lou wonder.

Both women wanted to be gone: they felt they had

already flown in spirit, and it was weary having the body left behind.

At last all was ready: they only awaited the telegram to say when their cargo-boat would sail. Trunks stood there packed, like great stones locked for ever. The Westminster house seemed already a shell. Rico wrote and telegraphed, tenderly, but there was a sense of relentless effort in it all, rather than of any real tenderness. He had taken his position.

Then the telegram came, the boat was ready to sail.

"There now!" said Mrs. Witt, as if it had been a sentence of death.

"Why do you look like that, mother?"

"I feel I haven't an ounce of energy left in my body."

"But how queer, for you, mother. Do you think you are ill?"

"No, Louise. I just feel that way: as if I hadn't an ounce of energy left in my body."

"You'll feel yourself again, once you are away."

"Maybe I shall."

After all, it was only a matter of telephoning. The hotel and the railway porters and taxi-men would do the rest.

It was a grey, cloudy day, cold even. Mother and daughter sat in a cold first-class carriage and watched the little Hampshire country-side go past: little, old, unreal it seemed to them both, and passing away like a dream whose edges only are in consciousness. Autumn! Was this autumn? Were these trees, fields, villages? It seemed but the dim, dissolving edges of a dream, without inward substance.

At Southampton it was raining: and just a chaos, till they stepped on to a clean boat, and were received by a clean young captain, quite sympathetic, and quite a gentleman. Mrs. Witt, however, hardly looked at him, but went down to her cabin and lay down in her bunk.

There, lying concealed, she felt the engines start, she knew the voyage had begun. But she lay still. She saw the clouds and the rain, and refused to be disturbed.

Lou had lunch with the young captain, and she felt she ought to be flirty. The young man was so polite and attentive. And she wished so much she were alone.

Afterwards, she sat on deck and saw the Isle of Wight
pass shadowly, in a misty rain. She didn't know it was
the Isle of Wight. To her, it was just the lowest bit of the
British Isles. She saw it fading away: and with it, her life,
going like a clot of shadow in a mist of nothingness. She
had no feelings about it, none: neither about Rico, nor
her London house, nor anything. All passing in a grey
curtain of rainy drizzle, like a death, and she with not a
feeling left.

They entered the Channel, and felt the slow heave
of the sea. And soon the clouds broke in a little wind. The
sky began to clear. By mid-afternoon it was blue summer,
on the blue, running waters of the Channel. And soon, the
ship steering for Santander, there was the coast of France,
the rock twinkling like some magic world.

The magic world! And back of it, that post-war Paris
which Lou knew only too well, and which depressed her
so thoroughly. Or that post-war Monte Carlo, the Riviera
still more depressing even than Paris. No, one must not
land, even on magic coasts. Else you found yourself in a
railway station and a "centre of civilization" in five minutes.

Mrs. Witt hated the sea, and stayed, as a rule, practically the whole time of the crossing, in her bunk. There
she was now, silent, shut up like a steel trap, as in her
tomb. She did not even read. Just lay and stared at the
passing sky. And the only thing to do was to leave her
alone.

Lewis and Phœnix hung on the rail, and watched
everything. Or they went down to see St. Mawr. Or they
stood talking in the doorway of the wireless operator's
cabin. Lou begged the captain to give them jobs to do.

The queer, transitory, unreal feeling, as the ship
crossed the great, heavy Atlantic. It was rather bad
weather. And Lou felt, as she had felt before, that this
grey, wolf-like, cold-blooded Ocean hated men and their
ships and their smoky passage. Heavy grey waves, a low-
sagging sky: rain: yellow, weird evening with snatches
of sun: so it went on. Till they got way South, into the
westward-running stream. Then they began to get blue
weather and blue water.

To go South! Always to go South, away from the arctic
horror as far as possible! That was Lou's instinct. To go
out of the clutch of greyness and low skies, of sweeping
rain, and of slow, blanketing snow. Never again to see the
mud and rain and snow of a northern winter, nor to feel
the idealistic, Christianized tension of the now irreligious
North.

As they neared Havana, and the water sparkled at night
with phosphorus, and the flying-fishes came like drops
of bright water, sailing out of the massive-slippery waves,
Mrs. Witt emerged once more. She still had that shut-up,
deadly look on her face. But she prowled round the deck,
and manifested at least a little interest in affairs not her
own. Here at sea, she hardly remembered the existence of
St. Mawr or Lewis or Phœnix. She was not very deeply
aware even of Lou's existence.—But, of course, it would
all come back, once they were on land.

They sailed in hot sunshine out of a blue, blue sea, past
the castle into the harbour at Havana. There was a lot of
shipping: and this was already America. Mrs. Witt had
herself and Lou put ashore immediately. They took a
motor-car and drove at once to the great boulevard that
is the centre of Havana. Here they saw a long rank of
motor-cars, all drawn up ready to take a couple of hundred American tourists for one more tour. There were the
tourists, all with badges in their coats, lest they should
get lost.

"They get so drunk by night," said the driver in Spanish, "that the policemen find them lying in the road—
turn them over, see the badge—and, hup!—carry them
to their hotel." He grinned sardonically.

Lou and her mother lunched at the Hotel d'Angleterre, and Mrs. Witt watched transfixed while a couple
of her countrymen, a stout successful man and his wife,
lunched abroad. They had cocktails—then lobster—and
a bottle of hock—then a bottle of champagne—then a
half-bottle of port.—And Mrs. Witt rose in haste as the
liqueurs came. For that successful man and his wife had
gone on imbibing with a sort of fixed and deliberate will,
apparently tasting nothing, but saying to themselves:
Now we're drinking Rhine wine! Now we're drinking

1912 champagne. Yah, Prohibition! Thou canst not put
it over me.—Their complexions became more and more
lurid. Mrs. Witt fled, fearing a Havana debacle. But she
said nothing.

In the afternoon, they motored into the country, to see
the great brewery gardens, the new villa suburb, and
through the lanes past the old, decaying plantations with
palm-trees. In one lane they met the fifty motor-cars with
the two hundred tourists all with badges on their chests
and self-satisfaction on their faces. Mrs. Witt watched in
grim silence.

"*Plus ça change, plus c'est la même chose,*" said Lou,
with a wicked little smile. "*On n'est pas mieux ici,*
mother."

"I know it," said Mrs. Witt.

The hotels by the sea were all shut up: it was not yet
the "season." Not till November. And then!—Why, then
Havana would be an American city, in full leaf of green
dollar bills. The green leaf of American prosperity shed-
ding itself recklessly, from every roaming sprig of a tourist, over this city of sunshine and alcohol. Green leaves
unfolded in Pittsburgh and Chicago, showering in winter
downfall in Havana.

Mother and daughter drank tea in a corner of the Hotel
d'Angleterre once more, and returned to the ferry.

The Gulf of Mexico was blue and rippling, with the
phantom of islands on the south. Great porpoises rolled
and leaped, running in front of the ship in the clear water,
diving, travelling in perfect motion, straight, with the tip
of the ship touching the tip of their tails, then rolling over,
corkscrewing, and showing their bellies as they went.
Marvellous! The marvellous beauty and fascination of
natural wild things! The horror of man's unnatural life, his
heaped-up civilization!

The flying-fishes burst out of the sea in clouds of silvery,
transparent motion. Blue above and below, the Gulf
seemed a silent, empty, timeless place where man did not
really reach. And Lou was again fascinated by the glamour
of the universe.

But bump! She and her mother were in a first-class hotel
again, calling down the telephone for the bell-boy and ice-

water. And soon they were in a Pullman, off towards San Antonio.

It was America, it was Texas. They were at their ranch, on the great level of yellow autumn, with the vast sky above. And after all, from the hot wide sky, and the hot, wide, red earth, there *did* come something new, something not used up. Lou *did* feel exhilarated.

The Texans were there, tall blond people, ingenuously cheerful, ingenuously, childishly intimate, as if the fact that you had never seen them before was as nothing compared to the fact that you'd all been living in one room together all your lives, so that nothing was hidden from either of you. The one room being the mere shanty of the world in which we all live. Strange, uninspired cheerfulness, filling, as it were, the blank of complete incomprehension.

And off they set in their motor-cars, chiefly high-legged Fords, rattling away down the red trails between yellow sunflowers or sere grass or dry cotton, away, away into great distances, cheerfully raising the dust of haste. It left Lou in a sort of blank amazement. But it left her amused, not depressed. The old screws of emotion and intimacy that had been screwed down so tightly upon her fell out of their holes, here. The Texan intimacy weighed no more on her than a postage stamp, even if, for the moment, it stuck as close. And there was a certain underneath recklessness, even a stoicism, in all the apparently childish people, which left one free. They might appear childish: but they stoically depended on themselves alone, in reality. Not as in England, where every man waited to pour the burden of himself upon you.

St. Mawr arrived safely, a bit bewildered. The Texans eyed him closely, struck silent, as ever, by anything pure-bred and beautiful. He was somehow too beautiful, too perfected, in this great open country. The long-legged Texan horses, with their elaborate saddles, seemed somehow more natural.

Even St. Mawr felt himself strange, as it were naked and singled out, in this rough place. Like a jewel among stones, a pearl before swine, maybe. But the swine were no fools. They knew a pearl from a grain of maize, and a grain of

maize from a pearl. And they knew what they wanted.
When it was pearls, it was pearls; though chiefly it was
maize. Which shows good sense. They could see St.
Mawr's points. Only he needn't draw the point too fine, or
it would just not pierce the tough skin of this country.

The ranch-man mounted him—just threw a soft skin
over his back, jumped on, and away down the red trail,
raising the dust among the tall wild yellow of sunflowers,
in the hot wild sun. Then back again in a fume, and the
man slipped off.

"He's got the stuff in him, he sure has," said the man.

And the horse seemed pleased with this rough han-
dling. Lewis looked on in wonder, and a little envy.

Lou and her mother stayed a fortnight on the ranch. It
was all so queer: so crude, so rough, so easy, so artificially
civilized, and so meaningless. Lou could not get over the
feeling that it all meant nothing. There were no roots of
reality at all. No consciousness below the surface, no
meaning in anything save the obvious, the blatantly obvious. It was like life enacted in a mirror. Visually, it was
wildly vital. But there was nothing behind it. Or like a
cinematograph: flat shapes, exactly like men, but without
any substance of reality, rapidly rattling away with talk,
emotions, activity, all in the flat, nothing behind it. No
deeper consciousness at all.—So it seemed to her.

One moved from dream to dream, from phantasm to
phantasm.

But at least this Texan life, if it had no bowels, no vitals,
at least it could not prey on one's own vitals. It was this
much better than Europe.

Lewis was silent, and rather piqued. St. Mawr had already made advances to the boss' long-legged, arched-
necked, glossy-maned Texan mare. And the boss was
pleased.

What a world!

Mrs. Witt eyed it all shrewdly. But she failed to par-
ticipate. Lou was a bit scared at the emptiness of it all,
and the queer, phantasmal self-consciousness. Cowboys
just as self-conscious as Rico, far more sentimental, inwardly vague and unreal. Cowboys that went after their
rows in black Ford motor-cars: and who self-consciously

saw Lady Carrington falling to them, as elegant young
ladies from the East fall to the noble cowboy of the films,
or in Zane Grey. It was all film-psychology.

And at the same time, these boys led a hard, hard life,
often dangerous and gruesome. Nevertheless, inwardly
they were self-conscious film-heroes. The boss himself, a
man over forty, long and lean and with a great deal
of stringy energy, showed off before her in a strong silent
manner, existing for the time being purely in his imagina-
tion of the sort of picture he made to her, the sort of impression he made on her.

So they all were, coloured up like a Zane Grey book-
jacket, all of them living in the mirror. The kind of picture
they made to somebody else.

And at the same time, with energy, courage, and a stoi-
cal grit getting their work done, and putting through what
they had to put through.

It left Lou blank with wonder. And in the face of this
strange cheerful living in the mirror—a rather cheap mirror at that—England began to seem real to her again.

Then she had to remember herself back in England.
And no, O God, England was not real either, except poi-
sonously.

What was real? What under heaven was real?

Her mother had gone dumb and, as it were, out of range.
Phœnix was a bit assured and bouncy, back more or less
in his own conditions. Lewis was a bit impressed by the
emptiness of everything, the *lack* of concentration. And
St. Mawr followed at the heels of the boss' long-legged
black Texan mare, almost slavishly.

What, in heaven's name, was one to make of it all?

Soon, she could not stand this sort of living in a film-
setting, with the mechanical energy of "making good,"
that is, making money, to keep the show going. The mystic
duty to "make good," meaning to make the ranch pay a
laudable interest on the "owners'" investment. Lou herself being one of the owners. And the interest that came
to her, from her father's will, being the money she spent
to buy St. Mawr and to fit up that house in Westminster.
Then also the mystic duty to "feel good." Everybody had
to *feel good, fine!* "How are you this morning, Mr.

Latham?"—"*Fine!* Eh! Don't you feel good out here, eh, Lady Carrington?"—"*Fine!*"—Lou pronounced it with the same ringing conviction. It was Coué all the time!

"Shall we stay here long, mother?" she asked.

"Not a day longer than you want to, Louise. I stay entirely for your sake."

"Then let us go, mother."

They left St. Mawr and Lewis. But Phœnix wanted to come along. So they motored to San Antonio, got into the Pullman, and travelled as far as El Paso. Then they changed to go North. Santa Fe would be at least "easy." And Mrs. Witt had acquaintances there.

They found the fiesta over in Santa Fe: Indians, Mexicans, artists had finished their great effort to amuse and attract the tourists. *Welcome, Mr. Tourist,* said a great board on one side of the high road. And on the other side, a little nearer to town: *Thank You, Mr. Tourist.*

"*Plus ça change——*" Lou began.

"*Ca ne change jamais*—except for the worse!" said Mrs. Witt, like a pistol going off. And Lou held her peace, after she had sighed to herself, and said in her own mind: "*Welcome Also Mrs. and Miss Tourist!*"

There was no getting a word out of Mrs. Witt, these days. Whereas Phœnix was becoming almost loquacious.

They stayed awhile in Santa Fe, in the clean, comfortable, "homely" hotel, where "every room had its bath": a spotless white bath, with very hot water night and day. The tourists and commercial travellers sat in the big hall down below, everybody living in the mirror! And, of course, they knew Lady Carrington down to her shoe-soles. And they all expected her to know them down to their shoe-soles. For the only object of the mirror is to reflect images.

For two days mother and daughter ate in the salad-bowl intimacy of the dining-room. Then Mrs. Witt struck, and telephoned down, every meal-time, for her meal in her room. She got to staying in bed later and later, as on the ship. Lou became uneasy. This was worse than Europe.

Phœnix was still there, as a sort of half-friend, half-servant retainer. He was perfectly happy, roving round among the Mexicans and Indians, talking Spanish all day, and telling about England and his two mistresses, rolling the ball of his own importance.

"I'm afraid we've got Phœnix for life," said Lou.

"Not unless we wish," said Mrs. Witt indifferently. And she picked up a novel which she didn't want to read, but which she was going to read.

"What shall we do next, mother?" Lou asked.

"As far as I am concerned, there is no next," said Mrs. Witt.

"Come, mother! Let's go back to Italy or somewhere, if it's as bad as that."

"Never again, Louise, shall I cross that water. I have come home to die."

"I don't see much home about it—the Gonzales Hotel in Santa Fe."

"Indeed not! But as good as anywhere else, to die in."

"Oh, mother, don't be silly! Shall we look for somewhere where we can be by ourselves?"

"I leave it to you, Louise. I have made my last decision."

"What is that, mother."

"Never, never to make another decision."

"Not even to decide to die?"

"No, not even that."

"Or *not* to die?"

"Not that either."

Mrs. Witt shut up like a trap. She refused to rise from her bed that day.

Lou went to consult Phœnix. The result was, the two set out to look at a little ranch that was for sale.

It was autumn, and the loveliest time in the South-west, where there is no spring, snow blowing into the hot lap of summer; and no real summer, hail falling in thick ice, from the thunderstorms: and even no very definite winter, hot sun melting the snow and giving an impression of spring at any time. But autumn there is, when the winds of the desert are almost still, and the mountains fume no clouds. But morning comes cold and delicate, upon the wild sunflowers and the puffing, yellow-flowered greasewood. For the desert blooms in autumn. In spring it is grey ash all the time, and only the strong breath of the summer sun, and the heavy splashing of thunder rain, succeed at last, by September, in blowing it into soft, puffy yellow fire.

It was such a delicate morning when Lou drove out with Phœnix towards the mountains, to look at this ranch that a Mexican wanted to sell. For the brief moment the high mountains had lost their snow: it would be back again in a fortnight: and stood dim and delicate with autumn haze. The desert stretched away pale, as pale as the sky, but silvery and sere, with hummock-mounds of shadow, and long wings of shadow, like the reflection of some great bird. The same eagle-shadows came like rude paintings of the outstretched bird, upon the mountains, where the aspens were turning yellow. For the moment, the brief moment, the great desert-and-mountain landscape had lost its certain cruelty, and looked tender, dreamy. And many, many birds were flickering around.

Lou and Phœnix bumped and hesitated over a long trail: then wound down into a deep canyon: and then the car began to climb, climb, climb, in steep rushes, and in long heart-breaking, uneven pulls. The road was bad, and driving was no joke. But it was the sort of road Phœnix was used to. He sat impassive and watchful, and kept on, till his engine boiled. He was *himself* in this country: impassive, detached, self-satisfied, and silently assertive. Guarding himself at every moment, but on his guard, sure of himself. Seeing no difference at all between Lou or Mrs. Witt and himself, except that they had money and he had none, while he had a native importance which they lacked. He depended on them for money, they on him for the power to live out here in the West. Intimately, he was as good as they. Money was their only advantage.

As Lou sat beside him in the front seat of the car, where it bumped less than behind, she felt this. She felt a peculiar tough-necked arrogance in him, as if he were asserting himself to put something over her. He wanted her to allow him to make advances to her, to allow him to suggest that he should be her lover. And then, finally, she would marry him, and he would be on the same footing as she and her mother.

In return, he would look after her, and give her his support and countenance, as a man, and stand between her and the world. In this sense, he would be faithful to her, and loyal. But as far as other women went, Mexican women or Indian women: why, that was none of her business. His marrying her would be a pact between two aliens, on behalf of one another, and he would keep his part of it all right. But himself, as a private man and a predative alien-blooded male, this had nothing to do with her. It didn't enter into her scope and count. She was one of these nervous white women with lots of money. She was very nice too. But as a *squaw*—as a real woman in a shawl whom a man went after for the pleasure of the night—why, she hardly counted. One of these white women who talk clever and know things like a man. She could hardly expect a half-savage male to acknowledge her as his female counterpart.—No! She had the bucks! And she had all the paraphernalia of the white man's civilization, which a savage can play with and so escape his own hollow boredom. But his own real female counterpart?—Phœnix would just have shrugged his shoulders, and thought the question not worth answering. How could there be any answer in *her* to the phallic male in him? Couldn't! Yet it would flatter his vanity and his self-esteem immensely, to possess her. That would be possessing the very clue to the white man's overwhelming world. And if she would let him possess her, he would be absolutely loyal to her, as far as affairs and appearances went. Only, the aboriginal phallic male in him simply couldn't recognize her as a woman at all. In this respect, she didn't exist. It needed the shawled Indian or Mexican women, with their squeaky, plaintive voices, their shuffling, watery humility, and the dark glances of their big, knowing eyes. When an Indian woman looked at him from under her black fringe, with dark, half-secretive suggestion in her big eyes: and when she stood before him hugged in her shawl, in such apparently complete quiescent humility: and when she spoke to him in her mousy squeak of a high, plaintive voice, as if it were difficult for her female bashfulness even to emit so much sound: and when she shuffled away with her legs wide apart, because of her wide-topped, white, high buckskin boots with tiny white feet, and her dark-knotted hair so full of hard, yet subtle lure: and when he remembered the almost watery softness of the Indian woman's dark, warm flesh: then he was a male, an old, secretive, rat-like male. But before Lou's straightforward-ness and utter sexual incompetence, he just stood in contempt. And to him, even a French *cocotte* was utterly devoid of the right sort of sex. She couldn't really move him. She couldn't satisfy the furtiveness in him. He needed this plaintive, squeaky, dark-fringed Indian quality. Something furtive and soft and rat-like, really to rouse him.

Nevertheless he was ready to trade his sex, which, in his opinion, every white woman was secretly pining for, for the white woman's money and social privileges. In the daytime, all the thrill and excitement of the white man's motor-cars and moving pictures and ice-cream sodas and so forth. In the night, the soft, watery-soft warmth of an Indian or half-Indian woman. This was Phœnix's idea of life for himself.

Meanwhile, if a white woman gave him the privileges of the white man's world, he would do his duty by her as far as all that went.

Lou, sitting very, very still beside him as he drove the car: he was not a very good driver, not quick and marvell-ous as some white men are, particularly some French chauffeurs she had known, but usually a little behindhand in his movements: she knew more or less all that he felt. More or less she divined as a woman does. Even from a certain rather assured stupidity of his shoulders, and a certain rather stupid assertiveness of his knees, she knew him.

But she did not judge him too harshly. Somewhere deep, deep in herself she knew she too was at fault. And this made her sometimes inclined to humble herself, as a woman, before the furtive assertiveness of this under-ground, "knowing" savage. He was so different from Rico.

Yet, after all, *was* he? In his rootlessness, his drifting, his real meaninglessness, was he different from Rico? And his childish, spellbound absorption in the motor-car, or in the moving pictures, or in an ice-cream soda—was it very different from Rico? Anyhow, was it really any better? Pleasanter, perhaps, to a woman, because of the childishness of it.

The same with his opinion of himself as a sexual male! So childish, really, it was almost thrilling to a woman. But then, so stupid also, with that furtive lurking in holes and imagining it could not be detected. He imagined he kept himself dark, in his sexual rat-holes. He imagined he was not detected!

No, no, Lou was not such a fool as she looked, in his eyes anyhow. She knew what she wanted. She wanted relief from the nervous tension and irritation of her life, she wanted to escape from the friction which is the whole stimulus in modern social life. She wanted to be still: only that, to be very, very still, and recover her own soul.

When Phœnix presumed she was looking for some secretly sexual male such as himself, he was ridiculously mistaken. Even the illusion of the beautiful St. Mawr was gone. And Phœnix, roaming round like a sexual rat in promiscuous back yards!—*Merci, mon cher!* For that was all he was: a sexual rat in the great barn-yard of man's habitat, looking for female rats!

Merci, mon cher! You are had.

Nevertheless, in his very mistakenness, he was a relief to her. His mistake was amusing rather than impressive. And the fact that one-half of his intelligence was a complete dark blank, that too was a relief.

Strictly, and perhaps in the best sense, he was a servant. His very unconsciousness and his very limitation served as a shelter, as one shelters within the limitations of four walls. The very decided limits to his intelligence were a shelter to her. They made her feel safe.

But that feeling of safety did not deceive her. It was the feeling one derived from having a *true* servant attached to one, a man whose psychic limitations left him incapable of anything but service, and whose strong flow of natural life, at the same time, made him need to serve.

And Lou, sitting there so very still and frail, yet self-contained, had not lived for nothing. She no longer wanted to fool herself. She had no desire at all to fool herself into thinking that a Phœnix might be a husband and a mate.

No desire that way at all. His obtuseness was a servant's obtuseness. She was grateful to him for serving, and she paid him a wage. Moreover, she provided him with something to do, to occupy his life. In a sense, she gave him his life, and rescued him from his own boredom. It was a balance.

He did not know what she was thinking. There was a certain physical sympathy between them. His obtuseness made him think it was also a sexual sympathy.

"It's a nice trip, you and me," he said suddenly, turning and looking her in the eyes with an excited look, and ending on a foolish little laugh.

She realized that she should have sat in the back seat.

"But it's a bad road," she said. "Hadn't you better stop and put the sides of the hood up? your engine is boiling."

He looked away with a quick switch of interest to the red thermometer in front of his machine.

"She's boiling," he said, stopping, and getting out with a quick alacrity to go to look at the engine.

Lou got out also, and went to the back seat, shutting the door decisively.

"I think I'll ride at the back," she said; "it gets so frightfully hot in front, when the engine heats up.—Do you think she needs some water? Have you got some in the canteen?"

"She's full," he said, peering into the steaming valve.

"You can run a bit out, if you think there's any need. I wonder if it's much further!"

"*Quien sabe!*" said he, slightly impertinent.

She relapsed into her own stillness. She realized how careful, how very careful she must be of relaxing into sympathy, and reposing, as it were, on Phœnix. He would read it as a sexual appeal. Perhaps he couldn't help it. She had only herself to blame. He was obtuse, as a man and a savage. He had only one interpretation, sex, for any woman's approach to him.

And she knew, with the last clear knowledge of weary disillusion, that she did not want to be mixed up in Phœnix's sexual promiscuities. The very thought was an insult to her. The crude, clumsy servant-male: no, no, not that. He was a good fellow, a very good fellow, as far as he went. But he fell far short of physical intimacy.

"No, no," she said to herself, "I was wrong to ride in the front seat with him. I must sit alone, just alone. Because sex, mere sex, is repellent to me. I will never prostitute myself again. Unless something touches my very spirit, the very quick of me, I will stay alone, just alone. Alone, and give myself only to the unseen presences, serve only the other, unseen presences."

She understood now the meaning of the Vestal Virgins, the Virgins of the holy fire in the old temples. They were symbolic of herself, of woman weary of the embrace of incompetent men, weary, weary, weary of all that, turning to the unseen gods, the unseen spirits, the hidden fire, and devoting herself to that, and that alone. Receiving thence her pacification and her fulfilment.

Not these little, incompetent, childish, self-opinionated men! Not these to touch her. She watched Phœnix's rather stupid shoulders, as he drove the car on between the piñon-trees and the cedars of the narrow mesa ridge, to the mountain foot. He was a good fellow. But let him run among women of his own sort. Something was beyond him. And this something must remain beyond him, never allow itself to come within his reach. Otherwise he would paw it and mess it up, and be as miserable as a child that has broken its father's watch.

No, no! She had loved an American, and lived with him for a fortnight. She had had a long, intimate friendship with an Italian. Perhaps it was love on his part. And she had yielded to him. Then her love and marriage to Rico.

And what of it all? Nothing. It was almost nothing. It was as if only the outside of herself, her top layers, were human. This inveigled her into intimacies. As soon as the intimacy penetrated, or attempted to penetrate, inside her, it was a disaster. Just a humiliation and a breaking down.

Within these outer layers of herself lay the successive inner sanctuaries of herself. And these were inviolable. She accepted it.

"I am not a marrying woman," she said to herself. "I am not a lover nor a mistress nor a wife. It is no good. Love can't really come into me from the outside, and I can never, never mate with any man, since the mystic new man will never come to me. No, no, let me know myself and my rôle. I am one of the eternal Virgins, serving the eternal fire. My dealings with men have only broken my stillness and messed up my doorways. It has been my own fault. I ought to stay virgin, and still, very, very still, and serve the most perfect service. I want my temple and my loneliness and my Apollo mystery of the inner fire. And with men, only the delicate, subtler, more remote relations. No coming near. A coming near only breaks the delicate veils, and broken veils, like broken flowers, only lead to rottenness."

She felt a great peace inside herself as she made this realization. And a thankfulness. Because, after all, it seemed to her that the hidden fire was alive and burning in this sky, over the desert, in the mountains. She felt a certain latent holiness in the very atmosphere, a young spring-fire of latent holiness, such as she had never felt in Europe, or in the East. "For me," she said, as she looked away at the mountains in shadow and the pale-warm desert beneath, with wings of shadow upon it: "For me, this place is sacred. It is blessed."

But as she watched Phœnix: as she remembered the motor-cars and tourists, and the rather dreary Mexicans of Santa Fe, and the lurking, invidious Indians, with something of a rat-like secretiveness and defeatedness in their bearing, she realized that the latent fire of the vast landscape struggled under a great weight of dirt-like inertia. She had to mind the dirt, most carefully and vividly avoid it and keep it away from her, here in this place that at last seemed sacred to her.

The motor-car climbed up, past the tall pine-trees, to the foot of the mountains, and came at last to a wire gate, where nothing was to be expected. Phœnix opened the gate, and they drove on, through more trees, into a clearing where dried-up bean-plants were yellow.

"This man got no water for his beans," said Phœnix. "Not got much beans this year."

They climbed slowly up the incline, through more pine-trees, and out into another clearing, where a couple of horses were grazing. And there they saw the ranch itself, little low cabins with patched roofs, under a few pine-trees, and facing the long twelve-acre clearing, or field, where the Michaelmas daisies were purple mist, and spangled with clumps of yellow flowers.

"Not got no alfalfa here neither!" said Phœnix, as the car waded past the flowers. "Must be a dry place up here. Got no water, sure they haven't."

Yet it was the place Lou wanted. In an instant, her heart sprang to it. The instant the car stopped, and she saw the two cabins inside the rickety fence, the rather broken corral beyond, and, behind all, tall, blue balsam pines, the round hills, the solid uprise of the mountain flank: and, getting down, she looked across the purple and gold of the clearing, downwards at the ring of pine-trees standing so still, so crude and untamable, the motionless desert beyond the bristles of the pine crests, a thousand feet below: and, beyond the desert, blue mountains, and far, far-off blue mountains in Arizona: *"This is the place,"* she said to herself.

This little tumble-down ranch, only a homestead of a hundred and sixty acres, was, as it were, man's last effort towards the wild heart of the Rockies, at this point. Sixty years before, a restless schoolmaster had wandered out from the East, looking for gold among the mountains. He found a very little, then no more. But the mountains had got hold of him, he could not go back.

There was a little trickling spring of pure water, a thread of treasure perhaps better than gold. So the schoolmaster took up a homestead on the lot where this little spring arose. He struggled, and got himself his log cabin erected, his fence put up, sloping at the mountain-side through the pine-trees and dropping into the hollows where the ghost-white mariposa lilies stood leafless and naked in flower, in spring, on tall invisible stems. He made the long clearing for alfalfa.

And fell so into debt, that he had to trade his homestead away, to clear his debt. Then he made a tiny living teaching the children of the few American prospectors who had squatted in the valleys, beside the Mexicans.

The trader who got the ranch tackled it with a will. He built another log cabin, and a big corral, and brought water from the canyon two miles and more across the mountain slope, in a little runnel ditch, and more water, piped a mile or more down the little canyon immediately above the cabins. He got a flow of water for his houses: for, being a true American, he felt he could not *really* say he had conquered his environment till he had got running water, taps, and wash-hand basins inside his house.

Taps, running water and wash-hand basins he accomplished. And, undaunted through the years, he prepared the basin for a fountain in the little fenced-in enclosure, and he built a little bath-house. After a number of years, he sent up the enamelled bath-tub to be put in the little log bath-house on the little wild ranch hung right against the savage Rockies, above the desert.

But here the mountains finished him. He was a trader down below, in the Mexican village. This little ranch was, as it were, his hobby, his ideal. He and his New England wife spent their summers there: and turned on the taps in the cabins and turned them off again, and felt really that civilization had conquered.

All this plumbing from the savage ravines of the canyons—one of them nameless to this day—cost, however, money. In fact, the ranch cost a great deal of money. But it was all to be got back. The big clearing was to be irrigated for alfalfa, the little clearing for beans, and the third clearing, under the corral, for potatoes. All these things the trader could trade to the Mexicans, very advantageously.

And, moreover, since somebody had started a praise of the famous goat's cheese made by Mexican peasants in New Mexico, goats there should be.

Goats there were: five hundred of them, eventually. And they fed chiefly in the wild mountain hollows, the no-man's-land. The Mexicans call them fire-mouths, because everything they nibble dies. Not because of their flaming mouths, really, but because they nibble a live plant down, down to the quick, till it can put forth no more.

So, the energetic trader, in the course of five or six years,

had got the ranch ready. The long three-roomed cabin was
for him and his New England wife. In the two-roomed
cabin lived the Mexican family who really had charge of
the ranch. For the trader was mostly fixed to his store,
seventeen miles away, down in the Mexican village.

The ranch lay over eight thousand feet up, the snows
of winter came deep and the white goats, looking dirty
yellow, swam in snow with their poor curved horns pok-
ing out like dead sticks. But the corral had a long, cosy,
shut-in goat-shed all down one side, and into this crowded
the five hundred, their acrid goat-smell rising like hot acid
over the snow. And the thin, pock-marked Mexican threw
them alfalfa out of the log barn. Until the hot sun sank
the snow again, and froze the surface, when patter-patter
went the two thousand little goat-hoofs, over the silver-
frozen snow, up at the mountain. Nibble, nibble, nibble,
the fire-mouths, at every tender twig. And the goat-bell
climbed, and the baa-ing came from among the dense and
shaggy pine-trees. And sometimes, in a soft drift under
the trees, a goat, or several goats, went through, into the
white depths, and some were lost thus, to reappear dead
and frozen at the thaw.

By evening, they were driven down again, like a dirty
yellowish-white stream carrying dark sticks on its yeasty
surface, tripping and bleating over the frozen snow, past
the bustling dark-green pine-trees, down to the trampled
mess of the corral. And everywhere, everywhere over the
snow, yellow stains and dark pills of goat-droppings melting into the surface crystal. On still, glittering nights, when
the frost was hard, the smell of goats came up like some
uncanny acid fire, and great stars sitting on the mountain's
edge seemed to be watching like the eyes of a mountain
lion, brought by the scent. Then the coyotes in the near
canyon howled and sobbed, and ran like shadows over the
snow. But the goat corral had been built tight.

In the course of years the goat-herd had grown from
fifty to five hundred, and surely that was increase. The
goat-milk cheeses sat drying on their little racks. In spring,
there was a great flowing and skipping of kids. In summer
and early autumn, there was a pest of flies, rising from all

that goat-smell and that cast-out whey of goats'-milk, after
the cheese-making. The rats came, and the pack-rats,
swarming.

And, after all, it was difficult to sell or trade the cheeses,
and little profit to be made. And, in dry summers, no water
came down in the narrow ditch-channel, that straddled in
wooden runnels over the deep clefts in the mountain-side.
No water meant no alfalfa. In winter the goats scarcely
drank at all. In summer they could be watered at the little
spring. But the thirsty land was not so easy to accommo-
date.

Five hundred fine white Angora goats, with their massive handsome padres! They were beautiful enough. And
the trader made all he could of them. Come summer, they
were run down into the narrow tank filled with the fiery
dipping fluid. Then their lovely white wool was clipped.
It was beautiful, and valuable, but comparatively little of
it.

And it all cost, cost, cost. And a man was always let
down. At one time no water. At another a poison-weed.
Then a sickness. Always, some mysterious malevolence
fighting, fighting against the will of man. A strange invisible influence coming out of the livid rock-fastnesses in
the bowels of those uncreated Rocky Mountains, preying
upon the will of man, and slowly wearing down his resistance, his onward-pushing spirit. The curious, subtle
thing, like a mountain fever, got into the blood, so that
the men at the ranch, and the animals with them,
had bursts of queer, violent, half-frenzied energy, in
which, however, they were wont to lose their wariness.
And then, damage of some sort. The horses ripped and
cut themselves, or they were struck by lightning, the men
had great hurts, or sickness. A curious disintegration working all the time, a sort of malevolent breath, like a stupe-
fying, irritant gas, coming out of the unfathomed mountains.

The pack-rats with their bushy tails and big ears came
down out of the hills, and were jumping and bouncing about: symbols of the curious debasing malevolence
that was in the spirit of the place. The Mexicans in charge,
good honest men, worked all they could. But they were

like most of the Mexicans in the South-west, as if they had
been pithed, to use one of Kipling's words. As if the invidious malevolence of the country itself had slowly taken
all the pith of manhood from them, leaving a hopeless sort
of corpus of a man.

And the same happened to the white men, exposed to
the open country. Slowly, they were pithed. The energy
went out of them. And, more than that, the interest. An
inertia of indifference invading the soul, leaving the body
healthy and active, but wasting the soul, the living interest, quite away.

It was the New England wife of the trader who put
most energy into the ranch. She looked on it as her home.
She had a little white fence put all round the two cabins:
the bright brass water-taps she kept shining in the two
kitchens: outside the kitchen door she had a little kitchen
garden and nasturtiums, after a great fight with invading
animals, that nibbled everything away. And she got so far
as the preparation of the round concrete basin which was
to be a little pool, under the few enclosed pine-trees between the two cabins, a pool with a tiny fountain jet.

But this, with the bath-tub, was her limit, as the five
hundred goats were her man's limit. Out of the mountains
came two breaths of influence: the breath of the curious,
frenzied energy, that took away one's intelligence as alcohol or any other stimulus does: and then the most strange
invidiousness that ate away the soul. The woman loved
her ranch, almost with passion. It was she who felt the
stimulus, more than the men. It seemed to enter her like a
sort of sex passion, intensifying her ego, making her full of
violence and of blind female energy. The energy, and the
blindness of it! A strange blind frenzy, like an intoxica-
tion while it lasted. And the sense of beauty that thrilled
her New England woman's soul.

Her cabin faced the slow down-slope of the clearing,
the alfalfa field: her long, low cabin, crouching under the
great pine-tree that threw up its trunk sheer in front of the
house, in the yard. That pine-tree was the guardian of the
place. But a bristling, almost demonish guardian, from
the far-off crude ages of the world. Its great pillar of pale,
flaky-ribbed copper rose there in strange callous indiffer-

ence, and the grim permanence, which is in pine-trees. A
passionless, non-phallic column, rising in the shadows of
the pre-sexual world, before the hot-blooded ithyphallic
column ever erected itself. A cold, blossomless, resinous
sap surging and oozing gum, from that pallid brownish
bark. And the wind hissing in the needles, like a vast nest
of serpents. And the pine cones falling plumb as the hail
hit them. Then lying all over the yard, open in the sun
like wooden roses, but hard, sexless, rigid with a blind
will.

Past the column of that pine-tree, the alfalfa field sloped
gently down, to the circling guard of pine-trees, from
which silent, living barrier isolated pines rose to ragged
heights at intervals, in blind assertiveness. Strange, those
pine-trees! In some lights all their needles glistened like
polished steel, all subtly glittering with a whitish glitter
among darkness, like real needles. Then again, at evening,
the trunks would flare up orange-red, and the tufts would
be dark, alert tufts like a wolf's tail touching the air. Again,
in the morning sunlight they would be soft and still, hardly
noticeable. But all the same, present, and watchful. Never
sympathetic, always watchfully on their guard, and resist-
ant, they hedged one in with the aroma and the power and
the slight horror of the pre-sexual primeval world. The
world where each creature was crudely limited to its
own ego, crude and bristling and cold, and then crowding
in packs like pine-trees and wolves.

But beyond the pine-trees, ah, there beyond, there was
beauty for the spirit to soar in. The circle of pines, with
the loose trees rising high and ragged at intervals, this was
the barrier, the fence to the foreground. Beyond was only
distance, the desert a thousand feet below, and beyond.

The desert swept its great fawn-coloured circle around,
away beyond and below like a beach, with a long mountain-side of pure blue shadow closing in the near corner,
and strange bluish hummocks of mountains rising like wet
rock from a vast strand, away in the middle distance, and
beyond, in the farthest distance, pale blue crests of mountains looking over the horizon, from the west, as if peering
in from another world altogether

Ah, that was beauty!—perhaps the most beautiful thing
in the world. It was pure beauty, *absolute* beauty! There!
That was it. To the little woman from New England, with
her tense, fierce soul and her egoistic passion of service,
this beauty was absolute, a *ne plus ultra*. From her doorway, from her porch, she could watch the vast, eagle-like
wheeling of the daylight, that turned as the eagles which
lived in the near rocks turned overhead in the blue, turning their luminous, dark-edged-patterned bellies and un-
der-wings upon the pure air, like winged orbs. So the daylight made the vast turn upon the desert, brushing the
farthest outwatching mountains. And sometimes the vast
strand of the desert would float with curious undulations
and exhalations amid the blue fragility of mountains,
whose upper edges were harder than the floating bases.
And sometimes she would see the little brown adobe
houses of the village Mexicans, twenty miles away, like
little cube crystals of insect-houses dotting upon the desert,
very distinct, with a cottonwood-tree or two rising near.
And sometimes she would see the far-off rocks, thirty miles
away, where the canyon made a gateway between the
mountains. Quite clear, like an open gateway out of a vast
yard, she would see the cut-out bit of the canyon-passage.
And on the desert itself, curious puckered folds of mesa-
sides. And a blackish crack which in places revealed the
otherwise invisible canyon of the Rio Grande. And beyond
everything, the mountains like icebergs showing up from
an outer sea. Then later, the sun would go down blazing
above the shallow cauldron of simmering darkness, and
the round mountain of Colorado would lump up into uncanny significance, northwards. That was always rather
frightening. But morning came again, with the sun peeping over the mountain slopes and lighting the desert away
in the distance long, long before it lighted on her yard.
And then she would see another valley, like magic and
very lovely, with green fields and long tufts of cottonwood-
trees, and a few long-cubical adobe houses, lying floating
in shallow light below, like a vision.

Ah! it was beauty, beauty absolute, at any hour of the
day: whether the perfect clarity of morning, or the moun-

tains beyond the simmering desert at noon, or the purple
lumping of northern mounds under a red sun at night. Or
whether the dust whirled in tall columns, travelling across
the desert far away, like pillars of cloud by day, tall, leaning pillars of dust hastening with ghostly haste: or
whether, in the early part of the year, suddenly in
the morning a whole sea of solid white would rise rolling below, a solid mist from melted snow, ghost-white under the mountain sun, the world below blotted out: or
whether the black rain and cloud streaked down, far across
the desert, and lightning stung down with sharp white
stings on the horizon: or the cloud travelled and burst
overhead, with rivers of fluid blue fire running out of
heaven and exploding on earth, and hail coming down like
a world of ice shattered above: or the hot sun rode in
again: or snow fell in heavy silence: or the world was
blinding white under a blue sky, and one must hurry under the pine-trees for shelter against that vast, white, back-
beating light which rushed up at one and made one almost
unconscious, amid the snow.

It was always beauty, *always!* It was always great, and
splendid, and, for some reason, natural. It was never
grandiose or theatrical. Always, for some reason, perfect.
And quite simple, in spite of it all.

So it was, when you watched the vast and living landscape. The landscape lived, and lived as the world of the
gods, unsullied and unconcerned. The great circling landscape lived its own life, sumptuous and uncaring. Man did
not exist for it.

And if it had been a question simply of living through
the eyes, into the *distance*, then this would have been
Paradise, and the little New England woman on her ranch
would have found what she was always looking for, the
earthly paradise of the spirit.

But even a woman cannot live only into the distance,
the beyond. Willy-nilly she finds herself juxtaposed to the
near things, the thing in itself. And willy-nilly she is caught
up into the fight with the immediate object.

The New England woman had fought to make the
nearness as perfect as the distance: for the distance was
absolute beauty. She had been confident of success. She

had felt quite assured, when the water came running out of her bright brass taps, the wild water of the hills caught, tricked into the narrow iron pipes, and led tamely to her kitchen, to jump out over her sink, into her wash-basin, at her service. *There!* she said. I have tamed the waters of the mountain to my service.

So she had, for the moment.

At the same time, the invisible attack was being made upon her. While she revelled in the beauty of the luminous world that wheeled around and below her, the grey, rat-like spirit of the inner mountains was attacking her from behind. She could not keep her attention. And, curiously, she could not keep even her speech. When she was saying something, suddenly the next word would be gone out of her, as if a pack-rat had carried it off. And she sat blank, stuttering, staring in the empty cupboard of her mind, like Mother Hubbard, and seeing the cupboard bare. And this irritated her husband intensely.

Her chickens, of which she was so proud, were carried away. Or they strayed. Or they fell sick. At first she could cope with their circumstances. But after a while, she couldn't. She couldn't care. A drug like numbness pos-sessed her spirit, and at the very middle of her, she couldn't care what happened to her chickens.

The same when a couple of horses were struck by light-ning. It frightened her. The rivers of fluid fire that sud-denly fell out of the sky and exploded on the earth near by, as if the whole earth had burst like a bomb, frightened her from the very core of her, and made her know, secretly and with cynical certainty, *that there was no mer-ciful God in the heavens.* A very tall, elegant pine-tree just above her cabin took the lightning, and stood tall and elegant as before, but with a white seam spiralling from its crest, all down its tall trunk, to earth. The perfect scar, white and long as lightning itself. And every time she looked at it, she said to herself, in spite of herself: *There is no Almighty loving God. The God there is shaggy as the pine-trees, and horrible as the lightning.* Outwardly, she never confessed this. Openly, she thought of her dear New England Church as usual. But in the violent under-current of her woman's soul, after the storms, she would look at that living seamed tree, and the voice would say in her, almost savagely: *What nonsense about Jesus and a God of Love, in a place like this! This is more awful and more splendid. I like it better.* The very chipmunks, in their jerky helter-skelter, the blue jays wrangling in the pine-tree in the dawn, the grey squirrel undulating to the tree-trunk, then pausing to chatter at her and scold her, with a shrewd fearlessness, as if she were the alien, the outsider, the creature that should not be permitted among the trees, all destroyed the illusion she cherished, of love, universal love. There was no love on this ranch. There was life, intense, bristling life, full of energy, but also with an undertone of savage sordidness.

The black ants in her cupboard, the pack-rats bouncing on her ceiling like hippopotamuses in the night, the two sick goats: there was a peculiar undercurrent of squalor, flowing under the curious *tussle* of wild life. That was it. The wild life, even the life of the trees and flowers, seemed one bristling, hair-raising tussle. The very flowers came up bristly, and many of them were fang-mouthed, like the dead-nettle: and none had any real scent. But they were very fascinating, too, in their very fierceness. In May, the curious columbines of the stream-beds, columbines scarlet outside and yellow in, like the red and yellow of a herald's uniform: farther from the dove nothing could be: then the beautiful rosy-blue of the great tufts of the flower they called bluebell, but which was really a flower of the snap-dragon family: these grew in powerful beauty in the little clearing of the pine-trees, followed by the flower the settlers had mysteriously called herb honeysuckle: a tangle of long drops of pure fire-red, hanging from slim invisible stalks of smoke-colour. The purest, most perfect vermilion scarlet, cleanest fire-colour, hanging in long drops like a shower of fire-rain that is just going to strike the earth. A little later, more in the open, there came another sheer fire-red flower, sparking, fierce red stars running up a bristly grey ladder, as if the earth's fire-centre had blown out some red sparks, white-speckled and deadly inside, puffing for a moment in the day air.

So it was! The alfalfa field was one raging, seething conflict of plants trying to get hold. One dry year, and the

bristly wild things had got hold: the spiky, blue-leaved
thistle-poppy with its moon-white flowers, the low clumps
of blue nettle-flower, the later rush, after the sereness of
June and July, the rush of red sparks and Michaelmas daisies, and the tough wild sunflowers, strangling and
choking the dark, tender green of the clover-like alfalfa!
A battle, a battle, with banners of bright scarlet and yellow.

When a really defenceless flower did issue, like the
moth-still, ghost-centred mariposa lily, with its inner
moth-dust of yellow, it came invisible. There was nothing
to be seen but a hair of greyish grass near the oak-scrub.
Behold, this invisible long stalk was balancing a white,
ghostly, three-petalled flower, naked out of nothingness.
A mariposa lily!

Only the pink wild roses smelled sweet, like the old
world. They were sweet brier-roses. And the dark-blue
harebells among the oak-scrub, like the ice-dark bubbles
of the mountain flowers in the Alps, the Alpenglocken.

The roses of the desert are the cactus flowers, crystal
of translucent yellow or of rose-colour. But set among
spines the devil himself must have conceived in a moment
of sheer ecstasy.

Nay, it was a world before and after the God of Love.
Even the very humming-birds hanging about the flowering
squawberry-bushes, when the snow had gone, in May,
they were before and after the God of Love. And the blue
jays were crested dark with challenge, and the yellow-
and-dark woodpecker was fearless like a warrior in war-
paint, as he struck the wood. While on the fence the hawks
sat motionless, like dark fists clenched under heaven, ig-
noring man and his ways.

Summer, it was true, unfolded the tender cottonwood
leaves, and the tender aspen. But what a tangle and
a ghostly aloofness in the aspen thickets high up on the
mountains, the coldness that is in the eyes and the long
cornelian talons of the bear.

Summer brought the little wild strawberries, with their
savage aroma, and the late summer brought the rose-jewel
raspberries in the valley cleft. But how lonely, how harsh-
lonely and menacing it was, to be alone in that shadowy,

steep cleft of a canyon just above the cabins, picking raspberries, while the thunder gathered thick and blue-purple
at the mountain tops. The many wild raspberries hanging
rose-red in the thickets. But the stream bed below all silent, waterless. And the trees all bristling in silence, and
waiting like warriors at an outpost. And the berries waiting for the sharp-eyed, cold, long-snouted bear to come
rambling and shaking his heavy sharp fur. The berries
grew for the bears, and the little New England woman,
with her uncanny sensitiveness to underlying influences,
felt all the time she was stealing. Stealing the wild raspberries in the secret little canyon behind her home. And
when she had made them into jam, she could almost taste
the theft in her preserves.

She confessed nothing of this. She tried even to confess
nothing of her dread. But she was afraid. Especially she
was conscious of the prowling, intense aerial electricity
all the summer, after June. The air was thick with wandering currents of fierce electric fluid, waiting to discharge
themselves. And almost every day there was the rage and
battle of thunder. But the air was never cleared. There
was no relief. However the thunder raged, and spent itself, yet, afterwards, among the sunshine was the strange
lurking and wandering of the electric currents, moving
invisible, with strange menace, between the atoms of the
air. She knew. Oh, she knew!

And her love for her ranch turned sometimes into a certain repulsion. The underlying rat-dirt, the everlasting
bristling tussle of the wild life, with the tangle and the
bones strewing. Bones of horses struck by lightning, bones
of dead cattle, skulls of goats with little horns: bleached,
unburied bones. Then the cruel electricity of the mountains. And then, most mysterious but worst of all, the ani-
mosity of the spirit of place: the crude, half-created spirit
of place, like some serpent-bird for ever attacking man, in
a hatred of man's onward-struggle towards further creation.

The seething cauldron of lower life, seething on the very
tissue of the higher life, seething the soul away, seething
at the marrow. The vast and unrelenting will of the swarm-

ing lower life, working for ever against man's attempt at a higher life, a further created being.

At last, after many years, the little woman admitted to herself that she was glad to go down from the ranch when November came with snows. She was glad to come to a more human home, her house in the village. And as winter passed by, and spring came again, she knew she did not want to go up to the ranch again. It had broken something in her. It had hurt her terribly. It had maimed her for ever in her hope, her belief in paradise on earth. Now, she hid from herself her own corpse, the corpse of her New England belief in a world ultimately all for love. The belief, and herself with it, was a corpse. The gods of those inner mountains were grim and invidious and relentless, huger than man, and lower than man. Yet man could never master them.

The little woman in her flower-garden away below, by the stream-irrigated village, hid away from the thought of it all. She would not go to the ranch any more.

The Mexicans stayed in charge, looking after the goats. But the place didn't pay. It didn't pay, not quite. It had paid. It might pay. But the effort, the effort! And as the marrow is eaten out of a man's bones and the soul out of his belly, contending with the strange rapacity of savage life, the lower stage of creation, he cannot make the effort any more.

Then also, the war came, making many men give up their enterprises at civilization.

Every new stroke of civilization has cost the lives of countless brave men, who have fallen defeated by the "dragon," in their efforts to win the apples of the Hesperides, or the fleece of gold. Fallen in their efforts to overcome the old, half-sordid savagery of the lower stages of creation, and win to the next stage.

For all savagery is half sordid. And man is only himself when he is fighting on and on, to overcome the sordidness.

And every civilization, when it loses its inward vision and its cleaner energy, falls into a new sort of sordidness, more vast and more stupendous than the old savage sort. An Augean stable of metallic filth.

And all the time, man has to rouse himself afresh, to cleanse the new accumulations of refuse. To win from the crude wild nature the victory and the power to make another start, and to cleanse behind him the century-deep deposits of layer upon layer of refuse: even of tin cans.

The ranch dwindled. The flock of goats declined. The water ceased to flow. And at length the trader gave it up.

He rented the place to a Mexican, who lived on the handful of beans he raised, and who was being slowly driven out by the vermin.

And now arrived Lou, new blood to the attack. She went back to Santa Fe, saw the trader and a lawyer, and bought the ranch for twelve hundred dollars. She was so pleased with herself.

She went upstairs to tell her mother.

"Mother, I've bought a ranch."

"It is just as well, for I can't stand the noise of automobiles outside here another week."

"It is quiet on my ranch, mother: the stillness simply speaks."

"I had rather it held its tongue. I am simply drugged with all the bad novels I have read. I feel as if the sky was a big cracked bell and a million clappers were hammering human speech out of it."

"Aren't you interested in my ranch, mother?"

"I hope I may be, by and by."

Mrs. Witt actually got up the next morning, and accompanied her daughter in the hired motor-car, driven by Phœnix, to the ranch: which was called Las Chivas. She sat like a pillar of salt, her face looking what the Indians call a False Face, meaning a mask. She seemed to have crystallized into neutrality. She watched the desert with its tufts of yellow greasewood go lurching past: she saw the fallen apples on the ground in the orchards near the adobe cottages: she looked down into the deep arroyo, and at the stream they forded in the car, and at the mountains blocking up the sky ahead, all with indifference. High on the mountains was snow: lower, blue-grey livid rock: and below the livid rock the aspens were expiring their daffodil-yellow, this year, and the oak-scrub was dark and reddish, like gore. She saw it all with a sort of stony indifference.

"Don't you think it's lovely?" said Lou.

"I can *see* it is lovely," replied her mother.

The Michaelmas daisies in the clearing as they drove up to the ranch were sharp-rayed with purple, like a coming night.

Mrs. Witt eyed the two log cabins, one of which was dilapidated and practically abandoned. She looked at the rather rickety corral, whose long planks had silvered and warped in the fierce sun. On one of the roof-planks a pack-rat was sitting erect like an old Indian keeping watch on a pueblo roof. He showed his white belly, and folded his hands and lifted his big ears, for all the world like an old immobile Indian.

"Isn't it for all the world as if *he* were the real boss of the place, Louise?" she said cynically.

And, turning to the Mexican, who was a rag of a man but a pleasant, courteous fellow, she asked him why he didn't shoot the rat.

"Not worth a shell!" said the Mexican, with a faint hopeless smile.

Mrs. Witt paced round and saw everything: it did not take long. She gazed in silence at the water of the spring, trickling out of an iron pipe into a barrel, under the cottonwood-tree in an arroyo.

"Well, Louise," she said, "I am glad you feel competent to cope with so much hopelessness and so many rats."

"But, mother, you must admit it is beautiful."

"Yes, I suppose it is. But, to use one of your Henry's phrases, beauty is a cold egg, as far as I am concerned."

"Rico never would have said that beauty was a cold egg to him."

"No, he wouldn't. He sits on it like a broody old hen on a china imitation.—Are you going to bring him here?"

"*Bring* him!—No. But he can come if he likes," stammered Lou.

"*Oh—h!* won't it be beau—ti—ful!" cried Mrs. Witt, rolling her head and lifting her shoulders in savage imitation of her son-in-law.

"Perhaps he won't come, mother," said Lou, hurt.

"He will most certainly come, Louise, to see what's doing: unless you tell him you don't want him."

"Anyhow, I needn't think about it till spring," said Lou, anxiously pushing the matter aside.

Mrs. Witt climbed the steep slope above the cabins, to the mouth of the little canyon. There she sat on a fallen tree, and surveyed the world beyond: a world not of men. She could not fail to be roused.

"What is your idea in coming here, daughter?" she asked.

"I love it here, mother."

"But what do you expect to achieve by it?"

"I was rather hoping, mother, to escape achievement. I'll tell you—and you mustn't get cross if it sounds silly. As far as people go, my heart is quite broken. As far as people go, I don't want any more. I can't stand any more. What heart I ever had for it—for life with people—is quite broken. I want to be alone, mother: with you here, and Phœnix perhaps to look after horses and drive a car. But I want to be by myself, really."

"With Phœnix in the background! Are you sure he won't be coming into the foreground before long?"

"No, mother, no more of that. If I've got to say it, Phœnix is a servant: he's really placed, as far as I can see. Always the same, playing about in the old back yard. I can't take those men seriously. I can't fool round with them, or fool myself about them. I can't and I won't fool myself any more, mother, especially about men. They don't count. So why should you want them to pay me out?"

For the moment, this silenced Mrs. Witt. Then she said:

"Why, *I* don't want it. Why should I? But after all you've got to live. You've never *lived* yet: not in my opinion."

"Neither, mother, in my opinion, have you," said Lou dryly.

And this silenced Mrs. Witt altogether. She had to be silent, or angrily on the defensive. And the latter she wouldn't be. She couldn't, really, in honesty.

"What do you call life?" Lou continued. "Wriggling half naked at a public show, and going off in a taxi to sleep with some half-drunken fool who thinks he's a man be-cause—oh, mother, I don't even want to think of it. I know you have a lurking idea that *that is life*. Let it be so then. But leave me out. Men in that aspect simply nauseate me: so grovelling and ratty. Life in that aspect simply drains all my life away. I tell you, for all that sort of thing, I'm broken, absolutely broken: if I wasn't broken to start with."

"Well, Louise," said Mrs. Witt after a pause, "I'm convinced that ever since men and women were men and women, people who took things seriously, and had time for it, got their hearts broken. Haven't I had mine broken? It's as sure as having your virginity broken: and it amounts to about as much. It's a beginning rather than an end."

"So it is, mother. It's the beginning of something else, and the end of something that's done with. I *know,* and there's no altering it, that I've got to live differently. It sounds silly, but I don't know how else to put it. I've got to live for something that matters, way, way down in me. And I think sex would matter, to my very soul, if it was really sacred. But cheap sex kills me."

"You have had a fancy for rather cheap men, perhaps."

"Perhaps I have. Perhaps I should always be a fool, where people are concerned. Now I want to leave off that kind of foolery. There's something else, mother, that I want to give myself to. I know it. I know it absolutely. Why should I let myself be shouted down any more?"

Mrs. Witt sat staring at the distance, her face a cynical mask.

"What is the something bigger? And *pray,* what is it bigger than?" she asked, in that tone of honeyed suavity which was her deadliest poison. "I want to learn. I am out to know. I'm terribly intrigued by it. Something bigger! Girls in my generation occasionally entered convents, for *something bigger.* I always wondered if they found it. They seemed to me inclined in the imbecile direction, but perhaps that was because I was *something less*——"

There was a definite pause between the mother and daughter, a silence that was a pure breach. Then Lou said:

"You know quite well I'm not conventy, mother, whatever else I am—even a bit of an imbecile. But that kind of religion seems to me the other half of men. Instead of running after them, you run away from them, and get the thrill that way. I don't hate men *because* they're men, as nuns do. I dislike them because they're not men enough: babies, and playboys, and poor things showing off all the time, even to themselves. I don't say I'm any better. I only wish, with all my soul, that some men *were* bigger and stronger and *deeper* than I am . . ."

"How do you know they're not?" asked Mrs. Witt.

"How *do* I know?——" said Lou mockingly.

And the pause that was a breach resumed itself. Mrs. Witt was teasing with a little stick the bewildered black ants among the fir-needles.

"And no doubt you are right about men," she said at length. "But at your age, the only sensible thing is to try and keep up the illusion. After all, as you say, you may be no better."

"I may be no better. But keeping up the illusion means fooling myself. And I won't do it. When I see a man who is even a bit attractive to me—even as much as Phœnix —I say to myself: *Would you care for him afterwards? Does he really mean anything to you, except just a sensation?*—And I know he doesn't. No, mother, of this I am convinced: either my taking a man shall have a meaning and a mystery that penetrates my very soul, or I will keep to myself.—And what I know is that the time has come for me to keep to myself. No more messing about."

"Very well, daughter. You will probably spend your life keeping to yourself."

"Do you think I mind! There's something else for me, mother. There's something else even that loves me and wants me. I can't tell you what it is. It's a spirit. And it's here, on this ranch. It's here, in this landscape. It's something more real to me than men are, and it soothes me, and it holds me up. I don't know what it is, definitely. It's something wild, that will hurt me sometimes and will wear me down sometimes. I know it. But it's something big, bigger than men, bigger than people, bigger than religion. It's something to do with wild America. And it's something to do with me. It's a mission, if you like. I am imbecile enough for that!—But it's my mission to keep myself for the spirit that is wild, and has waited so long here: even waited for such as me. Now I've come! Now I'm here. Now I am where I want to be: with the spirit that wants me.—And that's how it is. And neither Rico nor Phœnix nor anybody else really matters to me. They are in the world's back yard. And I am here, right deep in America, where there's a wild spirit wants me, a wild spirit more than men. And it doesn't want to save me either. It needs me. It craves for me. And to it, my sex is deep and sacred, deeper than I am, with a deep nature aware deep down of my sex. It saves me from cheapness, mother. And even you could never do that for me."

Mrs. Witt rose to her feet, and stood looking far, far away, at the turquoise ridge of mountains half sunk under the horizon.

"How much did you say you paid for Las Chivas?" she asked.

"Twelve hundred dollars," said Lou, surprised.

"Then I call it cheap, considering all there is to it: even the name."

The Man Who Died

Part One

There was a peasant near Jerusalem who acquired a young gamecock which looked a shabby little thing, but which put on brave feathers as spring advanced, and was resplendent with arched and orange neck by the time the fig-trees were letting out leaves from their end-tips.

This peasant was poor, he lived in a cottage of mud-brick, and had only a dirty little inner courtyard with a tough fig-tree for all his territory. He worked hard among the vines and olives and wheat of his master, then came home to sleep in the mud-brick cottage by the path. But he was proud of his young rooster. In the shut-in yard were three shabby hens which laid small eggs, shed the few feathers they had, and made a disproportionate amount of dirt. There was also, in a corner under a straw roof, a dull donkey that often went out with the peasant to work, but sometimes stayed at home. And there was the peasant's wife, a black-browed youngish woman who did not work too hard. She threw a little grain, or the remains of the porridge mess, to the fowls, and she cut green fodder with a sickle, for the ass.

The young cock grew to a certain splendour. By some freak of destiny, he was a dandy rooster, in that dirty little yard with three patchy hens. He learned to crane his neck and give shrill answers to the crowing of other cocks, beyond the walls, in a world he knew nothing of. But there was a special fiery colour to his crow, and the distant calling of the other cocks roused him to unexpected outbursts.

"How he sings," said the peasant, as he got up and pulled his day-shirt over his head.

"He is good for twenty hens," said the wife.

The peasant went out and looked with pride at his young rooster. A saucy, flamboyant bird, that has already made the final acquaintance of the three tattered hens. But the cockerel was tipping his head, listening to the challenge of far-off unseen cocks, in the unknown world. Ghost voices, crowing at him mysteriously out of limbo. He answered with a ringing defiance, never to be daunted.

"He will surely fly away one of these days," said the peasant's wife.

So they lured him with grain, caught him, though he fought with all his wings and feet, and they tied a cord round his shank, fastening it against the spur; and they tied the other end of the cord to the post that held up the donkey's straw pent-roof.

The young cock, freed, marched with a prancing stride of indignation away from the humans, came to the end of his string, gave a tug and a hitch of his tied leg, fell over for a moment, scuffled frantically on the unclean earthen floor, to the horror of the shabby hens, then with a sickening lurch, regained his feet, and stood to think. The peasant and the peasant's wife laughed heartily, and the young cock heard them. And he knew, with a gloomy, foreboding kind of knowledge, that he was tied by the leg.

He no longer pranced and ruffled and forged his feathers. He walked within the limits of his tether sombrely. Still he gobbled up the best bits of food. Still, sometimes, he saved an extra-best bit for his favourite hen of the moment. Still he pranced with quivering, rocking fierceness upon such of his harem as came nonchalantly within range, and gave off the invisible lure. And still he crowed defiance to the cock-crows that showered up out of limbo, in the dawn.

But there was now a grim voracity in the way he gobbled his food, and a pinched triumph in the way he seized upon the shabby hens. His voice, above all, had lost the full gold of its clangour. He was tied by the leg and he knew it. Body, soul and spirit were tied by that string.

Underneath, however, the life in him was grimly unbroken. It was the cord that should break. So one morning, just before the light of dawn, rousing from his slumbers with a sudden wave of strength, he leaped forward on his wings, and the string snapped. He gave a wild strange squawk, rose in one lift to the top of the wall, and there he crowed a loud and splitting crow. So loud, it woke the peasant.

At the same time, at the same hour before dawn, on the same morning, a man awoke from a long sleep in which he was tied up. He woke numb and cold, inside a carved hole in the rock. Through all the long sleep his body had been full of hurt, and it was still full of hurt. He did not open his eyes. Yet he knew that he was awake, and numb, and cold, and rigid, and full of hurt, and tied up. His face was banded with cold bands, his legs were bandaged together. Only his hands were loose.

He could move if he wanted: he knew that. But he had no want. Who would want to come back from the dead? A deep, deep nausea stirred in him, at the premonition of movement. He resented already the fact of the strange, incalculable moving that had already taken place in him: the moving back into consciousness. He had not wished it. He had wanted to stay outside, in the place where even memory is stone dead.

But now, something had returned to him, like a returned letter, and in that return he lay overcome with a sense of nausea. Yet suddenly his hands moved. They lifted up, cold, heavy and sore. Yet they lifted up, to drag away the cloth from his face, and to push at the shoulder bands. Then they fell again, cold, heavy, numb, and sick with having moved even so much, unspeakably unwilling to move further.

With his face cleared, and his shoulders free, he lapsed again, and lay dead, resting on the cold nullity of being dead. It was the most desirable. And almost, he had it complete: the utter cold nullity of being outside.

Yet when he was most nearly gone, suddenly, driven by an ache at the wrists, his hands rose and began pushing at the bandages of his knees, his feet began to stir, even while his breast lay cold and dead still.

And at last, the eyes opened. On to the dark. The same dark! yet perhaps there was a pale chink, of the all-disturbing light, prizing open the pure dark. He could not lift his head. The eyes closed. And again it was finished.

Then suddenly he leaned up, and the great world reeled.

Bandages fell away. And narrow walls of rock closed upon him, and gave the new anguish of imprisonment. There were chinks of light. With a wave of strength that came from revulsion, he leaned forward, in that narrow well of rock, and leaned frail hands on the rock near the chinks of light.

Strength came from somewhere, from revulsion; there was a crash and a wave of light, and the dead man was crouching in his lair, facing the animal onrush of light. Yet it was hardly dawn. And the strange, piercing keenness of daybreak's sharp breath was on him. It meant full awakening.

Slowly, slowly he crept down from the cell of rock, with the caution of the bitterly wounded. Bandages and linen and perfume fell away, and he crouched on the ground against the wall of rock, to recover oblivion. But he saw his hurt feet touching the earth again, with unspeakable pain, the earth they had meant to touch no more, and he saw his thin legs that had died, and pain unknowable, pain like utter bodily disillusion, filled him so full that he stood up, with one torn hand on the ledge of the tomb.

To be back! To be back again, after all that! He saw the linen swathing-bands fallen round his dead feet, and stooping, he picked them up, folded them, and laid them back in the rocky cavity from which he had emerged. Then he took the perfumed linen sheet, wrapped it round him as a mantle, and turned away, to the wanness of the chill dawn.

He was alone; and having died, was even beyond loneliness.

Filled still with the sickness of unspeakable disillusion, the man stepped with wincing feet down the rocky slope, past the sleeping soldiers, who lay wrapped in their woollen mantles under the wild laurels. Silent, on naked scarred feet, wrapped in a white linen shroud, he glanced down for a moment on the inert, heap-like bodies of the soldiers. They were repulsive, a slow squalor of limbs, yet he felt a certain compassion. He passed on towards the road, lest they should wake.

Having nowhere to go, he turned from the city that stood on her hills. He slowly followed the road away from the town, past the olives, under which purple anemones were drooping in the chill of dawn, and rich-green herb-age was pressing thick. The world, the same as ever, the natural world, thronging with greenness, a nightingale winsomely, wistfully, coaxingly calling from the bushes beside a runnel of water, in the world, the natural world of morning and evening, forever undying, from which he had died.

He went on, on scarred feet, neither of this world nor of the next. Neither here nor there, neither seeing nor yet sightless, he passed dimly on, away from the city and its precincts, wondering why he should be travelling, yet driven by a dim, deep nausea of disillusion, and a resolution of which he was not even aware.

Advancing in a kind of half-consciousness under the dry stone wall of the olive orchard, he was roused by the shrill wild crowing of a cock just near him, a sound which made him shiver as if electricity had touched him. He saw a black and orange cock on a bough above the road, then running through the olives of the upper level, a peasant in a gray woollen shirt-tunic. Leaping out of greenness, came the black and orange cock with the red comb, his tail-feathers streaming lustrous.

"O stop him, Master!" called the peasant. "My escaped cock!"

The man addressed, with a sudden flicker of smile, opened his great white wings of a shroud in front of the leaping bird. The cock fell back with a squawk and a flutter, the peasant jumped forward, there was a terrific beating of wings, and whirring of feathers, then the peasant had the escaped cock safely under his arm, its wings shut down, its face crazily craning forward, its round eyes goggling from its white chops.

"It's my escaped cock!" said the peasant, soothing the bird with his left hand, as he looked perspiringly up into the face of the man wrapped in white linen.

The peasant changed countenance, and stood trans-fixed, as he looked into the dead-white face of the man who had died. That dead-white face, so still, with the black beard growing on it as if in death; and those wide-open black sombre eyes, that had died! and those washed scars on the waxy forehead! The slow-blooded man of the field let his jaw drop, in childish inability to meet the situation.

"Don't be afraid," said the man in the shroud. "I am not dead. They took me down too soon. So I have risen up. Yet if they discover me, they will do it all over again. . . ."

He spoke in a voice of old disgust. Humanity! Especially humanity in authority! There was only one thing it could do. He looked with black, indifferent eyes into the quick, shifty eyes of the peasant. The peasant quailed, and was powerless under the look of deathly indifference, and strange cold resoluteness. He could only say the one thing he was afraid to say:

"Will you hide in my house, Master?"

"I will rest there. But if you tell anyone, you know what will happen. You will have to go before a judge."

"Me! I shan't speak. Let us be quick!"

The peasant looked round in fear, wondering sulkily why he had let himself in for this doom. The man with scarred feet climbed painfully up to the level of the olive garden, and followed the sullen, hurrying peasant across the green wheat among the olive trees. He felt the cool silkiness of the young wheat under his feet that had been dead, and the roughishness of its separate life was apparent to him. At the edges of rocks, he saw the silky, silvery-haired buds of the scarlet anemone bending downwards. And they too were in another world. In his own world he was alone, utterly alone. These things around him were in a world that had never died. But he himself had died, or had been killed from out of it, and all that remained now was the great void nausea of utter disillusion.

They came to a clay cottage, and the peasant waited dejectedly for the other man to pass.

"Pass!" he said. "Pass! We have not been seen."

The man in white linen entered the earthen room, taking with him the aroma of strange perfumes. The peasant closed the door, and passed through the inner doorway into the yard, where the ass stood within the high walls, safe from being stolen. There the peasant, in great disquietude, tied up the cock. The man with the waxen face sat down on a mat near the hearth, for he was spent and

barely conscious. Yet he heard outside the whispering of
the peasant to his wife, for the woman had been watching from the roof.

Presently they came in, and the woman hid her face.
She poured water, and put bread and dried figs on a
wooden platter.

"Eat, Master!" said the peasant. "Eat! No one has seen."

But the stranger had no desire for food. Yet he moistened a little bread in the water, and ate it, since life must
be. But desire was dead in him, even for food and drink.
He had risen without desire, without even the desire to
live, empty save for the all-overwhelming disillusion that
lay like nausea where his life had been. Yet perhaps,
deeper even than disillusion, was a desireless resoluteness,
deeper even than consciousness.

The peasant and his wife stood near the door, watching.
They saw with terror the livid wounds on the thin waxy
hands and the thin feet of the stranger, and the small lacerations in the still dead forehead. They smelled with terror the scent of rich perfumes that came from him, from
his body. And they looked at the fine, snowy, costly linen.
Perhaps really he was a dead king, from the region of terrors. And he was still cold and remote in the region of
death, with perfumes coming from his transparent body
as if from some strange flower.

Having with difficulty swallowed some of the moistened
bread, he lifted his eyes to them. He saw them as they
were: limited, meagre in their life, without any splendour
of gesture and of courage. But they were what they were,
slow inevitable parts of the natural world. They had no
nobility, but fear made them compassionate.

And the stranger had compassion on them again, for
he knew that they would respond best to gentleness,
giving back a clumsy gentleness again.

"Do not be afraid," he said to them gently. "Let me stay
a little while with you. I shall not stay long. And then I
shall go away forever. But do not be afraid. No harm will
come to you through me."

They believed him at once, yet the fear did not leave
them. And they said:

"Stay, Master, while ever you will. Rest! Rest quietly!"

But they were afraid.

So he let them be, and the peasant went away with the ass. The sun had risen bright, and in the dark house with the door shut, the man was again as if in the tomb. So he said to the woman, "I would lie in the yard."

And she swept the yard for him, and laid him a mat, and he lay down under the wall in the morning sun. There he saw the first green leaves spurting like flames from the ends of the enclosed fig-tree, out of the bareness to the sky of spring above. But the man who had died could not look, he only lay quite still in the sun, which was not yet too hot, and had no desire in him, not even to move. But he lay with his thin legs in the sun, his black perfumed hair falling into the hollows of his neck, and his thin colourless arms utterly inert. As he lay there, the hens clucked and scratched, and the escaped cock, caught and tied by the leg again, cowered in a corner.

The peasant woman was frightened. She came peeping, and, seeing him never move, feared to have a dead man in the yard. But the sun had grown stronger, he opened his eyes and looked at her. And now she was frightened of the man who was alive, but spoke nothing.

He opened his eyes, and saw the world again bright as glass. It was life, in which he had no share any more. But it shone outside him, blue sky, and a bare fig-tree with little jets of green leaf. Bright as glass, and he was not of it, for desire had failed.

Yet he was there, and not extinguished. The day passed in a kind of coma, and at evening he went into the house. The peasant man came home, but he was frightened, and had nothing to say. The stranger too ate of the mess of beans, a little. Then he washed his hands and turned to the wall, and was silent. The peasants were silent too. They watched their guest sleep. Sleep was so near death he could still sleep.

Yet when the sun came up, he went again to lie in the yard. The sun was the one thing that drew him and swayed him, and he still wanted to feel the cool air of morning in his nostrils, see the pale sky overhead. He still hated to be shut up.

As he came out, the young cock crowed. It was a di-

minished, pinched cry, but there was that in the voice of
the bird stronger than chagrin. It was the necessity to live,
and even to cry out the triumph of life. The man who had
died stood and watched the cock who had escaped and
been caught, ruffling himself up, rising forward on his
toes, throwing up his head, and parting his beak in another challenge from life to death. The brave sounds rang
out, and though they were diminished by the cord round
the bird's leg, they were not cut off. The man who had
died looked nakedly on life, and saw a vast resoluteness
everywhere flinging itself up in stormy or subtle wave-
crests, foam-tips emerging out of the blue invisible, a black
and orange cock or the green flame-tongues out of the ex-
tremes of the fig-tree. They came forth, these things and
creatures of spring, glowing with desire and with assertion. They came like crests of foam, out of the blue flood
of the invisible desire, out of the vast invisible sea
of strength, and they came coloured and tangible, evanes-
cent, yet deathless in their coming. The man who had
died looked on the great swing into existence of things
that had not died, but he saw no longer their tremulous
desire to exist and to be. He heard instead their ringing,
ringing, defiant challenge to all other things existing.

The man lay still, with eyes that had died now wide
open and darkly still, seeing the everlasting resoluteness
of life. And the cock, with the flat, brilliant glance, glanced
back at him, with a bird's half-seeing look. And always
the man who had died saw not the bird alone, but the
short, sharp wave of life of which the bird was the crest.
He watched the queer, beaky motion of the creature as it
gobbled into itself the scraps of food; its glancing of the
eye of life, ever alert and watchful, overweening and cau-
tious, and the voice of its life, crowing triumph and assertion, yet strangled by a cord of circumstance. He seemed
to hear the queer speech of very life, as the cock triumphantly imitated the clucking of the favourite hen, when
she had laid an egg, a clucking which still had, in the male
bird, the hollow chagrin of the cord round his leg. And
when the man threw a bit of bread to the cock, it called
with an extraordinary cooing tenderness, tousling and
saving the morsel for the hens. The hens ran up greedily,

and carried the morsel away beyond the reach of the string.

Then, walking complacently after them, suddenly the male bird's leg would hitch at the end of his tether, and he would yield with a kind of collapse. His flag fell, he seemed to diminish, he would huddle in the shade. And he was young, his tail-feathers, glossy as they were, were not fully grown. It was not till evening again that the tide of life in him made him forget. Then when his favourite hen came strolling unconcernedly near him, emitting the lure, he pounced on her with all his feathers vibrating. And the man who had died watched the unsteady, rocking vibration of the bent bird, and it was not the bird he saw, but one wave-tip of life overlapping for a minute another, in the tide of the swaying ocean of life. And the destiny of life seemed more fierce and compulsive to him even than the destiny of death. The doom of death was a shadow compared to the raging destiny of life, the determined surge of life.

At twilight the peasant came home with the ass, and he said: "Master! It is said that the body was stolen from the garden, and the tomb is empty, and the soldiers are taken away, accursed Romans! And the women are there to weep."

The man who had died looked at the man who had not died.

"It is well," he said. "Say nothing, and we are safe."

And the peasant was relieved. He looked rather dirty and stupid, and even as much flaminess as that of the young cock, which he had tied by the leg, would never glow in him. He was without fire. But the man who had died thought to himself: "Why, then, should he be lifted up? Clods of earth are turned over for refreshment, they are not to be lifted up. Let the earth remain earthy, and hold its own against the sky. I was wrong to seek to lift it up. I was wrong to try to interfere. The ploughshare of devastation will be set in the soil of Judæa, and the life of this peasant will be overturned like the sods of the field. No man can save the earth from tillage. It is tillage, not salvation. . . ."

So he saw the man, the peasant, with compassion; but the man who had died no longer wished to interfere in the soul of the man who had not died, and who could never die, save to return to earth. Let him return to earth in his own good hour, and let no one try to interfere when the earth claims her own.

So the man with scars let the peasant go from him, for the peasant had no re-birth in him. Yet the man who had died said to himself: "He is my host."

And at dawn, when he was better, the man who had died rose up, and on slow, sore feet retraced his way to the garden. For he had been betrayed in a garden, and buried in a garden. And as he turned round the screen of laurels, near the rock-face, he saw a woman hovering by the tomb, a woman in blue and yellow. She peeped again into the mouth of the hole, that was like a deep cupboard. But still there was nothing. And she wrung her hands and wept. And as she turned away, she saw the man in white, standing by the laurels, and she gave a cry, thinking it might be a spy, and she said:

"They have taken him away!"

So he said to her:

"Madeleine!"

Then she reeled as if she would fall, for she knew him. And he said to her:

"Madeleine! Do not be afraid. I am alive. They took me down too soon, so I came back to life. Then I was sheltered in a house."

She did not know what to say, but fell at his feet to kiss them.

"Don't touch me, Madeleine," he said. "Not yet! I am not yet healed and in touch with men."

So she wept because she did not know what to do. And he said:

"Let us go aside, among the bushes, where we can speak unseen."

So in her blue mantle and her yellow robe, she followed him among the trees, and he sat down under a myrtle bush. And he said:

"I am not yet quite come to. Madeleine, what is to be done next?"

"Master!" she said. "Oh, we have wept for you! And will you come back to us?"

"What is finished is finished, and for me the end is past," he said. "The stream will run till no more rains fill it, then it will dry up. For me, that life is over."

"And will you give up your triumph?" she said sadly.

"My triumph," he said, "is that I am not dead. I have outlived my mission, and know no more of it. It is my triumph. I have survived the day and the death of my interference, and am still a man. I am young still, Madeleine, not even come to middle age. I am glad all that is over. It had to be. But now I am glad it is over, and the day of my interference is done. The teacher and the saviour are dead in me; now I can go about my business, into my own single life."

She heard him, and did not fully understand. But what he said made her feel disappointed.

"But you will come back to us?" she said, insisting.

"I don't know what I shall do," he said. "When I am healed, I shall know better. But my mission is over, and my teaching is finished, and death has saved me from my own salvation. Oh, Madeleine, I want to take my single way in life, which is my portion. My public life is over, the life of my self-importance. Now I can wait on life, and say nothing, and have no one betray me. I wanted to be greater than the limits of my hands and feet, so I brought betrayal on myself. And I know I wronged Judas, my poor Judas. For I have died, and now I know my own limits. Now I can live without striving to sway others any more. For my reach ends in my finger-tips, and my stride is no longer than the ends of my toes. Yet I would embrace multitudes, I who have never truly embraced even one. But Judas and the high priests saved me from my own salvation, and soon I can turn to my destiny like a bather in the sea at dawn, who has just come down to the shore alone."

"Do you want to be alone henceforward?" she asked. "And was your mission nothing? Was it all untrue?"

"Nay!" he said. "Neither were your lovers in the past nothing. They were much to you, but you took more than you gave. Then you came to me for salvation from your own excess. And I, in my mission, I too ran to ex-

cess. I gave more than I took, and that also is woe and
vanity. So Pilate and the high priests saved me from my
own excessive salvation. Don't run to excess now in living,
Madeleine. It only means another death."

She pondered bitterly, for the need for excessive giving
was in her, and she could not bear to be denied.

"And will you not come back to us?" she said. "Have
you risen for yourself alone?"

He heard the sarcasm in her voice, and looked at her
beautiful face which still was dense with excessive need
for salvation from the woman she had been, the female
who had caught men at her will. The cloud of necessity
was on her, to be saved from the old, wilful Eve, who had
embraced many men and taken more than she gave. Now
the other doom was on her. She wanted to give without
taking. And that, too, is hard, and cruel to the warm body.

"I have not risen from the dead in order to seek death
again," he said.

She glanced up at him, and saw the weariness settling
again on his waxy face, and the vast disillusion in his dark
eyes, and the underlying indifference. He felt her glance,
and said to himself:

"Now my own followers will want to do me to death
again, for having risen up different from their expectation."

"But you will come to us, to see us, us who love you?"
she said.

He laughed a little and said:

"Ah, yes." Then he added, "Have you a little money?
Will you give me a little money? I owe it."

She had not much, but it pleased her to give it to him.

"Do you think," he said to her, "that I might come and
live with you in your house?"

She looked up at him with large blue eyes, that gleamed
strangely.

"Now?" she said, with peculiar triumph.

And he, who shrank now from triumph of any sort, his
own or another's, said:

"Not now! Later, when I am healed, and . . . and I
am in touch with the flesh."

The words faltered in him. And in his heart he knew

he would never go to live in her house. For the flicker of
triumph had gleamed in her eyes; the greed of giving. But
she murmured in a humming rapture:

"Ah, you know I would give up everything to you."

"Nay!" he said. "I didn't ask that."

A revulsion from all the life he had known came over
him again, the great nausea of disillusion, and the spear-
thrust through his bowels. He crouched under the myrtle
bushes, without strength. Yet his eyes were open. And
she looked at him again, and she saw that it was not the
Messiah. The Messiah had not risen. The enthusiasm and
the burning purity were gone, and the rapt youth. His
youth was dead. This man was middle-aged and disillusioned, with a certain terrible indifference, and a resoluteness which love would never conquer. This was not
the Master she had so adored, the young, flamy, unphys-
ical exalter of her soul. This was nearer to the lovers she
had known of old, but with a greater indifference to the
personal issue, and a lesser susceptibility.

She was thrown out of the balance of her rapturous,
anguished adoration. This risen man was the death of her
dream.

"You should go now," he said to her. "Do not touch
me, I am in death. I shall come again here, on the third
day. Come if you will, at dawn. And we will speak again."

She went away, perturbed and shattered. Yet as she
went, her mind discarded the bitterness of the reality, and
she conjured up rapture and wonder, that the Master was
risen and was not dead. He was risen, the Saviour, the
exalter, the wonder-worker! He was risen, but not as man;
as pure God, who should not be touched by flesh, and who
should be rapt away into Heaven. It was the most glorious
and most ghostly of the miracles.

Meanwhile the man who had died gathered himself together at last, and slowly made his way to the peasant's
house. He was glad to go back to them, and away from
Madeleine and his own associates. For the peasants had
the inertia of earth and would let him rest, and as yet,
would put no compulsion on him.

The woman was on the roof, looking for him. She was
afraid that he had gone away. His presence in the house

had become like gentle wine to her. She hastened to the
door, to him.

"Where have you been?" she said. "Why did you go
away?"

"I have been to walk in a garden, and I have seen a
friend, who gave me a little money. It is for you."

He held out his thin hand, with the small amount of
money, all that Madeleine could give him. The peasant's
wife's eyes glistened, for money was scarce, and she said:

"Oh, Master! And is it truly mine?"

"Take it!" he said. "It buys bread, and bread brings
life."

So he lay down in the yard again, sick with relief at being alone again. For with the peasants he could be alone,
but his own friends would never let him be alone. And in
the safety of the yard, the young cock was dear to him, as
it shouted in the helpless zest of life, and finished in the
helpless humiliation of being tied by the leg. This day the
ass stood swishing her tail under the shed. The man who
had died lay down and turned utterly away from life, in
the sickness of death in life.

But the woman brought wine and water, and sweetened
cakes, and roused him, so that he ate a little, to please her.
The day was hot, and as she crouched to serve him, he
saw her breasts sway from her humble body, under her
smock. He knew she wished he would desire her, and she
was youngish, and not unpleasant. And he, who had never
known a woman, would have desired her if he could. But
he could not want her, though he felt gently towards her
soft, crouching, humble body. But it was her thoughts,
her consciousness, he could not mingle with. She was
pleased with the money, and now she wanted to take more
from him. She wanted the embrace of his body. But her
little soul was hard, and short-sighted, and grasping, her
body had its little greed, and no gentle reverence of the
return gift. So he spoke a quiet, pleasant word to her, and
turned away. He could not touch the little, personal body,
the little, personal life of this woman, nor in any other. He
turned away from it without hesitation.

Risen from the dead, he had realised at last that the
body, too, has its little life, and beyond that, the greater

life. He was virgin, in recoil from the little, greedy life of the body. But now he knew that virginity is a form of greed; and that the body rises again to give and to take, to take and to give, ungreedily. Now he knew that he had risen for the woman, or women, who knew the greater life of the body, not greedy to give, not greedy to take, and with whom he could mingle his body. But having died, he was patient, knowing there was time, an eternity of time. And he was driven by no greedy desire, either to give himself to others, or to grasp anything for himself. For he had died.

The peasant came home from work, and said:

"Master, I thank you for the money. But we did not want it. And all I have is yours."

But the man who had died was sad, because the peasant stood there in the little, personal body, and his eyes were cunning and sparkling with the hope of greater rewards in money, later on. True, the peasant had taken him in free, and had risked getting no reward. But the hope was cunning in him. Yet even this was as men are made. So when the peasant would have helped him to rise, for night had fallen, the man who had died said:

"Don't touch me, brother. I am not yet risen to the Father."

The sun burned with greater splendour, and burnished the young cock brighter. But the peasant kept the string renewed, and the bird was a prisoner. Yet the flame of life burned up to a sharp point in the cock, so that it eyed askance and haughtily the man who had died. And the man smiled and held the bird dear, and he said to it:

"Surely thou art risen to the Father, among birds." And the young cock, answering, crowed.

When at dawn on the third morning the man went to the garden, he was absorbed, thinking of the greater life of the body, beyond the little, narrow, personal life. So he came through the thick screen of laurel and myrtle bushes, near the rock, suddenly, and he saw three women near the tomb. One was Madeleine, and one was the woman who had been his mother, and the third was a woman he knew, called Joan. He looked up, and saw them all, and they saw him, and they were all afraid.

He stood arrested in the distance, knowing they were there to claim him back, bodily. But he would in no wise return to them. Pallid, in the shadow of a gray morning that was blowing to rain, he saw them, and turned away. But Madeleine hastened towards him.

"I did not bring them," she said. "They have come of themselves. See, I have brought you money! . . . Will you not speak to them?"

She offered him some gold pieces and he took them, saying:

"May I have this money? I shall need it. I cannot speak to them, for I am not yet ascended to the Father. And I must leave you now."

"Ah! Where will you go?" she cried.

He looked at her, and saw she was clutching for the man in him who had died and was dead, the man of his youth and his mission, of his chastity and his fear, of his little life, his giving without taking.

"I must go to my Father!" he said.

"And you will leave us? There is your mother!" she cried, turning round with the old anguish, which yet was sweet to her.

"But now I must ascend to my Father," he said, and he drew back into the bushes, and so turned quickly, and went away, saying to himself:

"Now I belong to no one and have no connection, and mission or gospel is gone from me. Lo! I cannot make even my own life, and what have I to save? . . . I can learn to be alone."

So he went back to the peasant's house, to the yard where the young cock was tied by the leg, with a string. And he wanted no one, for it was best to be alone; for the presence of people made him lonely. The sun and the subtle salve of spring healed his wounds, even the gaping wound of disillusion through his bowels was closing up. And his need of men and women, his fever to have them and to be saved by them, this too was healing in him. Whatever came of touch between himself and the race of men, henceforth, should come without trespass or compulsion. For he said to himself:

"I tried to compel them to live, so they compelled me to

die. It is always so, with compulsion. The recoil kills the advance. Now is my time to be alone."

Therefore he went no more to the garden, but lay still and saw the sun, or walked at dusk across the olive slopes, among the green wheat, that rose a palm-breadth higher every sunny day. And always he thought to himself:

"How good it is to have fulfilled my mission, and to be beyond it. Now I can be alone, and leave all things to themselves, and the fig-tree may be barren if it will, and the rich may be rich. My way is my own alone."

So the green jets of leaves unspread on the fig-tree, with the bright, translucent, green blood of the tree. And the young cock grew brighter, more lustrous with the sun's burnishing; yet always tied by the leg with a string. And the sun went down more and more in pomp, out of the gold and red-flushed air. The man who had died was aware of it all, and he thought:

"The Word is but the midge that bites at evening. Man is tormented with words like midges, and they follow him right into the tomb. But beyond the tomb they cannot go. Now I have passed the place where words can bite no more and the air is clear, and there is nothing to say, and I am alone within my own skin, which is the walls of all my domain."

So he healed of his wounds, and enjoyed his immortality of being alive without fret. For in the tomb he had slipped that noose which we call care. For in the tomb he had left his striving self, which cares and asserts itself. Now his uncaring self healed and became whole within his skin, and he smiled to himself with pure aloneness, which is one sort of immortality.

Then he said to himself: "I will wander the earth, and say nothing. For nothing is so marvellous as to be alone in the phenomenal world, which is raging, and yet apart. And I have not seen it, I was too much blinded by my confusion within it. Now I will wander among the stirring of the phenomenal world, for it is the stirring of all things among themselves which leaves me purely alone."

So he communed with himself, and decided to be a physician. Because the power was still in him to heal any man or child who touched his compassion. Therefore he cut his hair and his beard after the right fashion, and smiled to himself. And he bought himself shoes, and the right mantle, and put the right cloth over his head, hiding all the little scars. And the peasant said:

"Master, will you go forth from us?"

"Yes, for the time is come for me to return to men."

So he gave the peasant a piece of money, and said to him:

"Give me the cock that escaped and is now tied by the leg. For he shall go forth with me."

So for a piece of money the peasant gave the cock to the man who had died, and at dawn the man who had died set out into the phenomenal world, to be fulfilled in his own loneliness in the midst of it. For previously he had been too much mixed up in it. Then he had died. Now he must come back, to be alone in the midst. Yet even now he did not go quite alone, for under his arm, as he went, he carried the cock, whose tail fluttered gaily behind, and who craned his head excitedly, for he too was adventuring out for the first time into the wider phenomenal world, which is the stirring of the body of cocks also. And the peasant woman shed a few tears, but then went indoors, being a peasant, to look again at the pieces of money. And it seemed to her, a gleam came out of the pieces of money, wonderful.

The man who had died wandered on, and it was a sunny day. He looked around as he went, and stood aside as the pack-train passed by, towards the city. And he said to himself:

"Strange is the phenomenal world, dirty and clean together! And I am the same. Yet I am apart! And life bubbles variously. Why should I have wanted it to bubble all alike? What a pity I preached to them! A sermon is so much more likely to cake into mud, and to close the fountains, than is a psalm or a song. I made a mistake. I understand that they executed me for preaching to them. Yet they could not finally execute me, for now I am risen in my own aloneness, and inherit the earth, since I lay no claim on it. And I will be alone in the seethe of all things; first and foremost, forever, I shall be alone. But I must toss this bird into the seethe of phenomena, for he must ride his wave. How hot he is with life! Soon, in some place, I shall leave him among the hens. And perhaps one evening, I shall meet a woman who can lure my risen body, yet leave me my aloneness. For the body of my desire has died, and I am not in touch anywhere. Yet how do I know! All at least is life. And this cock gleams with bright aloneness, though he answers the lure of hens. And I shall hasten on to that village on the hill ahead of me; already I am tired and weak, and want to close my eyes to everything."

Hastening a little with the desire to have finished going, he overtook two men going slowly, and talking. And being soft-footed, he heard they were speaking of himself. And he remembered them, for he had known them in his life, the life of his mission. So he greeted them, but did not disclose himself in the dusk, and they did not know him. He said to them:

"What then of him who would be king, and was put to death for it?"

They answered suspiciously: "Why ask you of him?"

"I have known him, and thought much about him," he said.

So they replied: "He has risen."

"Yea! And where is he, and how does he live?"

"We know not, for it is not revealed. Yet he is risen, and in a little while will ascend unto the Father."

"Yea! And where then is his Father?"

"Know ye not? You are then of the Gentiles! The Father is in Heaven, above the cloud and the firmament."

"Truly? Then how will he ascend?"

"As Elijah the Prophet, he shall go up in a glory."

"Even into the sky."

"Into the sky."

"Then is he not risen in the flesh?"

"He is risen in the flesh."

"And will he take flesh up into the sky?"

"The Father in Heaven will take him up."

The man who had died said no more, for his say was over, and words beget words, even as gnats. But the man asked him: "Why do you carry a cock?"

"I am a healer," he said, "and the bird hath virtue."

"You are not a believer?"

"Yea! I believe the bird is full of life and virtue."

They walked on in silence after this, and he felt they
disliked his answer. So he smiled to himself, for a dangerous phenomenon in the world is a man of narrow belief,
who denies the right of his neighbour to be alone. And
as they came to the outskirts of the village, the man who
had died stood still in the gloaming and said in his old
voice:

"Know ye me not?"

And they cried in fear: "Master!"

"Yea!" he said, laughing softly. And he turned suddenly away, down a side lane, and was gone under the
wall before they knew.

So he came to an inn where the asses stood in the yard.
And he called for fritters, and they were made for him. So
he slept under a shed. But in the morning he was wakened
by a loud crowing, and his cock's voice ringing in his ears.
So he saw the rooster of the inn walking forth to battle,
with his hens, a goodly number, behind him. Then the
cock of the man who had died sprang forth, and a battle
began between the birds. The man of the inn ran to save
his rooster, but the man who had died said:

"If my bird wins I will give him thee. And if he lose,
thou shalt eat him."

So the birds fought savagely, and the cock of the man
who had died killed the common cock of the yard. Then
the man who had died said to his young cock:

"Thou at least hast found thy kingdom, and the females
to thy body. Thy aloneness can take on splendour, polished
by the lure of thy hens."

And he left his bird there, and went on deeper into the
phenomenal world, which is a vast complexity of entan-
glements and allurements. And he asked himself a last
question:

"From what, and to what, could this infinite whirl be
saved?"

So he went his way, and was alone. But the way of the
world was past belief, as he saw the strange entanglement
of passions and circumstance and compulsion everywhere,
but always the dread insomnia of compulsion. It was fear,

the ultimate fear of death, that made men mad. So always he must move on, for if he stayed, his neighbours wound the strangling of their fear and bullying round him. There was nothing he could touch, for all, in a mad assertion of the ego, wanted to put a compulsion on him, and violate his intrinsic solitude. It was the mania of cities and societies and hosts, to lay a compulsion upon a man, upon all men. For men and women alike were mad with the egoistic fear of their own nothingness. And he thought of his own mission, how he had tried to lay the compulsion of love on all men. And the old nausea came back on him. For there was no contact without a subtle attempt to inflict a compulsion. And already he had been compelled even into death. The nausea of the old wound broke out afresh, and he looked again on the world with repulsion, dreading its mean contacts.

Part Two

The wind came cold and strong from inland, from the invisible snows of Lebanon. But the temple, facing south and west, towards Egypt, faced the splendid sun of winter as he curved down towards the sea, the warmth and radiance flooded in between the pillars of painted wood. But the sea was invisible, because of the trees, though its dashing sounded among the hum of pines. The air was turning golden to afternoon. The woman who served Isis stood in her yellow robe, and looked up at the steep slopes coming down to the sea, where the olive-trees silvered under the wind like water splashing. She was alone save for the goddess. And in the winter afternoon the light stood erect and magnificent off the invisible sea, filling the hills of the coast. She went towards the sun, through the grove of Mediterranean pine-trees and evergreen oaks, in the midst of which the temple stood, on a little, tree-covered tongue of land between two bays.

It was only a very little way, and then she stood among the dry trunks of the outermost pines, on the rocks under which the sea smote and sucked, facing the open where the bright sun gloried in winter. The sea was dark, almost indigo, running away from the land, and crested with white. The hand of the wind brushed it strangely with shadow, as it brushed the olives of the slopes with silver. And there was no boat out.

The three boats were drawn high up on the steep shingle of the little bay, by the small gray tower. Along the edge of the shingle ran a high wall, inside which was a garden occupying the brief flat of the bay, then rising in terraces up the steep slope of the coast. And there, some little way up, within another wall, stood the low white villa, white and alone as the coast, overlooking the sea. But higher, much higher up, where the olives had given way to pine-trees again, ran the coast road, keeping to the height to be above the gullies that came down to the bays.

Upon it all poured the royal sunshine of the January afternoon. Or rather, all was part of the great sun, glow and substance and immaculate loneliness of the sea, and pure brightness.

Crouching in the rocks above the dark water, which only swung up and down, two slaves, half naked, were dressing pigeons for the evening meal. They pierced the throat of a blue, live bird, and let the drops of blood fall into the heaving sea, with curious concentration. They were performing some sacrifice, or working some incantation. The woman of the temple, yellow and white and alone like a winter narcissus, stood between the pines of the small, humped peninsula where the temple secretly hid, and watched.

A black-and-white pigeon, vividly white, like a ghost escaped over the low dark sea, sped out, caught the wind, tilted, rode, soared and swept over the pine-trees, and wheeled away, a speck, inland. It had escaped. The priestess heard the cry of the boy slave, a garden slave of about seventeen. He raised his arms to heaven in anger as the pigeon wheeled away, naked and angry and young he held out his arms. Then he turned and seized the girl in an access of rage, and beat her with his fist that was stained with pigeon's blood. And she lay down with her face hidden, passive and quivering. The woman who owned them watched. And as she watched, she saw another onlooker, a stranger, in a low, broad hat, and a cloak of gray homespun, a dark bearded man standing on the little causeway of a rock that was the neck of her temple peninsula. By the blowing of his dark-gray cloak she saw him. And he saw her, on the rocks like a white-and-yellow narcissus, because of the flutter of her white linen tunic, below the yellow mantle of wool. And both of them watched the two slaves.

The boy suddenly left off beating the girl. He crouched over her, touching her, trying to make her speak. But she lay quite inert, face down on the smoothed rock. And he put his arms round her and lifted her, but she slipped back to earth like one dead, yet far too quickly for anything dead. The boy, desperate, caught her by the hips

and hugged her to him, turning her over there. There she
seemed inert, all her fight was in her shoulders. He twisted
her over, intent and unconscious, and pushed his hands
between her thighs, to push them apart. And in an instant he was covering her in the blind, frightened frenzy of
a boy's first passion. Quick and frenzied his young body
quivered naked on hers, blind, for a minute. Then it lay
quite still, as if dead.

And then, in terror, he peeped up. He peeped round,
and drew slowly to his feet, adjusting his loin-rag. He saw
the stranger, and then he saw, on the rocks beyond, the
Lady of Isis, his mistress. And as he saw her, his whole
body shrank and cowed, and with a strange cringing motion he scuttled lamely towards the door in the wall.

The girl sat up and looked after him. When she had
seen him disappear, she too looked round. And she saw
the stranger and the priestess. Then with a sullen movement she turned away, as if she had seen nothing, to the
four dead pigeons and the knife, which lay there on the
rock. And she began to strip the small feathers, so that they
rose on the wind like dust.

The priestess turned away. Slaves! Let the overseer
watch them. She was not interested. She went slowly
through the pines again, back to the temple, which stood
in the sun in a small clearing at the centre of the tongue
of land. It was a small temple of wood, painted all pink
and white and blue, having at the front four wooden pillars rising like stems to the swollen lotus-bud of Egypt at
the top, supporting the roof and open, spiky lotus-flowers
of the outer frieze, which went round under the eaves.
Two low steps of stone led up to the platform before the
pillars, and the chamber behind the pillars was open. There
a low stone altar stood, with a few embers in its hollow,
and the dark stain of blood in its end groove.

She knew her temple so well, for she had built it at her
own expense, and tended it for seven years. There it
stood, pink and white, like a flower in the little clearing,
backed by blackish evergreen oaks; and the shadow of
afternoon was already washing over its pillar-bases.

She entered slowly, passing through to the dark inner
chamber, lighted by a perfumed oil-flame. And once more

she pushed shut the door, and once more she threw a few grains of incense on a brazier before the goddess, and once more she sat down before her goddess, in the almost-darkness, to muse, to go away into the dreams of the goddess.

It was Isis; but not Isis, Mother of Horus. It was Isis Bereaved, Isis in Search. The goddess, in painted marble, lifted her face and strode, one thigh forward through the frail fluting of her robe, in the anguish of bereavement and of search. She was looking for the fragments of the dead Osiris, dead and scattered asunder, dead, torn apart, and thrown in fragments over the wide world. And she must find his hands and his feet, his heart, his thighs, his head, his belly, she must gather him together and fold her arms round the re-assembled body till it became warm again, and roused to life, and could embrace her, and could fecundate her womb. And the strange rapture and anguish of search went on through the years, as she lifted her throat and her hollowed eyes looked inward, in the tormented ecstasy of seeking, and the delicate navel of her bud-like belly showed through the frail, girdled robe with the eternal asking, asking, of her search. And through the years she found him bit by bit, heart and head and limbs and body. And yet she had not found the last reality, the final clue to him, that alone could bring him really back to her. For she was Isis of the subtle lotus, the womb which waits submerged and in bud, waits for the touch of that other inward sun that streams its rays from the loins of the male Osiris.

This was the mystery the woman had served alone for seven years, since she was twenty, till now she was twenty-seven. Before, when she was young, she had lived in the world, in Rome, in Ephesus, in Egypt. For her father had been one of Anthony's captains and comrades, had fought with Anthony and had stood with him when Cæsar was murdered, and through to the days of shame. Then he had come again across to Asia, out of favour with Rome, and had been killed in the mountains beyond Lebanon. The widow, having no favour to hope for from Octavius, had retired to her small property on the coast under Lebanon, taking her daughter from the world, a girl of nineteen, beautiful but unmarried.

When she was young the girl had known Cæsar, and
had shrunk from his eagle-like rapacity. The golden Anthony had sat with her many a half-hour, in the splendour
of his great limbs and glowing manhood, and talked with
her of the philosophies and the gods. For he was fascinated
as a child by the gods, though he mocked at them, and
forgot them in his own vanity. But he said to her:

"I have sacrificed two doves for you, to Venus, for I
am afraid you make no offering to the sweet goddess. Beware you will offend her. Come, why is the flower of you
so cool within? Does never a ray nor a glance find its way
through? Ah, come, a maid should open to the sun, when
the sun leans towards her to caress her."

And the big, bright eyes of Anthony laughed down on
her, bathing her in his glow. And she felt the lovely glow
of his male beauty and his amorousness bathe all her limbs
and her body. But it was as he said: the very flower of her
womb was cool, was almost cold, like a bud in shadow of
frost, for all the flooding of his sunshine. So Anthony, re-
specting her father, who loved her, had left her.

And it had always been the same. She saw many men,
young and old. And on the whole, she liked the old ones
best, for they talked to her still and sincere, and did not
expect her to open like a flower to the sun of their male-
ness. Once she asked a philosopher: "Are all women born
to be given to men?" To which the old man answered
slowly:

"Rare women wait for the re-born man. For the lotus,
as you know, will not answer to all the bright heat of the
sun. But she curves her dark, hidden head in the depths,
and stirs not. Till, in the night, one of these rare, invisible
suns that have been killed and shine no more, rises among
the stars in unseen purple, and like the violet, sends its
rare, purple rays out into the night. To these the lotus
stirs as to a caress, and rises upwards through the flood,
and lifts up her bent head, and opens with an expansion
such as no other flower knows, and spreads her sharp rays
of bliss, and offers her soft, gold depths such as no other
flower possesses, to the penetration of the flooding, violet-
dark sun that has died and risen and makes no show. But
for the golden brief day-suns of show such as Anthony,

and for the hard winter suns of power, such as Cæsar, the
lotus stirs not, nor will ever stir. Those will only tear open
the bud. Ah, I tell you, wait for the re-born and wait for
the bud to stir."

So she had waited. For all the men were soldiers or
politicians in the Roman spell, assertive, manly, splendid
apparently, but of an inward meanness, an inadequacy.
And Rome and Egypt alike had left her alone, unroused.
And she was a woman to herself, she would not give herself for a surface glow, nor marry for reasons. She would
wait for the lotus to stir.

And then, in Egypt, she had found Isis, in whom she
spelled her mystery. She had brought Isis to the shores of
Sidon, and lived with her in the mystery of search; whilst
her mother, who loved affairs, controlled the small estate
and the slaves with a free hand.

When the woman had roused from her muse and risen
to perform the last brief ritual to Isis, she replenished the
lamp and left the sanctuary, locking the door. In the outer
world, the sun had already set, and twilight was chill
among the humming trees, which hummed still, though
the wind was abating.

A stranger in a dark, broad hat rose from the corner of
the temple steps, holding his hat in the wind. He was dark-
faced, with a black pointed beard. "O Madam, whose shelter may I implore?" he said to the woman, who stood in
her yellow mantle on a step above him, beside a pink-
and-white painted pillar. Her face was rather long and
pale, her dusky blond hair was held under a thin gold net.
She looked down on the vagabond with indifference. It
was the same she had seen watching the slaves.

"Why come you down from the road?" she asked.

"I saw the temple like a pale flower on the coast, and
would rest among the trees of the precincts, if the lady
of the goddess permits."

"It is Isis in Search," she said, answering his first question.

"The goddess is great," he replied.

She looked at him still with mistrust. There was a faint
remote smile in the dark eyes lifted to her, though the

face was hollow with suffering. The vagabond divined her
hesitation, and was mocking her.

"Stay here upon the steps," she said. "A slave will show
you the shelter."

"The lady of Egypt is gracious."

She went down the rocky path of the humped peninsula, in her gilded sandals. Beautiful were her ivory feet,
beneath the white tunic, and above the saffron mantle her
dusky-blond head bent as with endless musings. A
woman entangled in her own dream. The man smiled a
little, half-bitterly, and sat again on the step to wait,
drawing his mantle round him, in the cold twilight.

At length a slave appeared, also in hodden gray.

"Seek ye the shelter of our lady?" he said insolently.

"Even so."

"Then come."

With the brusque insolence of a slave waiting on a vagabond, the young fellow led through the trees and down
into a little gully in the rock, where, almost in darkness,
was a small cave, with a litter of the tall heaths that grew
on the waste places of the coast, under the stone-pines.
The place was dark, but absolutely silent from the wind.
There was still a faint odour of goats.

"Here sleep!" said the slave. "For the goats come no
more on this half-island. And there is water!" He pointed
to a little basin of rock where the maidenhair fern fringed
a dripping mouthful of water.

Having scornfully bestowed his patronage, the slave
departed. The man who had died climbed out to the tip
of the peninsula, where the waves thrashed. It was rapidly
getting dark, and the stars were coming out. The wind was
abating for the night. Inland, the steep grooved upslope
was dark to the long wavering outline of the crest against
the translucent sky. Only now and then, a lantern flickered towards the villa.

The man who had died went back to the shelter. There
he took bread from his leather pouch, dipped it in the
water of the tiny spring, and slowly ate. Having eaten and
washed his mouth, he looked once more at the bright stars
in the pure windy sky, then settled the heath for his bed.

Having laid his hat and his sandals aside, and put his pouch under his cheek for a pillow, he slept, for he was very tired. Yet during the night the cold woke him, pinching wearily through his weariness. Outside was brilliantly starry, and still windy. He sat and hugged himself in a sort of coma, and towards dawn went to sleep again.

In the morning the coast was still chill in shadow, though the sun was up behind the hills, when the woman came down from the villa towards the goddess. The sea was fair and pale blue, lovely in newness, and at last the wind was still. Yet the waves broke white in the many rocks, and tore in the shingle of the little bay. The woman came slowly, towards her dream. Yet she was aware of an interruption.

As she followed the little neck of rock on to her peninsula, and climbed the slope between the trees to the temple, a slave came down and stood, making his obeisance. There was a faint insolence in his humility. "Speak!" she said.

"Lady, the man is there, he still sleeps. Lady, may I speak?"

"Speak!" she said, repelled by the fellow.

"Lady, the man is an escaped malefactor."

The slave seemed to triumph in imparting the unpleasant news.

"By what sign?"

"Behold his hands and feet! Will the lady look on him?"

"Lead on!"

The slave led quickly over the mound of the hill down to the tiny ravine. There he stood aside, and the woman went into the crack towards the cave. Her heart beat a little. Above all she must preserve her temple inviolate.

The vagabond was asleep with his cheek on his scrip, his mantle wrapped round him, but his bare, soiled feet curling side by side, to keep each other warm, and his hand lying loosely clenched in sleep. And in the pale skin of his feet, usually covered by sandal-straps, she saw the scars, and in the palm of the loose hand.

She had no interest in men, particularly in the servile class. Yet she looked at the sleeping face. It was worn, hollow, and rather ugly. But, a true priestess, she saw the other kind of beauty in it, the sheer stillness of the deeper life. There was even a sort of majesty in the dark brows, over the still, hollow cheeks. She saw that his black hair, left long, in contrast to the Roman fashion, was touched with gray at the temples, and the black pointed beard had threads of gray. But that must be suffering or misfortune, for the man was young. His dusky skin had the silvery glisten of youth still.

There was a beauty of much suffering, and the strange calm candour of finer life in the whole delicate ugliness of the face. For the first time, she was touched on the quick at the sight of a man, as if the tip of a fine flame of living had touched her. It was the first time. Men had roused all kinds of feeling in her, but never had touched her with the flame-tip of life.

She went back under the rock to where the slave waited.

"Know!" she said. "This is no malefactor, but a free citizen of the east. Do not disturb him. But when he comes forth, bring him to me; tell him I would speak with him."

She spoke coldly, for she found slaves invariably repellent, a little repulsive. They were so embedded in the lesser life, and their appetites and their small consciousness were a little disgusting. So she wrapped her dream round her, and went to the temple, where a slave-girl brought winter roses and jasmine, for the altar. But to-day, even in her ministrations, she was disturbed.

The sun rose over the hill, sparkling, the light fell triumphantly on the little pine-covered peninsula of the coast, and on the pink temple, in the pristine newness. The man who had died woke up, and put on his sandals. He put on his hat too, slung his scrip under his mantle, and went out, to see the morning in all its blue and its new gold. He glanced at the little yellow-and-white narcissus sparkling gaily in the rocks. And he saw the slave waiting for him like a menace.

"Master!" said the slave. "Our lady would speak with you at the house of Isis."

"It is well," said the wanderer.

He went slowly, staying to look at the pale blue sea like

a flower in unruffled bloom, and the white fringes among
the rocks, like white rock-flowers, the hollow slopes sheer-
ing up high from the shore, gray with olive-trees and
green with bright young wheat, and set with the white
small villa. All fair and pure in the January morning.

The sun fell on the corner of the temple, he sat down
on the step in the sunshine, in the infinite patience of
waiting. He had come back to life, but not the same life
that he had left, the life of little people and the little day.
Re-born, he was in the other life, the greater day of the
human consciousness. And he was alone and apart from
the little day, and out of contact with the daily people.
Not yet had he accepted the irrevocable noli me tangere
which separates the re-born from the vulgar. The separa-
tion was absolute, as yet here at the temple he felt peace,
the hard, bright pagan peace with hostility of slaves beneath.

The woman came into the dark inner doorway of the
temple, from the shrine, and stood there, hesitating. She
could see the dark figure of the man, sitting in that terrible stillness that was portentous to her, had something
almost menacing in its patience.

She advanced across the outer chamber of the temple,
and the man, becoming aware of her, stood up. She addressed him in Greek, but he said:

"Madam, my Greek is limited. Allow me to speak vulgar Syrian."

"Whence come you? Whither go you?" she asked,
with a hurried preoccupation of a priestess.

"From the east beyond Damascus—and I go west as
the road goes," he replied slowly.

She glanced at him with sudden anxiety and shyness.

"But why do you have the marks of a malefactor?" she
asked abruptly.

"Did the Lady of Isis spy upon me in my sleep?" he
asked, with a gray weariness.

"The slave warned me—your hands and feet—" she
said.

He looked at her. Then he said:

"Will the Lady of Isis allow me to bid her farewell, and
go up to the road?"

The wind came in a sudden puff, lifting his mantle and
his hat. He put up his hand to hold the brim, and she saw
again the thin brown hand with its scar.

"See! The scar!" she said, pointing.

"Even so!" he said. "But farewell, and to Isis my hom-
age and my thanks for sleep."

He was going. But she looked up at him with her wondering blue eyes.

"Will you not look at Isis?" she said, with sudden im-
pulse. And something stirred in him, like pain.

"Where then?" he said.

"Come!"

He followed her into the inner shrine, into the almost-
darkness. When his eyes got used to the faint glow of the
lamp, he saw the goddess striding like a ship, eager in the
swirl of her gown, and he made his obeisance.

"Great is Isis!" he said. "In her search she is greater
than death. Wonderful is such walking in a woman, wonderful the goal. All men praise thee, Isis, thou greater than
the mother unto man."

The woman of Isis heard, and threw incense on the
brazier. Then she looked at the man.

"Is it well with thee here?" she asked him. "Has Isis
brought thee home to herself?"

He looked at the priestess in wonder and trouble.

"I know not," he said.

But the woman was pondering that this was the lost
Osiris. She felt it in the quick of her soul. And her agita-
tion was intense.

He would not stay in the close, dark, perfumed shrine.
He went out again to the morning, to the cold air. He felt
something approaching to touch him, and all his flesh was
still woven with pain and the wild commandment: Noli
me tangere! Touch me not! Oh, don't touch me!

The woman followed into the open with timid eager-
ness. He was moving away.

"Oh stranger, do not go! O stay awhile with Isis!"

He looked at her, at her face open like a flower, as if a
sun had risen in her soul. And again his loins stirred.

"Would you detain me, girl of Isis?" he said.

"Stay! I am sure you are Osiris!" she said.

He laughed suddenly. "Not yet!" he said. Then he looked at her wistful face. "But I will sleep another night in the cave of the goats, if Isis wills it," he added.

She put her hands together with a priestess's childish happiness.

"Ah! Isis will be glad!" she said.

So he went down to the shore, in great trouble, saying to himself: "Shall I give myself into this touch? Shall I give myself into this touch? Men have tortured me to death with their touch. Yet this girl of Isis is a tender flame of healing. I am a physician, yet I have no healing like the flame of this tender girl. The flame of this tender girl! Like the first pale crocus of the spring. How could I have been blind to the healing and the bliss in the crocus-like body of a tender woman! Ah, tenderness! More terrible and lovely than the death I died—"

He pried small shell-fish from the rocks, and ate them with relish and wonder for the simple taste of the sea. And inwardly, he was tremulous, thinking: "Dare I come into touch? For this is further than death. I have dared to let them lay hands on me and put me to death. But dare I come into this tender touch of life? Oh, this is harder—"

But the woman went into the shrine again, and sat rapt in pure muse, through the long hours, watching the swirling stride of the yearning goddess, and the navel of the bud-like belly, like a seal on the virgin urge of the search. And she gave herself to the woman-flow and to the urge of Isis in Search.

Towards sundown she went on the peninsula to look for him. And she found him gone towards the sun, as she had gone the day before, and sitting on the pine-needles at the foot of the tree, where she had stood when first she saw him. Now she approached tremulously and slowly, afraid lest he did not want her. She stood near him unseen, till suddenly he glanced up at her from under his broad hat, and saw the westering sun on her nettled hair. He was startled, yet he expected her.

"Is that your home?" he said, pointing to the white low villa on the slope of olives.

"It is my mother's house. She is a widow, and I am her only child."

"And are these all her slaves?"

"Except those that are mine."

Their eyes met for a moment.

"Will you too sit to see the sun go down?" he said.

He had not risen to speak to her. He had known too much pain. So she sat on the dry brown pine-needles, gathering her saffron mantle round her knees. A boat was coming in, out of the open glow into the shadow of the bay, and slaves were lifting small nets, their babble coming off the surface of the water.

"And this is home to you," he said.

"But I serve Isis in Search," she replied.

He looked at her. She was like a soft, musing cloud, somehow remote. His soul smote him with passion and compassion.

"Mayst thou find thy desire, maiden," he said, with sudden earnestness.

"And art thou not Osiris?" she asked.

He flushed suddenly.

"Yes, if thou wilt heal me!" he said. "For the death aloofness is still upon me, and I cannot escape it."

She looked at him for a moment in fear, from the soft blue sun of her eyes. Then she lowered her head, and they sat in silence in the warmth and glow of the western sun: the man who had died, and the woman of the pure search.

The sun was curving down to the sea, in grand winter splendour. It fell on the twinkling, naked bodies of the slaves, with their ruddy broad hams and their small black heads, as they ran spreading the nets on the pebble beach. The all-tolerant Pan watched over them. All-tolerant Pan should be their god for ever.

The woman rose as the sun's rim dipped, saying:

"If you will stay, I shall send down victual and covering."

"The lady your mother, what will she say?"

The woman of Isis looked at him strangely, but with a tinge of misgiving.

"It is my own," she said.

"It is good," he said, smiling faintly, and foreseeing difficulties.

He watched her go, with her absorbed, strange motion

of the self-dedicate. Her dun head was a little bent, the white linen swung about her ivory ankles. And he saw the naked slaves stand to look at her, with a certain wonder, and even a certain mischief. But she passed intent through the door in the wall, on the bay.

The man who had died sat on at the foot of the tree overlooking the strand, for on the little shore everything happened. At the small stream which ran in round the corner of the property wall, women slaves were still washing linen, and now and again came the hollow chock! chock! chock! as they beat it against the smooth stones, in the dark little hollow of the pool. There was a smell of olive-refuse on the air; and sometimes still the faint rumble of the grindstone that was milling the olives, inside the garden, and the sound of the slave calling to the ass at the mill. Then through the doorway a woman stepped, a gray-haired woman in a mantle of whitish wool, and there followed her a bare-headed man in a toga, a Roman: probably her steward or overseer. They stood on the high shingle above the sea, and cast round a rapid glance. The broad-hammed, ruddy-bodied slaves bent absorbed and abject over the nets, picking them clean, the women washing linen thrust their palms with energy down on the wash, the old slave bent absorbed at the water's edge, washing the fish and the polyps of the catch. And the woman and the overseer saw it all, in one glance. They also saw, seated at the foot of the tree on the rocks of the peninsula, the strange man silent and alone. And the man who had died saw that they spoke of him. Out of the little sacred world of the peninsula he looked on the common world, and saw it still hostile.

The sun was touching the sea, across the tiny bay stretched the shadow of the opposite humped headland. Over the shingle, now blue and cold in shadow, the elderly woman trod heavily, in shadow too, to look at the fish spread in the flat basket of the old man crouching at the water's edge: a naked old slave with fat hips and shoulders, on whose soft, fairish-orange body the last sun twinkled, then died. The old slave continued cleaning the fish absorbedly, not looking up: as if the lady were the shadow of twilight falling on him.

Then from the gateway stepped two slave-girls with
flat baskets on their heads, and from one basket the terra-
cotta wine-jar and the oil-jar poked up, leaning slightly.
Over the massive shingle, under the wall, came the girls,
and the woman of Isis in her saffron mantle stepped in
twilight after them. Out at sea the sun still shone. Here
was shadow. The mother with gray head stood at the sea's
edge and watched the daughter, all yellow and white, with
dun blond head, swinging unseeing and unheeding after
the slave-girls, towards the neck of rock of the peninsula; the daughter, travelling in her absorbed other-world.
And not moving from her place, the elderly mother
watched that procession of three file up the rise of the
headland, between the trees, and disappear, shut in by
trees. No slave had lifted a head to look. The gray-haired
woman still watched the trees where her daughter had
disappeared. Then she glanced again at the foot of the
tree, where the man who had died was still sitting, incon-
spicuous now, for the sun had left him; and only the far
blade of the sea shone bright. It was evening. Patience!
Let destiny move!

The mother plodded with a stamping stride up the
shingle: not long and swinging and rapt, like the daughter,
but short and determined. Then down the rocks opposite
came two naked slaves trotting with huge bundles of dark
green on their shoulders, so their broad, naked legs twinkled underneath like insects' legs, and their heads were
hidden. They came trotting across the shingle, heedless
and intent on their way, when suddenly the man, the
Roman-looking overseer, addressed them, and they
stopped dead. They stood invisible under their loads, as
if they might disappear altogether, now they were arrested. Then a hand came out and pointed to the peninsula. Then the two green-heaped slaves trotted on, towards the temple precincts. The gray-haired woman
joined the man, and slowly the two passed through the
door again, from the shingle of the sea to the property of
the villa. Then the old, fat-shouldered slave rose, pallid
in the shadow, with his tray of fish from the sea, and the
women rose from the pool, dusky and alive, piling the wet
linen in a heap on to the flat baskets, and the slaves who

had cleaned the net gathered its whitish folds together. And the old slave with the fish basket on his shoulder, and the women slaves with the heaped baskets of wet linen on their heads, and the two slaves with the folded net, and the slave with oars on his shoulders, and the boy with the folded sail on his arm, gathered in a naked group near the door, and the man who had died heard the low buzz of their chatter. Then as the wind wafted cold, they began to pass through the door.

It was the life of the little day, the life of little people. And the man who had died said to himself: "Unless we encompass it in the greater day, and set the little life in the circle of the greater life, all is disaster."

Even the tops of the hills were in shadow. Only the sky was still upwardly radiant. The sea was a vast milky shadow. The man who had died rose a little stiffly, and turned into the grove.

There was no one at the temple. He went on to his lair in the rock. There, the slave-men had carried out the old heath of the bedding, swept the rock floor, and were spreading with nice art the myrtle, then the rougher heath, then the soft, bushy heath-tips on top, for a bed. Over it all they put a well-tanned white ox-skin. The maids had laid folded woollen covers at the head of the cave, and the wine-jar, the oil-jar, a terra-cotta drinking-cup, and a basket containing bread, salt, cheese, dried figs and eggs stood neatly arranged. There was also a little brazier of charcoal. The cave was suddenly full, and a dwelling-place.

The woman of Isis stood in the hollow by the tiny spring.

Only one slave at a time could pass. The girl-slaves waited at the entrance to the narrow place. When the man who had died appeared, the woman sent the girls away. The men-slaves still arranged the bed, making the job as long as possible. But the woman of Isis dismissed them too. And the man who had died came to look at his house.

"Is it well?" the woman asked him.

"It is very well," the man replied. "But the lady, your mother, and he who is no doubt the steward, watched while the slaves brought the goods. Will they not oppose you?"

"I have my own portion! Can I not give of my own? Who is going to oppose me and the gods?" she said, with a certain soft fury, touched with exasperation. So that he knew that her mother would oppose her, and that the spirit of the little life would fight against the spirit of the greater. And he thought: "Why did the woman of Isis relinquish her portion in the daily world? She should have kept her goods fiercely!"

"Will you eat and drink?" she said. "On the ashes are warm eggs. And I will go up to the meal at the villa. But in the second hour of the night I shall come down to the temple. O, then, will you come too to Isis?" She looked at him, and a queer glow dilated her eyes. This was her dream, and it was greater than herself. He could not bear to thwart her or hurt her in the least thing now. She was in the full glow of her woman's mystery.

"Shall I wait at the temple?" he said.

"O, wait at the second hour and I shall come." He heard the humming supplication in her voice and his fibres quivered.

"But the lady, your mother?" he said gently.

The woman looked at him, startled.

"She will not thwart me!" she said.

So he knew that the mother would thwart the daughter, for the daughter had left her goods in the hands of her mother, who would hold fast to this power.

But she went, and the man who had died lay reclining on his couch, and ate the eggs from the ashes, and dipped his bread in oil, and ate it, for his flesh was dry: and he mixed wine and water, and drank. And so he lay still, and the lamp made a small bud of light.

He was absorbed and enmeshed in new sensations. The woman of Isis was lovely to him, not so much in form, as in the wonderful womanly glow of her. Suns beyond suns had dipped her in mysterious fire, the mysterious fire of a potent woman, and to touch her was like touching the sun. Best of all was her tender desire for him, like sunshine, so soft and still.

"She is like sunshine upon me," he said to himself, stretching his limbs. "I have never before stretched my limbs in such sunshine as her desire for me. The greatest of all gods granted me this."

At the same time he was haunted by the fear of the outer world. "If they can, they will kill us," he said to himself. "But there is a law of the sun which protects us."

And again he said to himself: "I have risen naked and branded. But if I am naked enough for this contact, I have not died in vain. Before I was clogged."

He rose and went out. The night was chill and starry, and of a great wintery splendour. "There are destinies of splendour," he said to the night, "after all our doom of littleness and meanness and pain."

So he went up silently to the temple, and waited in darkness against the inner wall, looking out on a gray darkness, stars, and rims of trees. And he said again to himself: "There are destinies of splendour, and there is a greater power."

So at last he saw the light of her silk lanthorn swinging, coming intermittent between the trees, yet coming swiftly. She was alone, and near, the light softly swishing on her mantle-hem. And he trembled with fear and with joy, saying to himself: "I am almost more afraid of this touch than I was of death. For I am more nakedly exposed to it."

"I am here, Lady of Isis," he said softly out of the dark.

"Ah!" she cried, in fear also, yet in rapture. For she was given to her dream.

She unlocked the door of the shrine, and he followed after her. Then she latched the door shut again. The air inside was warm and close and perfumed. The man who had died stood by the closed door, and watched the woman. She had come first to the goddess. And dim-lit, the goddess-statue stood surging forward, a little fearsome like a great woman-presence urging.

The priestess did not look at him. She took off her saffron mantle and laid it on a low couch. In the dim light she was bare armed, in her girdled white tunic. But she was still hiding herself away from him. He stood back in shadow, and watched her slowly fan the brazier and fling on incense. Faint clouds of sweet aroma arose on the air. She turned to the statue in the ritual of approach, softly swaying forward with a slight lurch, like a moored boat, tipping towards the goddess.

He watched the strange rapt woman, and he said to himself: "I must leave her alone in her rapture, her female mysteries." So she tipped in her strange forward-swaying rhythm before the goddess. Then she broke into a murmur of Greek, which he could not understand. And, as she murmured, her swaying softly subsided, like a boat on a sea that grows still. And as he watched her, he saw her soul in its aloneness, and its female difference. He said to himself: "How different she is from me, how strangely different! She is afraid of me, and my male difference. She is getting herself naked and clear of her fear. How sensitive and softly alive she is, with a life so different from mine! How beautiful with a soft strange courage, of life, so different from my courage of death! What a beautiful thing, like the heart of a rose, like the core of a flame. She is making herself completely penetrable. Ah! how terrible to fail her, or to trespass on her!"

She turned to him, her face glowing from the goddess.

"You are Osiris, aren't you?" she said naïvely.

"If you will," he said.

"Will you let Isis discover you? Will you not take off your things?"

He looked at the woman, and lost his breath. And his wounds, and especially the death-wound through his belly, began to cry again.

"It has hurt so much!" he said. "You must forgive me if I am still held back."

But he took off his cloak and his tunic, and went naked towards the idol, his breast panting with the sudden terror of overwhelming pain, memory of overwhelming pain, and grief too bitter.

"They did me to death!" he said in excuse of himself, turning his face to her for a moment.

And she saw the ghost of the death in him, as he stood there thin and stark before her, and suddenly she was terrified, and she felt robbed. She felt the shadow of the gray, grisly wing of death triumphant.

"Ah, Goddess," he said to the idol, in the vernacular. "I would be so glad to live, if you would give me my clue again."

For here again he felt desperate, faced by the demand of life, and burdened still by his death.

"Let me anoint you!" the woman said to him softly. "Let me anoint the scars! Show me, and let me anoint them!"

He forgot his nakedness in this re-evoked old pain. He sat on the edge of the couch, and she poured a little ointment into the palm of his hand. And as she chafed his hand, it all came back, the nails, the holes, the cruelty, the unjust cruelty against him who had offered only kindness. The agony of injustice and cruelty came over him again, as in his death-hour. But she chafed the palm, murmuring: "What was torn becomes a new flesh, what was a wound is full of fresh life; this scar is the eye of the violet."

And he could not help smiling at her, in her naïve priestess's absorption. This was her dream, and he was only a dream-object to her. She would never know or understand what he was. Especially she would never know the death that was gone before in him. But what did it matter? She was different. She was woman: her life and her death were different from his. Only she was good to him.

When she chafed his feet with oil and tender, tender healing, he could not refrain from saying to her:

"Once a woman washed my feet with tears, and wiped them with her hair, and poured on precious ointment."

The woman of Isis looked up at him from her earnest work, interrupted again.

"Were they hurt then?" she said. "Your feet?"

"No, no! It was while they were whole."

"And did you love her?"

"Love had passed in her. She only wanted to serve," he replied. "She had been a prostitute."

"And did you let her serve you?" she asked.

"Yea."

"Did you let her serve you with the corpse of her love?"

"Ay!"

Suddenly it dawned on him: "I asked them all to serve me with the corpse of their love. And in the end I offered

them only the corpse of my love. This is my body—take
and eat—my corpse—"

A vivid shame went through him. "After all," he
thought, "I wanted them to love with dead bodies. If I
had kissed Judas with live love, perhaps he would never
have kissed me with death. Perhaps he loved me in the
flesh, and I willed that he should love me bodylessly, with
the corpse of love—"

There dawned on him the reality of the soft warm love
which is in touch, and which is full of delight. "And I told
them, blessed are they that mourn," he said to himself.
"Alas, if I mourned even this woman here, now I am in
death, I should have to remain dead, and I want so much
to live. Life has brought me to this woman with warm
hands. And her touch is more to me now than all my
words. For I want to live—"

"Go then to the goddess!" she said softly, gently pushing him towards Isis. And as he stood there dazed and
naked as an unborn thing, he heard the woman murmuring to the goddess, murmuring, murmuring with a plaintive appeal. She was stooping now, looking at the
scar in the soft flesh of the socket of his side, a scar deep
and like an eye sore with endless weeping, just in the soft
socket above the hip. It was here that his blood had left
him, and his essential seed. The woman was trembling
softly and murmuring in Greek. And he in the recurring
dismay of having died, and in the anguished perplexity of
having tried to force life, felt his wounds crying aloud, and
the deep places of the body howling again: "I have been
murdered, and I lent myself to murder. They murdered
me, but I lent myself to murder—"

The woman, silent now, but quivering, laid oil in her
hand and put her palm over the wound in his right side.
He winced, and the wound absorbed his life again,
as thousands of times before. And in the dark, wild pain
and panic of his consciousness rang only one cry: "Oh,
how can she take this death out of me? How can she take
from me this death? She can never know! She can never
understand! She can never equal it! . . ."

In silence, she softly rhythmically chafed the scar with
oil. Absorbed now in her priestess's task, softly, softly gath-

ering power, while the vitals of the man howled in panic. But as she gradually gathered power, and passed in a girdle round him to the opposite scar, gradually warmth began to take the place of the cold terror, and he felt: "I am going to be warm again, and I am going to be whole! I shall be warm like the morning. I shall be a man. It doesn't need understanding. It needs newness. She brings me newness—"

And he listened to the faint, ceaseless wail of distress of his wounds, sounding as if for ever under the horizons of his consciousness. But the wail was growing dim, more dim.

He thought of the woman toiling over him: "She does not know! She does not realise the death in me. But she has another consciousness. She comes to me from the opposite end of the night."

Having chafed all his lower body with oil, having worked with her slow intensity of a priestess, so that the sound of his wounds grew dimmer and dimmer, suddenly she put her breast against the wound in his left side, and her arms round him, folding over the wound in his right side, and she pressed him to her, in a power of living warmth, like the folds of a river. And the wailing died out altogether, and there was a stillness, and darkness in his soul, unbroken dark stillness, wholeness.

Then slowly, slowly, in the perfect darkness of his inner man, he felt the stir of something coming. A dawn, a new sun. A new sun was coming up in him, in the perfect inner darkness of himself. He waited for it breathless, quivering with a fearful hope . . . "Now I am not myself. I am something new . . ."

And as it rose, he felt, with a cold breath of disappointment, the girdle of the living woman slip down from him, the warmth and the glow slipped from him, leaving him stark. She crouched, spent, at the feet of the goddess, hiding her face.

Stooping, he laid his hand softly on her warm, bright shoulder, and the shock of desire went through him, shock after shock, so that he wondered if it were another sort of death: but full of magnificence.

Now all his consciousness was there in the crouching,

hidden woman. He stooped beside her and caressed her softly, blindly, murmuring inarticulate things. And his death and his passion of sacrifice were all as nothing to him now, he knew only the crouching fulness of the woman there, the soft white rock of life. . . . "On this rock I built my life." The deep-folded, penetrable rock of the living woman! The woman, hiding her face. Himself bending over, powerful and new like dawn.

He crouched to her, and he felt the blaze of his manhood and his power rise up in his loins, magnificent.

"I am risen!"

Magnificent, blazing indomitable in the depths of his loins, his own sun dawned, and sent its fire running along his limbs, so that his face shone unconsciously.

He untied the string on the linen tunic, and slipped the garment down, till he saw the white glow of her white-gold breasts. And he touched them, and he felt his life go molten. "Father!" he said, "why did you hide this from me?" And he touched her with the poignancy of wonder, and the marvellous piercing transcendence of desire. "Lo!" he said, "this is beyond prayer." It was the deep, interfolded warmth, warmth living and penetrable, the woman, the heart of the rose! "My mansion is the intricate warm rose, my joy is this blossom!"

She looked up at him suddenly, her face like a lifted light, wistful, tender, her eyes like many wet flowers. And he drew her to his breast with a passion of tenderness and consuming desire, and the last thought: "My hour is upon me, I am taken unawares—"

So he knew her, and was one with her.

Afterwards, with a dim wonder, she touched the great scars in his sides with her finger-tips, and said:

"But they no longer hurt?"

"They are suns!" he said. "They shine from your touch. They are my atonement with you."

And when they left the temple, it was the coldness before dawn. As he closed the door, he looked again at the goddess, and he said: "Lo, Isis is a kindly goddess; and full of tenderness. Great gods are warm-hearted, and have tender goddesses."

The woman wrapped herself in her mantle and went

home in silence, sightless, brooding like the lotus softly shutting again, with its gold core full of fresh life. She saw nothing, for her own petals were a sheath to her. Only she thought: "I am full of Osiris. I am full of the risen Osiris! . . ."

But the man looked at the vivid stars before dawn, as they rained down to the sea, and the dog-star green towards the sea's rim. And he thought: "How plastic it is, how full of curves and folds like an invisible rose of dark-petalled openness that shows where the dew touches its darkness! How full it is, and great beyond all gods. How it leans around me, and I am part of it, the great rose of Space. I am like a grain of its perfume, and the woman is a grain of its beauty. Now the world is one flower of many petalled darknesses, and I am in its perfume as in a touch."

So, in the absolute stillness and fulness of touch, he slept in his cave while the dawn came. And after the dawn, the wind rose and brought a storm, with cold rain. So he stayed in his cave in the peace and the delight of being in touch, delighting to hear the sea, and the rain on the earth, and to see one white-and-gold narcissus bowing wet, and still wet. And he said: "This is the great atonement, the being in touch. The gray sea and the rain, the wet narcissus and the woman I wait for, the invisible Isis and the unseen sun are all in touch, and at one."

He waited at the temple for the woman, and she came in the rain. But she said to him:

"Let me sit awhile with Isis. And come to me, will you come to me, in the second hour of night?"

So he went back to the cave and lay in stillness and in the joy of being in touch, waiting for the woman who would come with the night, and consummate again the contact. Then when night came the woman came, and came gladly, for her great yearning too was upon her, to be in touch, to be in touch with him, nearer.

So the days came, and the nights came, and days came again, and the contact was perfected and fulfilled. And he said: "I will ask her nothing, not even her name, for a name would set her apart."

And she said to herself: "He is Osiris. I wish to know no more."

Plum-blossom blew from the trees, the time of the narcissus was past, anemones lit up the ground and were
gone, the perfume of bean-field was in the air. All
changed, the blossom of the universe changed its petals
and swung round to look another way. The spring was fulfilled, a contact was established, the man and the woman
were fulfilled of one another, and departure was in the
air.

One day he met her under the trees, when the morning sun was hot, and the pines smelled sweet, and on the
hills the last pear-bloom was scattering. She came slowly
towards him, and in her gentle lingering, her tender hanging back from him, he knew a change in her.

"Hast thou conceived?" he asked her.

"Why?" she said.

"Thou art like a tree whose green leaves follow the blossom, full of sap. And there is a withdrawing about thee."

"It is so," she said. "I am with young by thee. Is it
good?"

"Yea!" he said. "How should it not be good? So the
nightingale calls no more from the valley-bed. But where
wilt thou bear the child, for I am naked of all but life."

"We will stay here," she said.

"But the lady, your mother?"

A shadow crossed her brow. She did not answer.

"What when she knows?" he said.

"She begins to know."

"And would she hurt you?"

"Ah, not me! What I have is all my own. And I shall be
big with Osiris. . . . But thou, do you watch her slaves."

She looked at him, and the peace of her maternity was
troubled by anxiety.

"Let not your heart be troubled!" he said. "I have died
the death once."

So he knew the time was come again for him to depart.
He would go alone, with his destiny. Yet not alone, for the
touch would be upon him, even as he left his touch on
her. And invisible suns would go with him.

Yet he must go. For here on the bay the little life of
jealousy and property was resuming sway again, as the
suns of passionate fecundity relaxed their sway. In the

name of property, the widow and her slaves would seek to be revenged on him for the bread he had eaten, and the living touch he had established, the woman he had delighted in. But he said: "Not twice! They shall not now profane the touch in me. My wits against theirs."

So he watched. And he knew they plotted. So he moved from the little cave, and found another shelter, a tiny cove of sand by the sea, dry and secret under the rocks.

He said to the woman:

"I must go now soon. Trouble is coming to me from the slaves. But I am a man, and the world is open. But what is between us is good, and is established. Be at peace. And when the nightingale calls again from your valley-bed, I shall come again, sure as Spring."

She said: "O don't go! Stay with me on half the island, and I will build a house for you and me under the pine-trees by the temple, where we can live apart."

Yet she knew that he would go. And even she wanted the coolness of her own air around her, and the release from anxiety.

"If I stay," he said, "they will betray me to the Romans and to their justice. But I will never be betrayed again. So when I am gone, live in peace with the growing child. And I shall come again; all is good between us, near or apart. The suns come back in their seasons: and I shall come again."

"Do not go yet," she said. "I have set a slave to watch at the neck of the peninsula. Do not go yet, till the harm shows."

But as he lay in his little cove, on a calm, still night, he heard the soft knock of oars, and the bump of a boat against the rock. So he crept out to listen. And he heard the Roman overseer say:

"Lead softly to the goat's den. And Lysippus shall throw the net over the malefactor while he sleeps, and we will bring him before justice, and the Lady of Isis shall know nothing of it . . ."

The man who had died caught a whiff of flesh from the oiled and naked slaves as they crept up, then the faint perfume of the Roman. He crept nearer to the sea. The slave who sat in the boat sat motionless, holding the oars, for the sea was quite still. And the man who had died knew him.

So out of the deep cleft of a rock he said, in a clear voice:

"Art thou not that slave who possessed the maiden under the eyes of Isis? Art thou not the youth? Speak!"

The youth stood up in the boat in terror. His movement sent the boat bumping against the rock. The slave sprang out in wild fear, and fled up the rocks. The man who had died quickly seized the boat and stepped in, and pushed off. The oars were yet warm with the unpleasant warmth of the hands of the slaves. But the man pulled slowly out, to get into the current which set down the coast, and would carry him in silence. The high coast was utterly dark against the starry night. There was no glimmer from the peninsula: the priestess came no more at night. The man who had died rowed slowly on, with the current, and laughed to himself: "I have sowed the seed of my life and my resurrection, and put my touch forever upon the choice woman of this day, and I carry her perfume in my flesh like essence of roses. She is dear to me in the middle of my being. But the gold and flowing serpent is coiling up again, to sleep at the root of my tree.

"So let the boat carry me. To-morrow is another day."

DAVID HERBERT LAWRENCE was born in the Nottinghamshire village of Eastwood on September 11, 1885, the son of a coal miner and a school teacher. A great deal of his life was spent outside England, including two years in New Mexico, and he died at Vence in France on March 2, 1930. He was the author of many novels and poems as well as books of travel and literary criticism. Among his most famous novels are Sons and Lovers, The Rainbow, Women in Love, The Plumed Serpent, *and* Lady Chatterley's Lover.

VINTAGE CRITICISM,
LITERATURE, MUSIC, AND ART